Acknowledgments and Thanks

I wish to thank the following people for their support and devotion as I wrote this novel.

- My God
- My Family
- My Country

The Blind Man's Rage

Skip

Coryell

Book 4 in The God Virus Series

Published by White Feather Press. (www.whitefeatherpress.com)

ISBN 978-1-61808-155-1

Printed in the United States of America

Cover photo mushroom cloud ©iStockphoto.com/ RomoloTavani

Cover photo of eyes ©iStockphoto.com/ RomoloTavani

Scripture taken from the HOLY BIBLE, NEW INTERNATIONAL VERSION®. NIV®. Copyright © 1973, 1978, 1984 by International Bible Society. Used by permission of Zondervan. All rights reserved worldwide.

Scriptures marked KJV are taken from the KING JAMES VERSION (KJV): KING JAMES VERSION, public domain.

White Feather Press

Reaffirming Faith in God, Family, and Country!

Books by Skip Coryell

We Hold These Truths
Bond of Unseen Blood
Church and State
Blood in the Streets
Laughter and Tears
RKBA: Defending the Right to Keep and Bear Arms
Stalking Natalie
The God Virus
The Shadow Militia
The Saracen Tide
The Blind Man's Rage
Civilian Combat - The Concealed Carry Book

For Sara, my dear wife,
whom I love and fight for.

And to my children.

What has gone before…

In book one of this series, *The God Virus*, a cyber ter-
rorist attack takes out the American power grid, leaving the
entire country in darkness, death and widespread chaos. Dan
Branch and his son, Jeremy, have to sojourn through Northern
Wisconsin to the Michigan Lower Peninsula to the safety of
his Uncle Rodney's home. Uncle Rodney, an eccentric, hard-
core prepper and Vietnam vet tries to rescue Dan but fails.

It takes Dan and his son six months to reach the safety of
the northern Lower Peninsula. On the way Dan is forced to
kill many men. He also rescues Jackie, a damsel in distress,
and marries her. When they finally reach Iroquois City, Uncle
Rodney reveals he is the commanding general of *The Shadow
Militia* and a mob of over a thousand cutthroats and thieves
will be attacking within the week.

In book two, *The Shadow Militia*, Dan Branch, Uncle
Rodney and Sheriff Leif lead the citizens of Iroquois county
into battle against thousands of vicious and deadly gang members hell-bent on destroying anyone who resists their quest for
power.

Through sheer tenacity and great sacrifice the army of
cutthroats is stopped, but not before they destroy much of
Iroquois City. Hundreds of townspeople are killed or wounded. The patriots of Iroquois county have earned a rest. But
repose is not in the cards, because a new, larger and deadlier
threat is on the way.

In book three, *The Saracen Tide*, the town is besieged with
a greater and deadlier threat as an army of 30,000 Jihadists
make their way north through Michigan, killing anyone who
will not convert to Islam. Uncle Rodney along with his family and The Shadow Militia defeat the jihadists, but Jared

Thompson, AKA, the Blind Man, is thirsty for blood and vengeance as he unleashes his nuclear arsenal on the Shadow Militia.

Will the Shadow Militia and the people of Iroquois, joined by patriots all over America, be able to defeat the Blind Man and his arsenal of hatred and insatiable lust for power?

The story begins where it left off. I am proud to give you … *The Blind Man's Rage*!

PROLOGUE

JARED **T**HOMPSON SAT ANXIOUSLY on the couch inside his spacious office deep in the underground complex somewhere near Spruce Mountain, West Virginia. This bunker was not quite as deep as his previous complex in western Pennsylvania, but that complex had been destroyed by ... The Blind Man didn't even want to think about the man's name right now. He couldn't recall a time in his life when he'd been this furious. Try as he might, he couldn't shake the anger and hatred he felt for General Rodney T. Branch of the Shadow Militia.

Spruce Mountain was nice, but much smaller and less technologically advanced than his previous headquarters. But, thanks to Rodney Branch, his underground Pennsylvania palace was now glowing in the dark for the next five thousand years.

Jared's back sank into the plushness of the corinthian leather couch as he gazed up, transfixed on the large video screen in his office. He propped up his feet onto the mahogany coffee table as the white-hot vortex of the nuclear explosion over Escanaba raced upward. Then, as it reached higher alti-

1

tudes, it began to cool, to billow outward, and then the mushroom cloud was formed.

The Blind Man loved a good mushroom cloud.

Strictly, from a tactical perspective, even as he was giving the order to vaporize the small city in Michigan's Upper Peninsula, Jared knew it wasn't the best use of his limited nuclear arsenal. But, for the first time in his life, he couldn't help himself. He had to do something. He demanded satisfaction. His usual patience was gone, and, in the aftermath and fury of his most recent defeat, Jared felt an uncontrollable urge to strike back at his enemy.

As he watched the mushroom cloud, race upward, billow, form and then spread out across the horizon, he achieved a perverse satisfaction, knowing that General Branch was watching it too, or, better yet ... maybe he was even dead, burned to death inside the heat of a thousand suns.

But, there was something that Jared did not know ...

St. Ignace, Upper Peninsula

SEVEN HUNDRED MILES AWAY FROM SPRUCE MOUNTAIN, General Rodney T. Branch watched the same mushroom cloud form over the now irradiated city of Escanaba. A soft smile touched his lips as he looked over at his friend Colonel MacPherson.

"Sorry Mac."

Colonel MacPherson, standing at attention as always, looked on and nodded. "You were right, general. He did exactly as you said he would. Thank God we were able to evacuate in time."

Uncle Rodney moved his hands behind his back and clasped them together as if in parade rest position. "The wind is from the southwest. We should be okay for now."

Mac relaxed his stance and turned his head to look at Rodney. "How did you know he would do this?"

The other man turned and met Mac's gaze. "I didn't. It was

just a hunch. Just human nature. We rattled him, thus forcing him to flex his muscles and reassert dominance."

The colonel's eyes narrowed. "But what if he'd chosen to flex his muscles here, in the Mackinaw straits?"

Uncle Rodney smiled. "Oops. I didn't think of that."

Mac looked at his friend in disbelief. "Oops? What do you mean oops? We could have all been melted where we stand."

The general put his hand on Mac's back and chuckled to himself. "Have I ever told you that you worry too much?"

Uncle Rodney turned to walk away and the colonel followed him. "Besides, now he feels vulnerable. He knows he's not 10 feet tall and bulletproof anymore."

Mac shook his head in disgust. "I think we just made him mad. Besides, he blew up my mansion. Where am I going to live now?"

Rodney laughed out loud. "I have an extra room in my basement. You're welcome to it."

Colonel MacPherson didn't answer his general. He just stoically trudged on behind his leader, all the while wondering ... where is he taking us now?

CHAPTER I

I T HAD BEEN ALMOST TWO WEEKS SINCE
Sammy Thurmond had watched in awe as the mighty
Mackinaw bridge had collapsed into the deep waters of
the Great Lakes. Now, he huddled beside the campfire overlooking the still-smoking rubble of Mackinaw City below.
Every morning for the past two weeks he'd watched the sun
rise over Lake Huron, and then each night he'd again watch
as the sun slowly slipped down into Lake Michigan, all the
while, the landscape around him soundless, except for the
birds and the rustling of the leaves on the breeze. On rough
days the white caps would kick up and lend beautiful contrast
to the blue of the straits, but Sammy didn't notice the beauty.
He had ceased to recognize natural beauty decades ago. His
one exception to that was the woman with the long, black hair
... Jackie Branch.

The day of the great battle for the straits of Mackinaw,
Sammy had called in on his satphone to report the results to
Jared Thompson, AKA, the Blind Man. His boss had been
stunned into silence for several seconds. Sammy had simply
waited through the silence, had, in fact even looked down at
his watch to time it. It had been fourteen seconds. And then
the swearing had unleashed itself. Sammy had listened dis-

passionately to his boss, almost amused at the childish lack of self-control. Then he'd looked down at the waters of the Great Lakes, still churning after the collapse of Mighty Mac, and, it was at that moment, on the fifteenth second after the great battle, that he'd decided to leave the Blind Man.

Sammy Thurmond had put the satphone down and climbed from his perch inside the bell tower of the church in Mackinaw City. Within a few hours he'd used his switchblade knife to cut open his right thigh and remove the tracking transponder inside the muscle.

That same evening he'd watched the night sky light up to the west and slightly north. It had been the unnatural light of the Blind Man's rage and had lasted for several minutes, illuminating the woods around him. Aside from a few isolated campfires of Shadow Militia soldiers, Sammy Thurmond was engulfed in darkness, and, that darkness, had brought light and clarity to his thinking. It was at that exact moment when Sammy Thurmond began contemplating his new life ... a life, without the Blind Man.

Iroquois City Rubble

NORMALLY, SHERIFF LEIF WOULD CALL A MEETING AT the courthouse, but that building, along with every other building in Iroquois had been razed to the ground. The sheriff wanted to blame Uncle Rodney, but he knew better. The town of Iroquois wasn't made of brick and stone; it was composed of flesh, blood, bone and spirit, and, because of General Rodney T. Branch, most of the people had been saved. Therefore, the town had been saved, despite its obvious lack of a skyline.

But his thoughts quickly moved to Escanaba and the brilliant flash of light they'd seen on the night of the great battle for the straits. It had been the final shot of the day, and everyone recognized that the fate of Iroquois could have been much worse.

The sheriff's thoughts were suddenly interrupted by the words of Dan Branch.

"What are we gonna do now, Joe?"

The sheriff had been in such deep thought that Dan's voice startled him. He looked over at his friend, Colonel Dan Branch, nephew to General Rodney T. Branch, commanding general of the Shadow Militia and shook his head back and forth. He answered Dan's question with one of his own.

"Where's your Uncle Rodney? Shouldn't we be asking him that question?"

Dan looked across the table at the sheriff, almost apologetically. "I think so. But he took Jackie and the baby fishing down at the Mill Pond."

The sheriff couldn't believe his ears. His head jerked up involuntarily as he spewed out a venomous response. "He's gone fishing! How is that possible? Why would he do that?"

Dan stood up and walked over to the Formica-topped counter of his Uncle Rodney's kitchen and poured himself another cup of coffee. "You want another cup?" The sheriff held his palm over the mouth of his coffee cup and shook his head. "Better not today. Cup's still half full. Besides, the caffeine gets me riled."

Dan smiled as he poured the black liquid into his cup. He was pretty sure there wasn't any caffeine in this coffee. "I think my uncle gets you riled more than anything else."

The muscles in Joe's face relaxed a bit before answering. "You got that right. I love that man like a brother, always have, but I swear to god some days ..." But Joe Leif bit his lip in restraint. "That man could make a nun swear like a drunken sailor."

Dan sat back down at the table and moved his chair forward. It scraped across the bare, wooden plank floor. Uncle Rodney didn't believe in anything fancy like carpeting or linoleum, so every room in his very modest home was bare wood. It was the same with the walls and ceiling ... just bare

7

planking or plywood or OSB, depending on what was on sale at the lumber yard or which decade he'd added that particular room. Uncle Rodney was a great general and warrior, but he'd never make a living as a carpenter.

"Escanaba is gone, Joe."

The sheriff nodded. "I know."

"Did you know that was Colonel MacPherson's home town? He grew up there and now his mansion is gone. He won't be able to replace that anytime soon."

Joe moved his hands up to the sides of his face and held them there. He massaged his temples trying to relieve the aching in his skull. "I don't understand how Rodney can go through all of this, two major battles in the matter of two months, watching thousands of people die, all the planning, the marching, all that stress and ... it's like he doesn't even feel it."

Dan smiled. He lifted the steaming cup of coffee to his lips and blew softly across the dark surface before taking a tiny sip. But Dan didn't say anything. In fact, many of the questions Joe was now asking he'd wondered about himself. How could Uncle Rodney do it all and make it look so easy, like it didn't even affect him.

"It's like the guy's a machine or something, Dan. Nothing gets to him. He just keeps right on a going like he's some deadly, nuclear-powered Everready battery or something. How does he do it? I don't get it."

Dan nodded. "I've been watching him around the baby. I think that's how he gets his batteries recharged. By playing with baby Donna. He's not nuclear charged. He's baby charged."

Joe dropped his hands to the table and met Dan's gaze. "He's baby charged? Did you just say that out loud?"

Dan laughed softly. "Yeah, it sounds stupid doesn't it. But I think it's true. I think it reminds him of why he's doing all this fighting. There are two sides to life, and baby Donna is the flip side of the coin. On one side is death and killing, misery, starvation and radiation poisoning. But, on the other, is a little baby who doesn't notice the suffering going on around her. All little children see are the good things in life. Like, playing with a stick on the ground, or eating dirt and then spitting it out cuz it doesn't taste so good."

Joe Leif turned away from the table and looked blankly at the wall. "Are all you Branch men crazy as loons?" Joe picked up his coffee mug and took a sip, but it was already cold. They called it coffee, but it was really chickory roots and a few other weeds that Joe didn't know the name of.

"Well ... I just hope he's having a good time fishing while we sit here worrying about the fate of the world." And then the eyes of the two men met again. Dan raised his coffee mug as if in toast. Joe lifted his as well and smiled sheepishly.

"To Uncle Rodney. May he catch a huge bass and figure out how to conquer the evil forces of the Blind Man in the process."

Joe nodded his head and both men took a sip of coffee in agreement. And then they talked about how much they missed real coffee, the kind from Columbia that used to be packed out on the mule of Juan Valdez. And they knew that real coffee would never come again, at least not in their lifetime.

But both men agreed that it could be worse. At least they were still alive and not glowing in the dark.

The Mill Pond

JACKIE BRANCH WATCHED FROM ACROSS THE POND AS Uncle Rodney held baby Donna on his lap with one hand and onto the old-fashioned cane fishing pole with the other. The old general was smiling as he looked down at the baby, and then Jackie saw him lightly kiss the top of her daughter's head. She had never seen him do that before. But then, this was really the first time since she'd known Uncle Rodney that she'd seen him in this type of relaxed and recreational setting.

9

Jackie looked out at the Mill Pond, at the shimmering sun on the surface of the calm water. It was a small body of water, and Dan had told her the history of it.

Iroquois City was first settled in 1867 by Major Jonathon Dremel who had served honorably for the Union Army during the Civil War between the states. He'd purchased a thousand acres of land, mostly virgin white pine forests, much of it with creeks and rivers running through the heart. Major Dremel had founded the town on his own property and built a sawmill on the Manistee River. The sawmill was the heart blood of the town, and it continued to grow and prosper all the way through the logging boom of the 1890s on up to the roaring twenties. Once the virgin pine forests were gone, the land lay desolate and exhausted of all its natural resources. Many people moved away, but some stayed on and Iroquois continued to limp along. Eventually the forests were replanted and harvested more responsibly.

At the time of the Fall just last year, the town had boasted 2,700 citizens and there was talk of putting in a WalMart. Of course, that would never happen now. This tiny Mill Pond and its mill race was the last remaining vestige of Major Jonathon Dremel and his grand vision of Iroquois City. Now, the city was in ruins, almost totally destroyed by the saracen army ... but the Mill Pond remained.

Dan had recounted beautiful stories to her about how he'd fished and swam in it as a boy, and how every generation of boy and girl had grown up around the banks of the Manistee River, swam there, fished trout, and grown to adulthood.

Jackie looked out at the peace and serenity of the pond and couldn't believe how it defied the onslaught and power of geopolitical dominance and tyranny. No matter what happened in the outside world, it remained unaffected.

She saw movement to her right and noticed Uncle Rodney and baby Donna moving toward her. Rodney sat down beside her, and the baby reached out to her. Jackie accepted her daughter readily and held the baby close, pressing her face against the top of her head, taking in the smells and feel of the child she loved the most.

"So, what do you think?"

Jackie nodded her head and smiled.

"It's beautiful, Uncle Rodney. I see why Dan was so keen on moving back here."

Uncle Rodney unfastened the top two buttons of his red flannel shirt and wiped his brow. "It's really hot today."

Jackie laughed. "Well, you are wearing a heavy, flannel shirt. Why do you do that so much?"

Rodney smiled. "Because I'm a man who knows what he likes and I'm set in my ways."

Jackie shook her head and let Donna grab onto her thumbs to play with. She took on a somber look.

"What's going to happen now, Uncle Rodney?"

But Rodney was silent. Jackie turned her head to face him.

"You already know what's going to happen to us don't you." She said it as a statement of fact and not a question at all. Rodney nodded slightly.

"I suppose I do."

"And I'm not going to like it, am I."

"Nope. I reckon you won't."

Jackie pulled her baby in tighter.

"Are we going to die?"

Uncle Rodney smiled and ran his right hand across the top of his head from front to back, wiping the sweat away from his short crew-cut hair.

"I heard an interesting statistic the other day. According to a recent study done by the federal government, one out of every one person is going to die at one time in their life."

Jackie looked over at him and shook her head.

"That's stupid."

Uncle Rodney looked off to one side at the grass and then back at the pond. "No, seriously, it was a very important study funded by the government. I guess it cost the tax payers pretty near a hundred million dollars to figure that out."

Jackie responded softly. "Well, at least they won't be wasting any more of our tax dollars for a very long time."

Uncle Rodney looked down at the ground between his legs. He was sitting with his butt planted firmly on the grassy, moist bank of the pond. "Well, truth is Jackie, we all know we're going to die. That's a given. We don't know when or where and we don't know how. But ... maybe the more important thing is to pick a cause worth dying for." And then he glanced down at Donna. "Like that little baby there."

Rodney reached up and stroked his chin and the left side of his face with his right hand. "I spent my whole life getting ready for this final moment in the world's history." He paused a few seconds. "Most people have the luxury of growing up and falling in love, getting married and then they spend the rest of their lives creating beautiful memories for their kids and grand kids."

He looked over at Jackie and their eyes locked.

"That didn't happen to us, Jackie. For whatever reason, it just didn't happen to us."

Jackie shrugged her shoulders lightly and looked back out at the water. "That sucks."

"It would appear that our job is to reset society to its place of normalcy. Our job is to win this war, defeat the tyrant, and rebuild."

Jackie nodded. "I suppose so." She waited a moment as if contemplating a higher question. "And what happens after that?"

Rodney's eyes took on a faraway gaze as he answered. "I don't know, Jackie. By then I'll be dead and you'll be an old woman. I guess the only one who can answer that question is the baby in your arms and the one still growing in your womb. After all, they can only build on what we leave them."

He waited a moment. "So ... let's leave them both the

ability to choose a good life and the freedom to start all over again."

Jackie kissed the top of baby Donna's head and looked out at the water. "I wish I had a boring life ... that all this conflict had never come to me."

She looked over to see Rodney smiling from ear to ear. "What? What did I say?"

He shook his head before speaking. "Look at what you've done in the past ten months little lady. You've lived a lifetime of adventure that few people in history ever experience. Some day, if humanity survives, future generations will be reading about you and Dan and I and everything we've done."

The old general looked down at the water ten feet in front of him. "That excites the hell outta me!"

And, it was at that moment, that very exact moment in time when Jackie finally understood her Uncle Rodney. She knew that he would never give up, that he would sooner die than give in to the Blind Man. It was as if Rodney had been pre-programmed before the dawn of time, before his birth, before the very foundations of the world to be exactly what and who he was at that very moment. And, if that were true, then she too, was destined to be sitting on the banks of the Mill Pond at this very moment, waiting patiently for the next battle, for the next round of killing and dying and overthrowing of tyranny.

She looked over at her uncle. "I suppose you're right."

Rodney smiled. "Jackie, when you get as old as I am, you realize that you're no longer fighting for your own future, but for the future of the ones you love, and, maybe, even for the future of strangers. Truth is I've got more life behind me than in front of me. I've lived a good life and it's been long. My only reason for existing right now is to kill the Blind Man."

That last sentence made Jackie want to cry, but she held it in, knowing instinctively that it wouldn't be appreciated. Jackie held baby Donna up to her face and kissed her on the forehead. Then, she girded up the loins of her heart to begin the next fight. She prayed to God she'd be equal to the challenge. She didn't want to let Uncle Rodney down. And she knew, in her heart of hearts, no matter what the task demanded of her, she knew that he was worthy of her devotion and sacrifice.

And through all these thoughts of profundity, the Mill Pond didn't care. It shimmered on, oblivious to the Blind Man and his evil, oblivious to the nobility and courage of Uncle Rodney.

CHAPTER 2

<u>*August 2 - Spruce Mountain*</u>

THE BLIND MAN WAS SITTING ON his couch, made of corinthian leather staring into the fireplace. It was a fake fire with just an electric log that glowed and dimmed in a preprogrammed sequence. If not for the Shadow Militia, he would already have the country pacified and he'd be living in the mansion of his choice by the seashore. He'd been looking at the map and plenty of photos, and had decided on somewhere in Florida. Problem was there was just too much resistance down south yet, and up north for that matter.

Things were definitely not going as planned. And now ... he'd lost his best and most trusted servant. Sammy Thurmond hadn't been heard from for over two weeks now, and that worried him. He looked down at the coffee table, and his eyes rested on the satellite phone. One of his Special Forces Teams had found it in a bell tower of a church overlooking Mackinaw City. He'd read the report a dozen times and even personally questioned the team leader. There were no signs of struggle, no blood, no notes, no clues of any kind as to the whereabouts of Sammy Thurmond. Even his tracking chip had stopped functioning.

Jared was a distrusting man by nature, that's how he'd managed to stay alive for so long in so dangerous a business, but ... he just couldn't imagine ... he let the thought pass him by in disbelief. Not Sammy. Not Sammy Thurmond. No ... never. He wouldn't do that. Perhaps he'd been captured by the Shadow Militia.

But the uneasy feeling in the pit of his stomach wouldn't go away. If the Shadow Militia had captured him ... the possibilities made him shiver. He reached down and picked up the decanter to pour himself another scotch. It would be so much better if Sammy was dead.

Yes, if General Branch had Sammy Thurmond ... it was a whole new ball game. He sipped the scotch, let it burn his throat and slip on down.

Shadow Militia Intelligence

Special Agent Jeff Arnett was a tall man, well over six feet, with a hawkish nose and eyes that could penetrate steel. He sat in the pole barn surrounded by desks and computers. There was a naked light bulb over his own desk that hurt his eyes, but was necessary if he was going to light up the darkness of the big room. He looked down at the thumb drive on the desk, as well as the rolled-up papers laid out before him. The container this information had been housed in was off to his left. It was a length of white, PVC pipe, about six inches long and an inch in diameter.

General Branch had given it to him shortly after returning from the Straits of Mackinaw. When he'd been told about how Sammy Thurmond had given it to Jackie with orders to give it directly to General Branch, he'd been miffed. *How could they have been so stupid?* It could have been a bomb, or a tracking device ... or both. But, luckily, it had been just a thumb drive with data. He picked up the stack of photographs. They were all pictures of Jared Thompson, AKA, the Blind Man. They appeared to be surveillance photos, all taken from different cameras and angles. In every picture but one, Jared was wearing dark sunglasses. And that's the picture that enthralled him the most. The man's eyes ... they were scary, deep and mystifying. He'd never seen Jared's eyes before. After all, they were always covered with dark glasses. But ... there was something spooky about this picture. The eyes ... the eyes ... what was it about those eyes. And then it hit him.

These eyes were not blind.

Jeff reached down and picked up a can of Mountain Dew soda. It was warm, and it was, so far as he knew, the last can of Dew in the county, or maybe even the state. Mountain Dew had always been his vice, but ... it just didn't taste so good when it was room temperature. He thought to himself, *probably just as well. If you can't pronounce the ingredients, it can't be good for you.*

But his dilemma remained. What to do about this thumb drive. He had to find out what was on it, but, ... it came from a hostile and unreliable source. For god's sake this man was Sammy Thurmond, the Blind Man's right-hand man, the only person in the world who had his trust. His imagination began to run wild. There could be all manner of malicious software on that drive. He couldn't very well open it with any of the machines connected to a network. He had to isolate it and then study it.

But one thing was certain. He had to find out what was on that drive. The Shadow Militia, if they were to defeat Jared Thompson, would need an edge they didn't presently have ... maybe ... even a miracle.

Marine in Love

THERE WAS AN INCREDIBLE SHORTAGE OF FAT PEOPLE IN the world these days. Sergeant Donny Brewster looked out across the encampment at the hundred or so Home Guard soldiers and couldn't help but notice how gaunt they all looked. He didn't think there was a fat body within five-hundred miles of here. Come to think of it, most of the people who were left, were all pretty lean and healthy. The diabetics were all dead. Anyone with heart disease or who depended on medication for survival had died long ago. Without the benefits of modern medicine, nature and law of the jungle had pretty much taken control and thinned the herd. Donny wondered if that was a good or a bad thing. He pretty much thought in black and white. On the one hand, it was good that people were strong, spirited and on their feet working again. Society before the Fall had become nothing but a culture of slackers and snowflakes ... weak, unmotivated ... a culture of selfish consumers and worthless eaters. But now ... now they were lean and strong and perhaps more alive than at any other time in their lives.

But ... at what cost?

So many millions had died. More than millions, hundreds of millions, maybe even billions across the globe. All because of what? Selfish men and their quests for power?

But society had always been like that, all throughout human history. There had always been one man who wanted to dominate another, the strong who controlled the weak and who were willing to kill and enslave to get and maintain that power.

And that's where Donny Brewster came in. He was strong, but he was different. He was willing to kill to protect the weak. He thought about it for a moment. No, he was more than willing. In times like these ... he was eager to kill.

"A penny for your thoughts, Marine."

Donny looked up and saw Lisa Vanderboeg, the woman of his dreams. And he thought to himself *What a terrible time to fall in love.* He stood up quickly, straight as an iron rod, to his full six feet of height and muscle, almost at position of attention. He saw her smile and the gleam in her eyes and began to relax. She put her arms around him and bent her head up to kiss him on the cheek.

"Nurse Vanderboeg. It's good to see you again."

The pretty, young woman, in her late twenties, kicked him

in the left shin and squeezed him tighter.

"Don't be stoic with me, Donny! You know you love me and I own you now. So tell me ..." She pulled him closer. "What were you thinking about?"

Donny smiled and looked down at the beautiful woman. Her blonde hair had lengthened since their first meeting, and it fell down onto her shoulders again. The Marine sniper reached up and touched her face with his left hand. A month ago she'd acted like she hated him, and now ... it was like she'd always loved him, like she'd been born and bred for him specifically. He didn't understand women.

"And why should I tell you what I'm thinking? I'm a Marine. I'm stoic, remember?"

Lisa's smile broadened. "It's because I'll kick you in the shin again if you don't do as I say."

Donny laughed out loud for the first time since the Battle of Mackinaw. "That tells me that you trust me."

The petite blonde pushed away just far enough to look him in the eyes, but still held on to his waist.

"How so, Marine?"

Donny's handsome face and white teeth shone in the mid-day summer sunlight. "Because I'm bigger and stronger than you. I could crush the life out of you with my bare hands, but still ... you trust me enough to kick me in the shins. You know I won't hurt you and I respect that."

Lisa cocked her head slightly to one side as if perplexed. "You are in dire need of therapy, young man." And then without warning, she kicked him again.

This time it hurt, but Donny didn't show it. "Wow! You must really be stuck on me!" And then he put his arms around her and pulled her closer. "Tell me you love me."

Donny felt her body tense up and pull away. Without warning or hesitation, she turned and walked back the same way she had come, leaving him alone with this awkward moment. Just then Jason Little walked up. Jason was six and a half feet tall, an accountant before the Fall, but now cross-trained into something useful, an infantry officer.

"What was that all about?"

Donny shrugged, still looking after her as she stomped away from them. "She just loves me, that's all."

"Oh." Jason looked confused. "It looked to me like she got mad at you, kicked you and walked away."

Donny turned and strode over to teach his class on close quarters combat. "I know. Ain't love grand?"

Jason followed him, all the while shaking his head more confused than ever.

August 3 - Near Pellston, Michigan

SAMMY THURMOND HAD BEEN ON THE ROAD FOR TWO weeks now. After ditching his satphone and digging the tracker out of his leg, he'd wasted no time in traveling west down Wilderness Park Drive and then to the south. He'd stayed east of the Lake Michigan shoreline, traveling only at night and sleeping during the day. He ate mostly roots, berries and edible plants. At first he'd tried to forage from nearby houses, but there was just no food to be found. When he got really hungry, he shot a rabbit or squirrel and ate that. He didn't take a chance on building a fire - he just ate the meat raw. It felt good to be out on his own again, not beholden to the Blind Man or the government or anyone else.

Sammy was in no hurry. He just took his time, taking in the water of the many lakes and ponds and streams along the way, the sunrise, the sunset, the smells of the woods and the darkness of the night. It gave him time to think and time to plan. But most of all - he thought of her. That woman. The special one. She intrigued him, enthralled him, consumed his every waking moment. And he knew where she would be, where she must be.

For the very first time in his life, Sammy had no detailed plans. All he knew was that he wanted to see Jackie Branch again, and that he wanted to meet Rodney T. Branch, commanding general of the Shadow Militia.

Iroquois County

"WOMEN AREN'T LIKE THAT, DONNY! YOU CAN'T TELL them you can crush the life out of them and expect a good response!"

Dan Branch and Donny Brewster were practicing hand-to-hand combat in a small clearing behind Uncle Rodney's house. It was early afternoon, and the sun was beating down hard on them both, causing sweat to bead up and quickly run off their faces and backs in tiny rivers. Dan faked with a left jab and came across hard with his right fist. The padded glove struck Donny on the left side of his face sending him crashing to the ground.

"Come on, Donny. You're not even trying today! Will you please try to focus."

The marine sniper shook his head from side to side. He got up doggedly to his feet and held up his gloves again.

"I can't help it, Dan. I just keep thinking about her. I want to fix it, but I don't know how. It's like if things aren't right with her then nothing else in my life is right either."

Dan lowered his gloves. "Really? It's that bad?"

His friend nodded and then walked over to the old oak stump ten feet away and sat down. Dan walked over too, rolled an oak log about 24 inches long onto its end and sat down beside him.

"It sounds like you're in love, Donny. That's the only thing that can mess up a man that much."

"Well, I don't much like it, Dan." Then he thought for a moment and shook his head as if trying to clear away the cobwebs in his mind. "Actually, I am in love with her. I want to marry her. And I'd be happy about it if she wanted to marry me too. But ... something's holding her back. It's like she loves me and hates me at the same time. It's confusing."

Dan Branch laughed out loud. "So she hates you one day and loves you the next. That sounds pretty normal to me."

Donny shook his head from side to side and then spit some phlegm off to his right. "No. That's not it. She doesn't hate me one day and love me the next, it's like she hates me and loves me simultaneously. It's like she's two women trapped in the same body."

Dan thought for a moment. "Didn't her husband die just a few days after the Fall?"

The birds were singing in the trees about fifty yards to the left. They sounded beautiful, and Donny wanted to shoot them all.

"Yeah, something like that. He was killed by some neanderthal thugs in Grand Rapids. I guess it was pretty hard on her and it took a while to get over it."

Dan glanced up and over at his friend. "Donny that was less than a year ago. She's not over it yet - not by a long shot."

Donny raised his head and looked over at Dan. "Really?"

Dan nodded. "Yup."

"So how long does it take? It won't be too long will it?"

Dan Branch smiled sympathetically and looked back down at the grass in front of them."It might take the rest of her life, Donny. People just don't get over things like that."

Donny bent his neck down and held his head between his hands. He rubbed his temples as if he had a migraine.

"I don't think I can wait that long, Dan."

Dan reached over and placed his hand on Donny's back and patted it firmly.

"You won't have to Donny boy. But you will have to be patient and try to understand her point of view."

Donny grunted. "So what's her point of view?"

With his free hand, Dan rubbed his aching knee from front to back while gathering his thoughts. His knee had been bothering him ever since the march back from Mackinaw City.

"My first wife killed herself right after the Fall."

Donny's back stiffened. "Really?"

Dan nodded. "She was cheating on me again, and Jeremy and I were coming to get her on our way to Iroquois. We found her in bed with her lover. He was already dead and she tried to shoot me with a shotgun when I came to rescue her."

Donny looked on in disbelief.

"An hour later she died of an overdose."

All of a sudden Donny felt very clumsy and needed to get away, but he forced himself to engage at least on a surface level for his friend.

"Sorry, man. I don't know what to say about that."

"You don't have to say anything, Donny. You just have to listen and try to understand." Dan rubbed his chin a moment before moving on. "Lisa still loves her husband just the same way that I still love Debbie."

Donny interrupted him. "You still love Debbie ... even after she cheated on you?"

Dan nodded. "So imagine how much Lisa still loves her husband after having a child with her. They had a happy family. She was forced to watch him die and there was nothing she could do to save him, even though she was a nurse."

Donny looked out into the woods and sighed. "She must feel terrible."

"It's worse than that, Donny. She feels terrible about losing the love of her life. She lost her home. Her daughter lost her daddy. She's been forced to kill to stay alive. That doesn't come natural to her. And some goon like you comes along and she falls in love again before she's ready. And that makes her feel guilty, because she knows she should still be grieving for the loss of her husband."

Donny felt blown away. "How do women feel so many things at the same time? I think my head would explode."

Dan shook his head in frustration. "I don't know. It boggles the mind."

"So what should I do?"

For the longest while Dan didn't answer him, and, when he did, it was in a hushed voice, forcing Donny to perk up and listen to every word.

"Don't talk so much. Just listen to her. Be patient. Don't talk about love. Let her have control of the relationship. Just take your cues from her and everything will be alright."

Donny stood up abruptly. "I guess I should go talk to her now."

"No! That's exactly what you shouldn't do." Dan motioned with his hand for him to sit back down. "You need to think about this for a while first. Give it a day or two. Go slow. Slow is good - fast is bad. That's your new mantra."

Donny nodded his head up and down. "Something tells me this is going to be tougher than a fifteen-hundred yard head shot."

Dan agreed in silence. They both stood up now and began walking back to the house.

"You might talk to Jackie about it too. She seems to understand women better than I do, and she's been through the same things as Lisa."

Donny nodded. "Yeah. Kind of like being on an intelligence-gathering operation."

Dan reached over and slapped the other man on the left shoulder. "Donny, welcome to the female world."

And then to himself he added, *This woman has you, and you don't stand a chance.*

CHAPTER 3

August 4 - the Blind Man's Lair

"I WANT YOU TO HUNT HIM DOWN AND bring him back to me!" Jared Thompson looked dispassionately into the face of the man before him. Jared waited only briefly for a response before lashing out.

"Do you understand!?"

The young lieutenant, a former Special Ops soldier from France, nodded his head, snapped to attention and rendered his best salute.

"Yes, sir! It will be done, sir!"

Jared didn't return the salute. He never did. That was beneath him. "Do you have any questions?"

The lieutenant hesitated but then finally spit it out. "What should we do, sir, if ... Mr. Thurmond resists us?"

A smile moved over Jared's face like plastic melting in the hot July sun. When he answered, it was a venomous spewing. "I never said he had to be alive. I just want him back."

The young officer nodded before executing a perfect about-face and exiting the room. Once the door to the Blind Man's lair closed shut behind him, he stopped and looked down at the floor. *Why was the Blind Man doing this?* But he quickly shook the thought out of his mind before striding away in a military fashion.

"It's none of my business. Just do your job. Follow orders. Do your job and don't ask questions."

The young officer wiped the ambivalence from his mind, already starting to plan the details of the coming rescue operation, or assassination, or ... whatever it turned out to be.

The French lieutenant had always been a practical man, bent on success and a rapid rise in the ranks. His home country was in chaos, as was the rest of Europe. When he'd gotten this opportunity in America, he'd jumped at the chance. But ... he was slowly figuring out that America wasn't much better off than the rest of the world.

But ... at least here he had creature comforts and he could practice his trade. That was something to build on ... at least for now.

Young Sniper's Remorse

JEREMY BRANCH SAT ON THE HARD, WOODEN BENCH beside the grave of his grandfather. This was his father's father, a man he'd never met and knew very little about. But today, the relative stranger would be his closest friend.

"You've never met me, but I'm Jeremy Branch, Dan's boy. I guess I'm your grandson, technically I'm not cuz your son isn't really my dad, but ..." Jeremy looked off across the spattering of granite and marble headstones to make sure no one was listening or watching.

"Family life today is pretty complicated. Your son married my mom, and I was already born at the time. So I guess technically I'm your step-grandson and you're my step-grandad."

Jeremy was wearing faded, blue, cut-off shorts, with the hem of the pant legs frayed and blowing slightly in the gentle, July breeze.

"My dad still loves you. I thought you might want to know that. He didn't always understand you, but ... I think that's pretty normal in the whole father-son thing."

Jeremy looked down at an ant crawling up his ankle. He

moved his hand down to squash it, but then stopped. He looked at the ant, moved his left hand up to it, and the tiny ant crawled on top of his hand and across his palm without so much as a hesitation. Jeremy watched the tiny bug for a few seconds and then gently laid him back on the grass beside his feet.

"I needed someone to talk to, someone I didn't know and who could keep a confidence. I figure since you're dead that wouldn't be a problem for you." Jeremy smiled sadly. "After all, you've got plenty of time and it's not like you're going anywhere real soon." The noon sun was high in the sky, and Jeremy was grateful for the relative cool of the shade. "And it's not likely you'll gossip to anyone about this - at least not with anyone I know."

There was a white pine tree off to his left about twenty-four inches in diameter, then an oak tree straight behind him about ten feet away.

"I like to come here. It's peaceful and no one interrupts my thoughts." Jeremy ran his left hand through his scalp from front to back. A residue of grease and sweat was left on his hand, so he wiped it off on his t-shirt. "I'm only sixteen years old, but I've learned that the dead can be very polite and accommodating. And ..." He hesitated before coming to the crux of the matter. "... very non judgmental."

"I've done a lot of bad things in my life. I took advantage of Tonya, our neighbor girl from Wisconsin. At the time I thought it was okay - that I deserved to make myself happy. But ... since then I've learned that it's not okay to be selfish if it hurts other people."

Jeremy wrung his hands together nervously. "I've killed a lot of people. If my count is correct, about 47 so far." He looked up at the sky. "I want you to know that I didn't enjoy it, that it's killing a part of me to do it, and that I'll probably have to do it again."

Jeremy looked down at the granite head stone, then back

up at the sky, as if suddenly realizing he was talking to a dead person when he should be talking to the living God. He glanced back up into the sky and thought a moment.

"What should I do?"

There was no answer.

"Can you tell me what to do?"

There was a loud buzzing noise of a cicada coming from way up in the oak tree behind him. The breeze suddenly picked up, and it caressed his face softly, easing his tension, encouraging him and causing him to open up and talk more about his heart.

"I felt terrible when I shot that first man, but ..." Tears welled up into his eyes. "But if I hadn't, then, my dad would probably be dead right now. I felt like I didn't have a choice."

The cicada stopped buzzing, and another ant crawled up his ankle, the right one this time. He looked down and watched it. The ant's tiny legs tickled his skin.

"I don't think I'm a very good soldier. I'm not like Donny, or my dad or my Uncle Rodney." He paused. "They seem to do it so gracefully, like it's second nature to them, like it doesn't bother them at all."

Jeremy propped his right ankle atop his left knee and watched the ant's progress from a closer vantage point. He was amazed at how resilient the little insect was. It just kept crawling over one obstacle after another, never giving up, never hesitating, almost as if every time it faced a challenge, it became stronger and more determined to move forward.

And then it hit him. He was describing his Uncle Rodney. General Rodney T. Branch was like the ant. Always slugging along, never stopping, never pausing, never hesitating to mourn. He simply, in machine-like fashion, overcame the next challenge and then moved on.

"I just have to get through this next battle don't I. I just have to keep fighting until the bad guys are all dead, and then I can rest and maybe get back to normal." But, in his heart,

Jeremy knew there was no normal - not anymore. But he needed to believe that it could happen again, that he could regain his innocence, that some day he could go back on the playground and take up where he left off before the Fall and finish recess.

He glanced over at his M4 carbine leaning against the bench beside him. Just a few months ago he would have been honored and yearning to carry that gun. But now ... it was a curse to him, a burden that weighed a million pounds.

He looked back up at God. "Lord, if you're up there, if you really do care about me, then please help me get through this last battle. I need to stay human, and I need a reason to live."

The cicada started buzzing again, so Jeremy stood resolutely to his feet, leaned over and picked up his carbine. With one fluid movement, the action of a seasoned warrior, Jeremy slung it on his back and marched away. Almost casually, he turned his head and called out behind him.

"Nice meeting you, Gramps."

And then the boy, now a man unaware, trudged off through the cemetery, down the hill and back to Uncle Rodney's house.

The cicada looked down at the grave and wondered if God would answer the boy's prayer. But it was just a cicada, just a bug, and in a bug's life things like that were unimportant. The cicada ceased its buzzing. The ant looked up and the breeze became silent again.

Uncle Rodney HQ

"SO WHY DO YOU WANT ME TO LOCATE THIS MAN? I don't get it. Why is he so important?"

Special Agent, Jeff Arnett, head of the Shadow Militia intelligence gathering unit, bore his hawk-like eyes into the hard skull of General Rodney T. Branch. Rodney met the tall man's gaze with a casual air that he wasn't used to. Most people were intimidated by his demeanor and presence, but not Uncle Rodney. He just soaked it all in as if amused.

"That's a good question, Jeff." The general was dressed in a red flannel shirt and faded, dirty blue jeans. He'd just been hoeing the tomatoes in his small garden on the south side of his house and hadn't cleaned up yet.

"I strongly believe this man is the key to final victory in our fight against the Blind Man."

Jeff Arnett's staunch eyes perked up and he leaned in closer. "I'm listening."

Uncle Rodney leaned over in his chair to the left so he could remove a knife from his right pocket. Jeff saw the knife come out and instinctively moved back a hair. Uncle Rodney pretended not to notice.

"He's a weapons designer that Mac used to know 20 years ago." With a flick of his right wrist, the knife blade came out, and Rodney began to clean the black dirt of his garden out from under his finger nails.

"Okay. I can see where that would be helpful. But, we already have tons of weapon's designs, but they're useless without the industrial capacity to manufacture them."

Rodney nodded. "Correct. And that's what makes this man so important. He specializes in nineteenth-century weapons manufacture. He can design weapons that can be mass produced and built without electricity."

Jeff was interested now. "What kind of weapons systems?"

Rodney reached down to pick up his mug of tea. He took a sip and placed the mug back onto the table. It really wasn't tea in the traditional sense. It was made from the red berries of staghorn sumac, and had a distinct lemony flavor to it. Rodney had shown Jackie how to find and harvest the berries. At first he hadn't liked the beverage, but had eventually gotten used to it. It was true, he still had a few hundred pounds of coffee and black tea in storage, but he wanted to live like everyone else, lest jealousy set in and become a wedge to weaken his leadership.

"Mortars, rockets, cannons ..." then he hesitated before

continuing. "Atomic bombs."

Jeff Arnett's eyes jerked up and met Rodney's gaze.

"Did you say atomic bombs?"

Rodney nodded. Jeff Arnett leaned forward and placed both elbows on the Formica top of Uncle Rodney's kitchen table.

"Since when are atomic bombs nineteenth-century weapons?"

Uncle Rodney smiled. "Well, atoms have been around a long time, Mr. Arnett. And this guy is a man of many talents."

The tall man, suddenly grasping the importance, placed his chin atop his fists as he spoke.

"So what's this guy's name?"

Rodney took another sip from his mug before answering him.

"His name is Justice ... Justice Reed."

August 4, Coker Creek, Tennessee

JUSTICE REED LIVED A FEW MILES UP THE MOUNTAIN IN the heart of the Chippewa National Forest near a tiny town called Coker Creek. He lived there by design, to get away from people and all things modern. Tellico Mountain was just to the north, and Farner Mountain was to the south. He was at a place near where Georgia, Tennessee and North Carolina all converged in the southeast corner of the state. The trout fishing was good, and no one bothered him here. Justice planned on dying here on his porch, whenever God saw fit to take him. If he became sick, he wouldn't fight the inevitable, he'd just let life take its natural course, and one-hundred years from now he imagined some weary traveler would find his dried-out body still attached to this very porch swing.

Right now Justice Reed's only goal in life was to drink himself into a belated grave.

He took a drink of his dandelion wine and placed the Mason jar back on his lap. Then he began to rock slowly back and forth in the shade of his porch swing. No one knew he was up here. He closed his eyes and listened to the birds. It was hot on the mountain, but a little cooler in the shade of his cabin. Justice Reed was seventy-six years old, and he hadn't ventured down the mountain in over seven years. He didn't have to. Everything he needed was right here at his homestead.

Every night he listened to his solar-powered radio for the news. Well, every night until over a year ago when everything suddenly went silent. He knew what had happened, and he was probably the only person on the planet who wasn't adversely affected by it. He grew his own food, had running water, minimal power requirements, and had neither need nor desire for human companionship.

The old man looked ancient and frail, not an ounce over one-hundred and thirty-five pounds soaking wet. The skin on his face appeared to be draped over his skull and then pasted down with Elmer's glue and then stapled on the very edges. He looked out at the kudzu vines growing anywhere they could find sunlight and couldn't help but wonder, *can I make wine out of that?*

Justice Reed was a certified genius. A nuclear physicist with advanced degrees in Chemical Engineering, Electrical Engineering, Aerospace Technology, Military History and Mechanical Engineering. It had always been his goal to be a well-rounded scientist, but to also be practical. That's why he'd diversified his education more than others. Over the years, before his failed life-long experiment with inebriation, Justice had worked at a lot of different jobs: Chief Engineer of a nuclear power plant, advanced weapons designer for the Department of Defense, as well as a short stint as an illegal arms dealer.

It was that last one which had caused him most of his grief. In fact, he'd spent several years in a federal prison before being pardoned by the last president, in return for a five-year commitment to help design a miniaturized atomic weapons system. That had been fifteen years ago, and he hadn't enjoyed it at all, aside from the challenge of it and the unlimited budget.

The problem was this: Justice Reed liked to work alone, and he just didn't work and play well with others. That, and his addictive personality. He took another drink of the wine, this time letting it linger at the back of his throat before swallowing.

There was movement to his right, down at floor level, and Justice looked down to see a small mouse scamper across the broken-down porch floor of his house. He didn't like mice; they carried too many diseases and they pooped all over everything. They bred like rabbits, and if he didn't do anything about it, they'd soon over-run him from his own home.

He made a mental note to build a better mouse trap.

There was a book beside him, a hardback, and he picked it up and opened it to his bookmark. He read it out loud to himself.

1 Peter 4:2-3
New International Version (NIV)

2 As a result, they do not live the rest of their earthly lives for evil human desires, but rather for the will of God.
3 For you have spent enough time in the past doing what pagans choose to do—living in debauchery, lust, drunkenness, orgies, carousing and detestable idolatry.

Justice put the Bible back down on the bench and looked out at the woods around him. And then he said out loud, "That about sums it up for me."

Indeed, he had spent enough time on drunkenness and debauchery, that was true enough and he couldn't deny it. He wondered what would have happened with his life if he'd not given himself over to the bottle, had not dived headlong into immorality for all those years. And now ... now he was old and all used up. And he wondered ... was the part in the Bible about grace and forgiveness really true? He understood the law and justice and wrath, but ... Justice did not fully understand Jesus. And, most of all, he wondered if it was too late for him to change course.

He decided that he regretted his youthful indiscretions, and would try to do it different in another life, if it was given to him.

Then he thought about verse 2, about doing the will of God, and he wondered, how does anyone know the will of God. Does He tell them in dreams or visions? He just didn't know these things, but had a desire to find out. He made a mental note to himself: *After I finish that mouse trap I'll find out what is the will of God.*

He thought about the state of the world, the anarchy, the chaos, the violence and the mayhem ... about what he would cook for dinner tonight. And then it occurred to him that none of these things really mattered ... except for the dinner.

Justice picked up the Mason jar and drank until it consumed him. He fell asleep on the porch swing, and slept right on through dinner, unaware that the mouse had gone inside his home and had eaten his fill with impunity.

Lake Michigan - 50 miles offshore

JEFF ARNETT SAT IN THE CAPTAIN'S CHAIR ON THE SMALL charter fishing boat with the laptop on his thighs. The thumb drive from Sammy Thurmond was in his right hand, poised over the USB port on the side.

He wanted to put it in the computer. The curiosity was driving him crazy, and General Branch had ordered him in the most clear terms to do so, but ... it just didn't make any sense to him. Why would the Blind Man's right-hand man give them anything of value? The spook part of him distrusted ... but the human part of him hoped.

In the end, he inserted the thumb drive into the USB port

and waited for the hard drive to be erased or for a cruise missile to come crashing down on him. If he was the Blind Man, that's what he'd have done ... given them a carrot of hope, a deadly carrot to annihilate them once and for all.

But there was no virus - no sirens, no bells or whistles, not even a cruise missile. Just a prompt that said:

"Enter Code Key."

The sun was shining down on him, making it hard to see past the glare of the laptop screen. He typed in a few random keys and pressed enter. Almost immediately the screen shot back:

"Incorrect Code Key."

He tried another with the same results.

Then, he entered a third sequence and the response surprised him.

"Patience is a virtue."

Jeff Arnett swore under his breath. He didn't have time for patience or virtues or some smart-aleck software programmer with a perverse sense of humor. He didn't have time for anything except quick and easy success. He thought for a moment, and finally closed the laptop and stood to his feet. He would need his lab to break the code, but at least he knew it was safe to work with back at Iroquois.

Jeff motioned for his bodyguard to tell the captain they were heading back to land. He looked over the side of the boat and felt a sudden queasiness. The motion of the boat, rocking up and down on the swells caused the bile to rise in his throat. He leaned over the railing and emptied the contents of his stomach into the water. He suddenly felt very, very poorly. And then he thought to himself ... *What hope do we have of winning? We don't have a chance.*

CHAPTER 4

GENERAL RODNEY T. BRANCH, flanked on the left by Colonel MacPherson, moved on down the line from one soldier to the next. If the Blind Man knew the condition of the men opposing him, he would laugh out loud and be renewed with confidence.

"What's your name corporal?"

The man in front of him was about sixty-five years old, but, based on the way he looked, Rodney guessed he didn't have too many more winters in front of him.

"Eric Olsen, suh." The man's voice was raspy and old, like worn out sandpaper. Most of his teeth were rotting or missing completely.

Rodney nodded. "What's your job, soldier?"

The old man's eyes darted back and forth for just a second, then fixed back down on the general's collar button. Rodney noticed the nervousness.

"My job's ta try'n stay alive 'n send my men back ta the ones that love 'em."

The general smiled and then nodded. The man was a soldier, but he had no uniform - none of them did. They were dressed in various shades and designs of camouflage, denim and canvas. Most of them had been farmers and blue-collar workers before the Fall.

"Sounds like we got the same job, corporal." He thought he saw the corporal's weary eyes almost smile.

Then he paused. "So, corporal, do you have any advice for the general?"

The old soldier wasn't sure he was hearing correctly, so he paused for a full ten seconds before answering.

"Well, suh, the way I see it we got two choices. We kin kick this Blind Dude's ass or he kin kick ours. I perfer we kick his. I just wanna gitter dun so's I kin get back home 'n pick my corn."

The general nodded his head in thanks and then moved on down the line with the colonel in tow closely behind him. Every so often he would stop and converse briefly. His intent was to assess the individual character of the men which always gave him a good assessment of the fighting capability of the unit as a whole.

When they were done, the troops were dismissed and Rodney and Mac returned to the command tent. Major General Masbruch was already there waiting for them.

Rodney returned his salute sharply, and then the two men hesitated briefly before sitting down at the folding table in front of them.

"It's good to see you again, Dale. You've done a great job building up this army down here and to the east."

General Masbruch's hard, green eyes looked first at Colonel MacPherson and then back at his commanding general. "Well, Rodney, it's not like I had much of a choice. We didn't have squat six months ago. We had to do something."

Uncle Rodney nodded and smiled. "And now, thanks to you and your staff, we have twenty-thousand men, all trained and battle-ready."

Mac chimed in from the left side of the table. "You did a hell of a job, General Masbruch."

At first, General Masbruch smiled, but then the smile slowly faded as he began to slowly sense they were about to tell him things he didn't already know.

"Why are you two being so nice to me? And since when does Mac address me as "general?" What's going on that I don't know about?"

And then he rose to his feet, the chair almost falling down behind him. "What the hell are you two up to now?"

Rodney looked up at him and his eyes squinted tensely. "Just calm down, Dale, and sit back at the table."

Colonel MacPherson smiled and then looked down at the white, plastic folding table. "There's just a few logistical and strategic details we need to fill you in on."

Dale's green eyes narrowed fiercely, then he broke eye contact and looked out at the training camp around him. Many of his amateur soldiers were sleeping under lean-to's made of sticks, branches and moss. They couldn't even afford tents. Suddenly, General Masbruch began to understand George Washington's predicament at Valley Forge.

"All right, Rodney, give it to me straight. What are we in for?"

As General Branch spoke softly and methodically, Dale's old face sagged, then his head hung down almost until his chin touched his chest. His bald head was tanned and glistening with sweat from the severe heat and humidity of the southern summer.

Rodney pulled out some intelligence papers and maps and showed him the plan, but it did little to ease the old soldier's pain. If anything, he became even more skeptical and distraught.

Finally, General Masbruch lifted his head back up and looked Rodney square in the eyes.

"Have you completed a risk assessment of this plan, Rodney?"

Rodney said nothing.

"Hell, Rodney, you got more holes in this plan than you've got plan. It's too complicated, and there's just way too many things that can go wrong!" He was raising his voice now without even knowing it. All three men were silent for a full minute. Then General Masbruch regained his composure and looked off in the distance.

"Dale, you've got good men here. They've got spirit and they'll fight for you."

Dale looked him in the eye again. "I know that." And then he paused before getting to the heart of the matter. "They are good men. Excellent men, the best I've ever trained or served with. I know they don't look like much, but they've got more piss and vinegar than any army on this planet." He paused, looked over at Mac and then back at Rodney.

"Rodney, I want you to give me your word that my men won't die in vain. This plan of yours doesn't have much more than a snowball's chance in hell of success, so I want your very best promise that you'll do everything you can to keep my men from dying without purpose."

General Branch looked down and then over at Mac before speaking out loud. The two seemed to read each other's thoughts, and that had always bothered Masbruch. It felt like they were speaking a foreign language right there in front of him and he felt left out of the conversation. General Branch finally looked back over at him.

"You have my word of honor that your men will have a fighting chance of success, and, even if they die, it will not be in vain."

General Masbruch lowered his head again, then came back up, drew a handkerchief out of his pocket and then wiped his brow with it.

"Rodney, you are one crazy son of a bitch, but ..."

And then, it was as if a switch tripped on deep inside him and he remembered who he was. "If it can be humanly done, then we will accomplish the mission, general."

And then he stood to his feet and rendered his best military salute. Colonel MacPherson rose to his feet and saluted as well. Rodney stood slowly, as if he held the weight of the world on his shoulders, and then he summoned all his energy and saluted sharply and crisply.

After formal good byes, Rodney and Mac got in their helicopter and flew away.

General Masbruch, old, tired, worn down to the bone, sagged back down into his chair. After a few moments of rest he yelled for his aid and summoned a staff meeting. With renewed energy, he kicked himself into high gear, and it was as if he'd never been discouraged.

CHAPTER 5

Coker Creek Tennessee

HE **UH60** HELICOPTER HOVERED
two hundred feet above the clearing on the side of
the mountain. The pilot had told them to acceler-
ate their descent because of dangerous and shifting thermal
currents, so Dan Branch hesitated for just a moment before
rappeling down. He glanced over at Sergeant Donny Brewster
who was grinning from ear to ear at his longer than normal
pause. Donny lived for the excitement of danger, but Dan had
been out of the Marine Corps for many years and, to be quite
frank, never had relished jumping out of aircraft.

"Do you want me to go first and show you how it's done
old man?"

Dan grimaced and pushed himself out the door and down
the rope. It's not like he hadn't done this before; it's just that
he'd only done it a few times and he didn't enjoy heights.
About half way down the rope Donny Brewster passed him.
Dan thought to himself, *why is everything a competition to
him?* But that thought quickly left him as he looked down and
watched Donny disappear into the brush below. Dan was surprised when his legs crashed into mountain laurel and he was
turned upside down before landing on his head. Fortunately,
thick kudzu vines softened his fall, and his neck didn't break.
He felt Donny Brewster's strong hand lift him up and set him

back on his feet.

The two men quickly unhooked from the rope and the helicopter raced away to the rendezvous point several miles away.

"This stuff is so thick I can't even see through it!"

Donny nodded in agreement and quickly pulled out his machete. "It's that way, to the east." And then he began swinging his blade with enthusiasm. Dan Branch backed away just in time to keep from getting hit with it.

"Careful marine!"

But Donny just laughed and kept swinging. "Lead, follow or get out of the way, colonel."

Dan shook his head from side to side, adjusted his M4 to ride better on his front and then tightened the straps on his light pack. "Good thinking, sergeant. I think I'll just get out of the way and follow."

Donny hacked through the kudzu vines and laurel for about fifty yards before it finally gave way to pine trees and a more open terrain. They both sat down on a log to rest.

"How much further, Donny?"

The sergeant looked over at his friend with his young, green eyes and smiled. "What's the problem old man? Tired already?"

Dan frowned. He hated it when Donny made cracks about his age. "I'm not old! I'm only thirty five!"

Donny laughed out loud. "Sorry colonel. Didn't realize you were getting so cranky."

Dan took off his olive drab boonie hat and used it to wipe the sweat off his brow. The summer heat and humidity were nearly unbearable here in the mountains of Tennessee. Dan took a moment to regain his self-control.

"Stop calling me colonel when we're alone. You know I don't like that." Then he looked over at the kudzu they'd just hacked through. "So how old are you, Donny?"

Donny's green eyes seemed to sparkle in the mid-day sun.

"I'm old enough to know better."

Dan looked over at his friend and gave him a quizzical smile. "What kind of answer is that?"

Donny fished his compass out of a cargo pocket and took a compass reading. "We need to go that way, about another mile."

Donny stood up to march away, but Dan reached out and grabbed his arm. "Hold on there, sergeant. Just exactly how old are you?"

Donny smiled. "Are you pulling rank on me over a silly, little thing like my age?"

But then it was Dan's turn to laugh and he let Donny's arm go. "If it's such a silly, little thing then you certainly won't mind telling me."

"Do you really want to know?"

"Yer darn right I want to know."

Donny hesitated before answering.

"I'm thirty-five years old."

Dan's eyes opened wide with surprise. "You're the same age as me?"

Donny shook his head back and forth. "No way. You're two months older than me. I checked your records."

Dan threw his hat down on the ground before raising his voice. "For the past three months you've been calling me an old man and you're the same age as me!"

"But we're not the same age. You've got two months on me." His green eyes glanced over into the woods ahead, looking for danger. "Besides, look at you and then look at me. I'm obviously the younger, finer masculine specimen."

Dan couldn't believe he was hearing these words. "A finer, masculine specimen?" He turned his head and spit onto the ground a few feet away. "I can't believe you said that."

Donny laughed, but then his eyes narrowed and he grew strangely quiet. Dan looked at him, trying to figure out what was wrong.

"What are you thinking now?"

Donny shrugged. "Nothing."

"Nothing? You're thinking nothing?"

Donny turned to walk away and this time Dan picked up his hat, put it back on his head and followed him. They walked another half mile before Dan spoke again.

"You don't look thirty-five years old. You could pass for twenty-five with no problem."

Donny stopped walking and turned to meet his friend. "Why thank you, colonel. If it's any consolation to you, you don't look your age either."

Dan smiled. "Thanks."

"Right. You could pass for forty-five in a heartbeat."

Dan reared his right hand back to slap his friend on the head, but then quickly stopped.

"Do you hear that?"

Donny turned his head toward the sound and nodded. "Yeah. We must be closer than I thought."

"What is it?"

They crept forward through the pine needles another hundred yards. The pines gave way to laurel and kudzu, forcing them to pick their way carefully and quietly through the dense underbrush. It took them another thirty minutes to make their way through the dense undergrowth. Finally, they peered out into the clearing up ahead to a small cabin with a back porch and a rocking chair.

Justice Reed was stark naked, drinking wine and singing at the top of his voice.

"Swing low ... sweet chariot."

He took another drink of dandelion wine.

"A comin' for ta carry me ... home."

Dan Branch reached into his left, breast pocket and pulled out the plastic bag containing the picture. He looked at it briefly and then handed it to Donny.

"Hmm, he looks different without clothes."

Dan nodded. "Uncle Rodney says our fate lies in this man's hands."

His voice boomed out louder. His voice cracked and he went suddenly way off key. "Swing low ... sweet chariot. A comin' for ta carry me home."

Justice looked out and saw both soldiers stand up and step away from the cover of the brush into his back yard. He took another long drink and didn't stop until the bottle was drained. He passed out and the Mason jar slipped out of his hand and hit the wooden planking with a crash and a shatter of glass.

His last thoughts before fading off to sleep were, *They've found me and I'm going back to prison.*

Dan crept up to the back porch while Donny circled the house on a quick perimeter check. Donny came through the front door, which was unlocked and then cleared each room. When he reached the back porch, he saw Dan still staring down at the naked old man. Donny broke the silence first.

"Why does your Uncle Rodney want this guy so much?"

Dan shook his head from side to side. "I don't know. But if this guy is our last hope then ..."

Donny finished the sentence for him. "Then we're in a world of shit."

Dan didn't disagree with him. The two men wrapped Justice in an old blanket, then searched the house and gathered up anything they thought would be of interest to General Branch and Jeff Arnett.

Three hours later they were on board the Blackhawk and on their way back to Iroquois.

Justice Reed and his needs

RODNEY BRANCH LOOKED OVER AT JUSTICE REED AND smiled. The man was sitting in a straight-backed folding chair in his kitchen, drinking staghorn sumac tea that Jackie had given him. Jackie sat off to the side now, fascinated by the frail, old man. He couldn't be more than five feet four inches tall, skinny as a rail, with the malnourishment typical of many alcoholics. His hair, what was left of it, was disheveled and silver, sticking up at odd angles all around the sides of his head. And, quite possibly, the most unusual thing about him was his obvious lack of clothing.

"Why is this man naked, Sergeant Brewster?"

Donny, who was off to the side, up against the wall answered abruptly. "We gave him clothes, sir, but he refused to wear them."

Colonel Branch had a fly swatter in his hand as he walked around the room, sneaking up on house flies and then dispatching them with a quick flick of his wrist. Justice Reed appeared to be watching Dan with interest. And then he spoke for the first time since being in the room.

"It's very important to kill the flies as early in the day as possible, because they tend to gather in groups. I studied flies every day for several months before coming to that conclusion. They really bother me when they land on me. Very dirty animals they are. Yes, very dirty. It gives me the heebies when they get on my skin."

Dan Branch smiled and killed another fly. "I hate them too. Nasty little buggers. Drive me crazy as a loon."

Justice smiled as if he'd just found a new friend. And then he nodded and turned back to looking at the table in front of him. Uncle Rodney hesitated and then spoke softly.

"Do you know why we brought you here, Dr. Reed?"

The frail, old man looked up from the table and then out the window, watching a robin on the ground in the front yard, as it hopped from one stick to another. Then it pecked the ground.

"You want me to build killing machines."

Uncle Rodney, dressed in olive drab utilities, with three stars on his collar, nodded his head. "Yes, that is correct."

Justice looked Rodney in the eye and held his gaze. Rodney returned it and his own eyes softened. He saw the pain, the brokenness, the despair, and then ... just a tiny spark of life. And that tiny spark caused him to have a glimmer of hope.

"I don't like to kill people, General Branch. I don't like it at all."

Rodney nodded. "Neither do I." He looked down, breaking the man's gaze, but then quickly back up again. "But ... I don't see a way out of this one. We have to kill to survive. Kill to maintain our freedom."

Justice laughed out loud, a boisterous, full-bodied roar that originated in his gut and was forced out his throat by his diaphragm. Rodney raised one eyebrow, but didn't say anything.

"Freedom. That's funny. You kidnapped me from my home. Stuck me in a helicopter and flew me hundreds of miles away against my will ... and you dare talk about freedom?"

A smile touched Rodney's lips. "You make a good point. I guess that gets us off on the wrong foot, doesn't it. I guess that makes us hypocrites."

The smile on Justice' face hardened, then dropped off like a dead bird falling from the sky. "Yes, I suppose it does. But, you see, I'm a hypocrite too, so I don't judge you. I am not righteous. There is none righteous, no not even one."

Rodney nodded. "Romans chapter three."

Justice Reed smiled again. "Yes. You are a follower of The Way, general?"

The general shrugged. "I am a man of war. I study a bit of everything. It helps me know myself, helps me know my enemy ... It gives me the edge."

Justice crossed his arms and seemed intrigued. Then he put his right forefinger to his lips and held it there. "If you know the enemy and know yourself, you need not fear the result of a hundred battles. If you know yourself but not the enemy, for every victory gained you will also suffer a defeat. If you know neither the enemy nor yourself, you will succumb in every battle."

Justice and Rodney locked eyes, like two sumo wrestlers

engaged in combat, neither one giving an inch to the other.

"I see you know your Sun Tzu, Dr. Reed."

The naked professor nodded before continuing.

"And who is your enemy, General Branch?"

"My enemy is the Blind Man and his rage."

Justice shook his head from side to side. "Yes, to be sure, the Blind Man is your enemy, but his rage is your friend. His anger will aid you in his own demise."

Rodney thought about it a moment before answering. Dan Branch stopped pacing back and forth looking for flies to kill. Jackie held baby Donna close to her breast for all she was worth, while Donny Brewster looked on at the intellectual duel in fascination.

"Point well taken, Dr Reed. Do you know the Blind Man?"

Justice nodded.

"How?"

The old man hesitated, as if counting the personal cost of his reply; it was the hesitation of a man about to lose his life, but couldn't decide whether to fight or surrender. Finally, he spoke softly, barely a whisper, and every other voice in the room silenced as every ear strained to hear.

"Jared Thompson once owned me."

CHAPTER 6

August 7, A Tough Nut to Crack

JEFF SHOOK HIS HEAD FROM SIDE TO side. "I'm sorry, general. Not at this time. We're still trying to decipher the data on the thumb drive given to us from Sammy Thurmond, but ... let's just say that it's slow going."

Rodney looked Jeff in the eyes before replying. "How slow?"

A slight hint of a smile toyed with the corners of Jeff's mouth. "You've heard the phrase 'slower than molasses in January?' Well, we're just a little bit faster than that. But we'll break it eventually ... just a matter of time."

General Branch leaned back in his chair, then placed his hands behind his head, interlaced. "Forgive me, Jeff, but it seems like it's taking a long time. What exactly is the hold-up?"

Jeff Arnett didn't like the general's tone, but ...it was understandable, given the gravity of the situation. He placed his hands up on the table and leaned in before answering. "It's not like I'm back at Langley, general. I've got a bunch of laptops and desktop PCs networked together. What I'm used to working with, what I really need to do this job efficiently, is a supercomputer the size of a warehouse where I have nearly unlimited speed and processing power."

Jeff leaned forward even farther. "This is not the easiest task, general, and my people are working on it twenty-four seven."

Uncle Rodney smiled and then nodded his head. "I'm sure you are Agent Arnett. Forgive my impatience." Then he stood up slowly, stretched his arms and then his legs. Lastly, he arched his back to take out a few of the kinks. He hated getting old, but he just needed to last a little bit longer ... just this one, last mission, and then he could rest.

Jeff Arnett jumped up quickly for a man of his size, nodded his head and quickly walked away without speaking again. Uncle Rodney watched him leave, staring after him, wondering ... can this man do the job I need him to do? But he filed the question away for another time. Jeff Arnett would just have to crack the code and access the files as best he could. And the sooner - the better.

In the meantime, Rodney's job was to try and come up with an alternative plan, just in case Jeff Arnett failed. But how could he do that? How could he defeat a man who held all the cards, who had all the power, and who seemed to have all the time in the world? Offhand he didn't know. But he would think on it, and, rest assured, Uncle Rodney would come up with a workable alternative to help them all defeat the Blind Man, come hell or high water. After all, what choice did he have?

August 7, What Women Want

"I HAVE NO IDEA, DONNY. I REALLY DON'T KNOW HER that well." Jackie Branch looked over at Donny Brewster, but his muscular, shoulders sagged at her reply.

"But ... you're a woman, you have to know what's going on with her! She's just not making any sense. One minute she's kissing me and the next she's slapping me across the face. Just tell me what I'm supposed to do!"

Deep inside Jackie felt sad for the poor man. And then she

thought to herself, *Why is it men can do so many great and wonderful things, Edison invented the light bulb, Einstein the theory of relativity, but when it comes to understanding women ... they were all morons.* She smiled sympathetically, wondering how she could put it into terms he could understand.

"Donny, have you studied Sun Tzu and *The Art of War*?"

Donny looked up and scoffed. "Of course I have. Hasn't everyone?"

Jackie thought to herself but said nothing out loud. *The man is so clueless about normal people.*

"Donny, perhaps you need to work on your timing a little bit. I think she loves you and that you love her, but ... maybe this just isn't the right time for her to make a commitment."

Donny nodded. "Okay, Dan said something like that too. Something about her feelings I think. But what does that have to do with Sun Tzu?"

Jackie looked off into the distance. They were on Uncle Rodney's small front porch. The baby was playing down on the ground below them. "Donny, sometimes the direct frontal attack isn't the best option."

Donny nodded. "Sure, I know that." But he said nothing more. Jackie tried to coax him along.

"So what do you do when your frontal attack is repelled? Do you just give up or do you try a different tactic?"

The marine shrugged his shoulders. "You back off, gather more intelligence, and then try things from a different angle. Maybe probe the flanks a bit and test for weakness."

Jackie nodded. "Yes, and then?"

"Well, when you find a weakness in the line, you plan a coordinated attack, amass your forces and attack the weakness and continue to hammer it until you break through. After that it's just a matter of mopping up resistance. You know, taking prisoners, rendering aid to the wounded, interrogating their officers, setting up a defensive perimeter, you know ... stuff like that."

Jackie smiled softly. "That's right. And capturing a woman's heart is a little like a military campaign. It could take many battles to win her over, but you never should keep doing things that aren't working for you. After all, you have plenty of options, right?"

Donny hacked up some phlegm and spit off to the side. It made her think *I hope he isn't doing that in front of Lisa and her daughter.*

"Yeah, Sun Tzu says, 'In military strategy, there is only the direct and the oblique, but between them they offer an inexhaustible range of tactics.'"

Jackie smiled again. "That's right, and what does Sun Tzu say about timing?"

Donny thought for a moment. He looked out across the yard, now grown over with weeds, waist high of every kind. "He says there are roads that should not be followed and there are enemies that should not be attacked."

Jackie glanced down at her baby who was putting sticks in her mouth and chewing with delight. "And what else?"

"Well, Sun Tzu says you should only attack when you are sure of your direction, that you should be patient, that you should wait for exactly the right moment when success is assured."

Jackie's face beamed. "That's right. I think you've figured it out now."

Donny turned his head to one side in confusion. "I have?" He reached up his left hand to stroke his cleanly shaven face. "So what should I do?"

The woman felt like reaching over and slapping him up side the head. But she took a deep breath and remained calm. "The timing isn't right, Donny. You have to wait for her. Don't talk so much. Let her talk about her feelings. Let her laugh and let her cry. Don't try to understand her, because it's way above your pay grade." She paused a moment, searching his face to see if any of it was sinking in.

Donny had a blank look on his face. "So what should I say to her to get her to fall in love with me?"

Jackie thought about that for a moment, and then she replied. "Well, Donny, I think ... in your case perhaps less is more."

He cocked his head to the right and raised an eyebrow. "Excuse me?"

Jackie sighed. "Just say things like, 'Oh, I see.' Or maybe 'So how did that make you feel?' or maybe 'That must have been terrible for you.' or something like 'Well, you're going to be okay' or 'These things just take time.' You know, simple little things like that."

Donny quickly reached up into his left breast pocket of his camo shirt and pulled out a small, green spiral notebook and a blank ink pen. He began to write furiously.

"This is good stuff, Jackie! What was that last one again?"

Jackie took a deep breath and repeated all of them over again as he wrote. And then she thought to herself, *This is amazing, so truly amazing.* Here before her was a powerful man, a great leader, a highly skilled military fighter, but he was intimidated and reduced to blubbering incoherence by a woman half his size and strength. Donny Brewster could reach over and snap her neck with one twist. He could shoot an adversary in the head at one thousand yards. He could hike nonstop for days and knife a man in the liver, slicing all the way around his rib cage. But, despite all that, he trembled beside the woman of his dreams ... all one-hundred-and-ten pounds of her.

Justice Reed looked General Branch straight in the eyes and refused him point blank. "I won't do it!"

Rodney glanced over at Colonel MacPherson and then quickly back at the frail scientist sitting before him. He'd expected some resistance, but not the massive vehemence being exhibited by the man before him. Rodney stared over at Justice from the other side of his kitchen table. Roger MacPherson stood to his left and slightly abreast with his hands folded behind him. A tired sigh escaped Rodney's mouth and his head sagged just a little.

"Please tell me why, Dr. Reed."

The old man was wearing clothes now, a pair of faded blue jeans, white t-shirt with a brown flannel shirt over it. Justice glanced off to his left, looking over the sink and through the window that was now open. A tiny breeze came in, caressing his face before fading into calm.

"I'm retired."

Rodney broke into a sudden laugh. His left hand moved up to his clean-shaven face where he rubbed it harshly before suppressing his smile. "Dr. Reed, you aren't retired, you are in hiding. There's a difference."

Justice smiled softly. He was more interested in the two black squirrels scampering about on the lawn than he was the battle plans of General Branch. "I have no desire to help you recommission twelve tactical nuclear devices."

"And why not?"

"Because I'm obstinate, Mr. Branch! Because I don't like being kidnapped at gunpoint and taken from my home."

That was the first time the doctor had raised his voice, and Rodney took careful note of it. Apparently this wasn't going to be as easy as he'd originally hoped.

The two squirrels disappeared around the oak tree and then spiraled back around and on up into the canopy out of sight. Justice looked back into the room. "I was happy, Mr. Branch. I was about to begin work on a very important project when you invaded my life and took me captive."

Ranger MacPherson spoke for the first time in the conversation, his voice low and without a lot of feeling. "And what project was that, Dr. Reed?"

Justice looked back out the window, but he could no longer find the squirrels and that perturbed him to no end. *Where did the squirrels go? I want the squirrels to come back so I can watch them!* He looked up at the colonel. "I was about to devise a new type of mouse trap. I've always wanted to do that."

Uncle Rodney smiled again. He placed his hands up on the Formica table top and joined them with his fingers interlaced. He looked down at his joined hands and then back up. He searched the bloodshot eyes of Justice Reed before speaking.

"So how do you know this new mousetrap will work?"

It was Justice Reed's turn to smile now. "I don't." He looked down at the red Formica, connecting the silver specks with his eyes in a geometrical pattern. "And that's half the fun, general. I never know what will work and what will not. And that's the fun of it all." He paused. "It's the journey, General Branch ... not the destination."

Rodney Branch nodded his head. He was finally beginning to understand the old scientist. He turned slightly in his chair and spoke directly to Colonel MacPherson.

"Mac, I want you to provide Dr. Reed with everything he needs to build a better mouse trap. Make sure he has decent quarters, plenty of food, supplies, whatever he wants we give it to him, provided we have the power to do so."

Rodney paused. "And make sure he has adequate protection. Even if he won't work for us ... we can't have him falling into the hands of Jared Thompson. That would be most unfortunate."

Justice looked up from the Formica and stared into Rodney's eyes. Rodney held his gaze and gave it back to him double. Finally, Justice nodded.

"Thank you, General Branch."

Rodney stood up and reached across the kitchen table, extending his right hand to Justice as he did so. The old scientist hesitated, but then reached out his own right hand and grasped the olive branch extended to him. They locked eyes for just a tiny moment and then Justice smiled and turned away to leave the room.

Colonel MacPherson turned to follow, but then hesitated and turned back toward his general. "What the hell are you doing, Rodney?"

General Branch was surprised by the colonel's question. Mac hadn't spoken to him that way in many years. He was usually all polish, military precision and bourgeois refinement. Rodney hesitated before answering, looking Mac straight in the eyes, assessing the man's question.

"Colonel MacPherson, you are to follow through with my orders in all haste and without question. It is extremely important that Dr. Reed complete his mousetrap as quickly as possible."

The colonel nodded and then snapped to attention before turning to leave the room.

"Oh, and one more thing, colonel." Colonel MacPherson stopped near the door but didn't turn his body toward the general. "You are to compose a memo to the general staff, informing them of this Top Secret project, which shall be called Project White Horseman."

Mac raised his brow and then turned his head back to General Branch. "You'd like me to help Dr. Reed, a devout, possibly insane scientist, some would call him a mad scientist ... you'd like me to help him build a better mousetrap?"

General Branch nodded. "And then you'd like me to distribute a memo detailing this Top Secret project to the general staff, and it is to be named Project White Horseman? Is that correct, sir?"

Rodney smiled and nodded his head. "That is correct, colonel. But under no circumstances are the details of this project to be revealed to anyone. Only say that the project will be the culmination of many centuries of scientific venture, that it will result in the loss of many lives, vermin who have plagued mankind, and it will bring a quick end to the Blind Man and his diabolical plans."

Colonel MacPherson smiled and shook his head from side to side. He didn't speak for a moment, then he turned, snapped to attention and saluted.

"It shall be done, sir, exactly as you ordered."

General Branch returned the colonel's crisp salute with

one of his own. Ranger MacPherson strode quickly out of the room, on his way to building a better mousetrap, leaving General Branch to his own thoughts.

CHAPTER 7

August 8, The Prophet

SPARKY **F**ILLMORE WAS A VERY nondescript man. He'd never done anything great, at least not by the world's standards, but one thing he'd always done consistently, was to obey the Lord and all His commands. But when God came to him on that particular day, after the apocalypse, while he was milking the cow, Sparky had questioned the Lord.

"Are you sure this is what you want me to do? You want me to leave my wife and all I've built up here, in a hometown my family has lived in for generations, and you'd like me to walk halfway across the country just to give some stranger a message?"

God had never spoken to Sparky before ... well, at least not in this way; the Lord's voice was almost audible, and the feeling he got was like he was standing on holy ground, like the very air around him had suddenly been transformed into something other-worldly, like a spiritual electricity had been infused into the space around him. When the message came to him he half expected to see a burning bush, or, in this case, a burning bale of hay or straw.

Sparky had been a deacon in the local church for much of his adult life. He'd even done a bit of preaching from time to time, especially when the little congregation was between pastors, as happened occasionally with many small country churches. He read his Bible everyday, even studied it with his wife, Edna. She was his childhood sweetheart, and they'd been married for fifty-three years. Their three children had been successful as adults, two of them moving across the country, one as a doctor and the other as an engineer. The third owned a farm just a few miles from Sparky's own home in western Kansas.

A million questions and thoughts and concerns all competed for voice as the old man contemplated his answer to the Lord. He knew that God loved him, but he also knew, from his immense study of the scripture that to question God rarely ended well. One man in particular came to his mind as God waited for Sparky to give account. It was the story of Zechariah. The angel Gabriel had gone to him and told him his wife would give birth in her old age. But Zechariah, had doubted the angel and been struck mute until after the birth of his son, who was later known as "John the Baptist."

And Moses had also questioned God but to no avail. The Bible was filled with stories of people questioning the commission of God, so, no matter how crazy it might sound, Sparky uttered his reply.

"Command me Lord and I shall go."

So the Lord commanded Sparky Fillmore, a man of little consequence to travel to Michigan in search of a man named General Rodney T. Branch. God didn't give him the message, but simply demanded that Sparky trust Him in all things. And so, Sparky believed and obeyed the Lord, and it was credited to him as righteousness.

And Sparky left that very same day, with nothing but the clothes on his back and a lunch of raspberry jam and peanut butter sandwiches that his wife had fixed for him. He also brought one can of Spam, just in case, and hoped that God wouldn't see that as a lack of faith on his part. And Sparky wondered, in his heart of hearts. *Will I surely die?*

But the Lord was with him in all that he did.

August 8, The Woods of Iroquois County

Sammy Thurmond had been watching the remains of Iroquois City for the past two days, but had seen nothing to impress him. In fact, he'd seen very little of anything. The town per se had been almost totally destroyed by the saracen army weeks before on their march to Mackinaw City. He sat perched atop the burnt-out shell of an Abrams tank on the hill overlooking the town. An oak tree was off to his left; it was a full three feet in diameter, and the bark about head high was charred from the same battle that had killed the tank. Despite the damage, the tree was doing its best to recover and live. Its leaves were green and hardy, and Sammy respected the tree for fighting so hard to stay alive.

Sammy had read all the reports of the first battle for Iroquois City, as it had come to be called, and he was in awe of the incredible leadership skills and military tactics of General Branch. He'd even seen the video footage from the drones as the three cars had raced up the hill to try and destroy the tanks, and he wondered to himself, *how do you convince people to give up their lives in a battle that can't possibly be won*? Because Rodney Branch should not have won that battle. He'd been outgunned, outnumbered and outmaneuvered. The Shadow Militia and the Iroquois County Home Guard should have been soundly defeated and every last man, woman and child killed. But they weren't. They had won ... not only won, but gloriously and soundly they had destroyed every last attacker, almost to the man. Sammy wanted to meet the person who'd conceived of that victory, the man who'd inspired these farmers and shopkeepers and factory workers to rise up and fight against hopeless odds.

So Sammy watched now, trying to figure out a way to find the general. A year ago he could have simply done an internet records search and gotten his home address through the county clerk's records, but that was no longer possible. For all intents and purposes, the internet was dead, and would not be resurrected for many years to come, maybe even decades.

And then there was the question of Jackie Branch, the woman he'd become enamored with. Women had always been mere objects to him, things to be possessed, to be exploited, mere toys he could play with for his own amusement and distraction. But Jackie ... Jackie Branch had been different. He'd tried to play with her, but had been flummoxed. There was some inner strength she possessed that made her unconquerable, indomitable and unyielding. She had a quality that intrigued Sammy Thurmond. And it was that undefinable quality that had caused him to set her free, had indeed inspired him to leave the Blind Man and come to Iroquois, what was left of it.

It was odd for Sammy to contemplate what he was doing, because it defied logic. The Blind Man held all the cards, all the power, all the means to come out on top in this fight. But still ... Sammy had left him, had deserted the obvious winner, and with it, fortune and power and a sure future. But still ... there was a muse drawing him here, the muse of a strong, beautiful woman, and the sirens of General Rodney T. Branch. General Branch, who was not supposed to win, indeed it had been impossible for him to win, against the cutthroat murderer named Manny with his three thousand barbarians, and then again against the saracen tide of tens of thousands, backed up with military armor and F18 fighter jets. Still, the general had won.

So Sammy Thurmond waited now for what he knew not, for whatever would happen next. He simply released his grip on the bank of life and let the river take him, and suddenly, he believed in fate, and maybe ... even a higher power.

August 9, Five Miles East of Hays, Kansas 8AM

SPARKY FILLMORE DIDN'T FEEL LIKE A PROPHET, BUT

when he examined it closely, which, he had plenty of time to do while walking down the incredibly hot West Kansas pavement, he couldn't help but see some similarities. Throughout the Bible, prophets had been simply ordinary people whom God had called to give messages to people or to nations, sometimes messages that were not well received, and could even cause the death of the messenger. Sparky couldn't help but be mindful of the words of Jesus Christ when talking about the prophets of old.

> *"Jerusalem, Jerusalem, you who kill the prophets
> and stone those sent to you, how often I have
> longed to gather your children together, as a hen
> gathers her chicks under her wings, and you were
> not willing."*

> *Luke 13:34 (NIV)*

Sparky desperately wanted to be well received by who ever God was sending him to meet. And he hoped above all else that he was giving them good news. He hated so much to be a bearer of ill omen. With feet hurting, hot and sweaty, with a lower back that cried out for him to collapse on the side of the road, Sparky plodded on. The heat in Western Kansas this time of year was oppressive, but the old man had grown up here and was used to it, as much as anyone could be. But still ... walking almost a thousand miles in the scorching heat was different than working for a few hours at his son's farm or hoeing the vegetable garden.

Funny, but it hadn't occurred to Sparky to question whether or not he'd actually be able to walk that far at his age. Sure, he'd wondered about a violent death, being robbed, beaten and left to die on the side of the road, because Sparky was not a violent man. He didn't even own a gun. Other than a few years in the army back during the Vietnam War, Sparky had never taken up arms. What would happen to him if someone attacked? Would God protect him or would he be killed? In his mind's eye, Sparky saw his body lying motionless on the side of the road, bloated in the intense heat of the day, as a turkey vulture circled overhead.

But Sparky knew this mission, or quest, or whatever it was had come from God, not just because God had spoken to him, because something like that had never happened before, but because of the way his wife had responded to him. When Sparky had told Edna that he was going to walk from Kansas to Michigan to give a message from God to a man that he hadn't met, and that he had no idea what the message was, she had simply said, "I know." And then she'd packed him the lunch and sent him on his way the very same hour. Sparky hadn't even said good bye to his children. He'd thought about it, but then asked the question "why?" After all, they would just call him crazy and try to talk him out of it, and, to be honest with himself, he didn't think he'd be able to withstand any kind of peer pressure, that he could have been very easily persuaded to stay home, that this venture was ludicrous and dangerous and the ravings of a crazy man. So, Sparky had left his home and the wife he loved that very hour.

And now, alone with nothing but his own thoughts ... he wondered about his own sanity. But, regardless of whether he was sane or stark, raving mad, there was nothing left for him to do but to walk on. After all, what else could he do? Could he turn around and go back to his wife and home? What would he tell her; that he'd been afraid, or foolish, or that his feet hurt?

And then he was reminded of the story of Christian, in the book *Pilgrim's Progress*, written by John Bunyan, and of the many hardships that had been encountered. He kind of felt like Christian in that story, like he was going against the grain of everything that made sense. So, renewed in his purpose, the old man kept going. And then, way up ahead, shimmering off the waves of heat coming up off the hot asphalt, Sparky saw something and quickened his pace.

Uncle Rodney's kitchen

"Gentlemen, we are here this morning to talk about who is going to lead the new America once we've defeated the Blind Man." Uncle Rodney was standing before them at the head of the red, Formica-topped table in his kitchen. Seated around it were Colonel MacPherson, Jeff Arnett, Dan Branch, and Sheriff Joe Leif, while Jackie Branch and baby Donna were seated off to the side.

The intense and sad irony of the situation didn't escape Dan, nor did it elude anyone else around the table. Just over a year ago this type of high-level meeting wouldn't be held in a run-down kitchen of a private home, but in the halls of congress or in the White House itself. But now ... so much had changed. Here they were, just a ragtag group of citizens, deciding who the next leader of the free world would be.

Just a year ago Dan had been in a failed marriage, awaiting his inevitable divorce, working in a factory for a mere penance as a wage. But now, he was a colonel in the Shadow Militia, commanding thousands of seasoned combat veterans and presiding over the only force on the planet capable of defeating the next tyrant, Jared Thompson, also known as the Blind Man, the person who had orchestrated the demise of the United States, and, for that matter, the entire world. His plan had proceeded almost flawlessly, and half of America had already been pacified, but there was only one thing standing in his way of continental domination, and that was ... Rodney T. Branch and the handful of people sitting around the table.

As Dan looked back on the past year, he recalled the horrors of battle and the butchery he'd witnessed; it was more than any one man could ever want, but still ... if he had to do it all over again, he would act with even less hesitation than before. Dan had gained confidence as a military leader, even though he'd been a mere sergeant in the Marine corps in what seemed like a distant life. But still ... one thing was there that he could not deny ... what they had done ... they had done. It was there, staring him and all the others in the face as they presided over what might become the most important meeting they'd ever had. And it was all being decided over a red, Formica table top dating back to the nineteen-fifties, and they were sipping casually on sumac-berry tea and chickory-based coffee. All this ... and there was no ice to cool their tea.

"Uncle Rodney." Dan placed his tea down on the table in front of him before continuing. "I just assumed that you'd be leading America once the Blind Man was out of the picture."

General Branch was already shaking his head from side to side before Dan could even finish his statement. "No. It can't be that way. Though I appreciate your vote of confidence. The succession of power has to be as outlined in the US constitution. That's the way the Founding Fathers wanted it, and nothing has changed in that regard."

Joe Leif chimed in. "That's right. The country may be down and out right now, but we still have to maintain the rule of law, and the constitution is the supreme law of the land."

Colonel MacPherson and Jeff Arnett nodded their heads in approval before Uncle Rodney continued. "We will be proceeding with the continuity of government plan that was in place at the time of the Fall, over a year ago. Agent Jeff Arnett will brief us on the details." Rodney nodded to Jeff, who then stood and moved to the kitchen wall behind him. A large chalkboard, taken from the debris of a local elementary school had been nailed there. Uncle Rodney took his seat.

Jeff Arnett picked up a piece of white chalk and wrote the letters C - O - G in big letters near the top of the old-fashioned chalkboard. "Continuity of Government, gentlemen, that's what we are here to decide." He looked around the room, meeting each person's gaze one at a time before going on. "First, a little background information. Continuity of government establishes defined procedures which allow a government to continue its essential operations in case of a catastrophic event such as nuclear war, or, in our case, a wide-spread and open-ended long-term power loss."

Dan Branch had always been impressed by the professional bearing of Agent Jeff Arnett. He was always prepared, always formal, and seemed to radiate confidence whenever he spoke to a group.

"COG was first created by the British government before and throughout World War II to meet certain threats, for example, the Luftwaffe bombing during the Battle of Britain. After that, the necessity for continuity of government gained new expediency with nuclear proliferation following World War Two.

"During and after the Cold War many countries developed contingency plans to minimize chaos and disorder during a power vacuum in the event of a nuclear attack.

"Here in America, COG is no longer limited to nuclear emergencies, as it was activated following the September 11 attacks on New York City."

Jeff scanned the room to see if there were any questions. Seeing no quizzical looks, he pressed on.

"The US plan sets up a line of succession that allows for certain elected officials, and, some appointed officials to be included in the presidential line of succession. And they are as follows:" Jeff moved closer to the chalkboard.

"If the president is no longer able to perform his duties, the vice president will be sworn in as president. If the VP and president are deemed unable to lead, then the following offices will be named as acting president of the United States. Number three in the line of succession is the Speaker of the House, Number four is the president pro tempore of the Senate, followed by cabinet positions in the following order: the Secretary of State, then by Secretary of the Treasury, Secretary of Defense, Attorney General, Secretary of the Interior, Secretary of Agriculture, Secretary of Commerce, Secretary of Labor, Secretary of Health and Human Services, Secretary of Housing and Urban Development, Secretary of

Transportation, Secretary of Energy, Secretary of Education, Secretary of Veterans Affairs, and then Secretary of Homeland Security."

Jeff looked up from the list he was reading and quickly scanned the room. He had everyone's attention, and no one seemed to have any questions at this point, so he quickly moved on. "Our best intelligence tells us that the president, vice president, speaker of the house along with the president pro tempore of the senate are no longer alive. Also, the following people in this line of succession have met with an untimely demise:

Secretary of State
Secretary of the Treasury
Secretary of Defense
Attorney General
Secretary of the Interior
Secretary of Agriculture
Secretary of Commerce
Secretary of Labor
Secretary of Health and Human Services
Secretary of Transportation
Secretary of Energy
Secretary of Education
Secretary of Veterans Affairs
Secretary of Homeland Security"

Jeff Arnett paused to let the message sink in. Sheriff Joe Leif was the first to ask the obvious question. "So ... how did all these people die?"

Jeff answered the question promptly and without emotion. "The majority were killed when the Blind Man attacked the designated underground strongholds of Cheyenne Mountain, Mount Weather and Raven Rock. These underground facilities were hardened against nuclear attack and highly fortified, and previously considered impregnable to nuclear attack. However, the Blind Man somehow pumped vast amounts of deadly nerve agents into the ventilating systems of these complexes and killed every last inhabitant.

"That occurred just a few days after the nationwide power loss. There were only four people in the presidential line of succession to survive after that. The secretary of state, secretary of education, secretary of transportation and the secretary of veterans affairs."

Joe Leif followed up with another question. "So where are these people now? Why didn't they assume command?"

Jeff Arnett paused a moment, as if girding up the loins of his mental strength to continue on. "The secretary of state was shot in the head with a pistol at close range. The secretary of education died of food poisoning, and the secretary of transportation was attacked via a predator drone attack. That last one wasn't confirmed visually, but we assume he is dead, since no one has seen or heard from him since."

There was a deathly silence in the room. Dan looked over at Joe. Colonel MacPherson didn't move, standing ramrod straight and at the position of attention behind General Branch. Joe Leif was the first to talk.

"I don't understand what the big deal is, Rodney. There's only one of these guys left, the Secretary of the Department of Veteran Affairs. It sounds like the Blind Man is way ahead of us on this one. He probably already knows where this person is, because he's systematically exterminated anyone who could possibly lead the United States out of this mess."

Dan Branch nodded his head in agreement. "He's right, Uncle Rodney. The Blind Man has effectively eliminated all the competition. Besides, even if we could locate the secretary, what would that gain us? The Blind Man has taken control of what's left of the US military. The secretary of Veteran's Affairs would just be a symbol without any real power."

General Branch stood to his feet and glanced around the room before speaking. Then he nodded to Colonel MacPherson, who immediately stepped forward. "That's not entirely true, Colonel Branch. There are still many isolated pockets of Army, Navy, Marine and Air Force resistance who are holding out against the Blind Man. However, they are not actively fighting against him, because no one is holding legitimate constitutional power who can order them to attack."

Uncle Rodney interrupted. "It's not like the Shadow Militia can take control of US Military bases. We can't do that. It would be wrong and we'd have to kill American military warriors to do that." There was a momentary silence before Rodney continued. "However, if we can find the secretary of Veteran Affairs before the Blind Man, then we can link him up to military bases across the country, re-establish command and control and we will unite beside them. Our combined forces might be enough to win the day."

Dan Branch took a sip of his tea before speaking. "So who exactly is the Blind Man getting to fight for him, if not the US military?"

Colonel MacPherson nodded to Jeff Arnett, who began speaking immediately. "Some of the American forces lined up behind him, but he also has a combination of Caribbean, Central and South American, as well as western and eastern European military personnel. Most of them came on board shortly after the collapse. But it was orchestrated from the beginning. The Blind Man had his military forces organized on paper before the attack, then he simply mobilized them in the ensuing chaos and aftermath. The bulk of their equipment and arsenal was captured within a few days of the collapse from existing armories across the country. One weakness the Blind Man has is airpower. He has a limited number of trained pilots and operational planes. That's how we've been able to stay in the fight as long as we have. He is hesitant to commit his airpower because it is irreplaceable. His nuclear arsenal is also limited."

Sheriff Joe Leif mumbled under his breath. "Tell that to the residents of Escanaba."

Dan ignored Joe's comment. "So, do we know where this guy is?"

Jeff moved to the chalkboard and wrote the name 'Joseph Donnelly.' Dan's hand moved up to his chin and stroked it thoughtfully. "That name sounds familiar to me."

Jeff Arnett nodded his head. "Yes, you probably heard his name in the news. Just a few weeks before the collapse it was announced that the FBI was investigating him on possible misuse of government funds."

Jeff let the indictment hang in the air, like the smell of burning rubber in a closed room. Joe Leif moved both his hands up to the sides of his head and sighed. "So he's a crook?"

General Branch took a step closer. "He's a politician, Joe. But he's the only politician who can legally take control of what's left of the US government."

The baby began to cry, and Jackie hushed her, picked her up and rocked her back and forth. "So, General Branch, where is the secretary now? Do we even know where he might be?"

Turning to the chalkboard, Jeff Arnett wrote in big letters. "HAITI"

Jackie's heart leaped into her throat. She looked down at her baby girl, with black skin and black, kinky hair. She'd spent a lot of time in Haiti with her first husband on mission trips. They'd also spent time in neighboring Dominican Republic. She knew the island well. But ... there was a darkness in her past, and it centered on an island just 800 miles from Miami, Florida.

She looked over at Dan. His head was down, and there was a sadness about him. She looked up at General Branch, and he was looking directly at her. Jackie looked down at her baby, then back up to Dan, who refused to make eye contact with her. She let out a deep breath, then sucked it back in, establishing eye contact with her Uncle Rodney.

It was at that moment in time she began to understand the bond between Uncle Rodney and Ranger MacPherson, the way they could talk with each other without speaking, the way they always seemed to know what the other was thinking. She took one last look at her husband, begging for help, but none was forthcoming. Resolved, she glanced back at General Branch and nodded her head slightly.

Jackie Branch would leave her baby and travel across the country, back in time to the land of her nightmares. It was a decision that broke her heart.

CHAPTER 8

August 10, Jackie Prepares to Leave

DAN BRANCH WAS NOT A HAPPY camper. The last time his Uncle Rodney had sent his wife on a secret mission she'd been raped, tortured and hung on a cross to die. And to be quite honest, Jackie was not happy either. She was now three months pregnant with Dan's baby, and she wanted so much to give birth, and raise their child, to love and cuddle, and watch both her babies grow up. Jackie reached down and felt the bump on her stomach.

She so much wanted the chance to grow old.

Of all the places to be sent, this was the last place on earth she wanted to go. It felt to her like returning to the scene of the crime, like a constant reminder of her life's greatest sin, like a reminder of the evil she'd perpetrated against a good and godly man.

And then there was her baby, little baby Donna, almost a year old now, but still a baby to her mother. It pained her to leave the little girl she loved. Against the saracen tide, Jackie had been eager to get into the fight, to be a spy in their camp, and she had indeed killed thousands of the enemy, but ... her eagerness to battle had turned to sand in her mouth as the reality and horror of war had taken hold. She had been content to sit this one out, to simply stay home with her baby and let the men go off and do all the fighting this time around, but ...

that was not in the cards, and she couldn't argue with Uncle Rodney. This mission was crucial to the cause, and it stood a higher chance for success with her as its leader.

Baby Donna was already with Marge Leif for the next few days; they'd said their good byes, and, of course the baby had no idea what was going on, that her mother may never return, that she could be an orphan soon. Jackie thought about that for a moment. *But wasn't that always true, especially these days?* Even before the collapse, life had been precarious, but now ... the Blind Man could find them and kill them at any moment, and they wouldn't even know it was coming. And then she silently rebuked herself. She should have more faith in Uncle Rodney ... and in God. Both had never let her down.

She looked over at her husband sitting on the edge of the bed as she finished filling her backpack.

"I don't like this, Jackie. Last time you almost died."

Jackie paused a moment, but then forced her hands to keep working. "I don't like it either. But the logic is sound."

Dan wanted to argue, but he couldn't in any reasonable way. The mission was sound, and it was necessary. And then Dan surprised her. "I want you to know how proud I am of you for doing this."

Jackie stopped and turned to face him. Tears ran down her cheeks as she moved across the bed to embrace him. "Thank you, honey. I really don't want to go this time. I just want to stay home and take care of the baby and let other people do the work. I'm not ashamed of thinking that way either."

This seemed to surprise Dan, but he let it go. "You need to be careful, Jackie. You need to come home to me and Jeremy and Donna." He reached down and rubbed the small bump on her stomach. "We need you here."

Jackie reached up and touched Dan's cheek. She ran her thumb across his face from up to down and then back to his ear. Then she pressed her own lips against his in a passionate embrace. Jackie pushed him down on his back and made love to him like it was going to be the very last time.

An hour later Dan drove her to the rally point, where they said goodbye. Dan waved as the helicopter faded into the night sky. It would be days, perhaps weeks before they saw each other again.

August 11, A Bicycle Built for One

THE KANSAS PROPHET PEDALED AS FAST AS HIS 72-YEAR-old legs would carry him, though that wasn't really all that fast. He should have been singing a great hymn of the faith, like *How Great thou Art* or perhaps *A Mighty Fortress is Our God*, but no, Sparky Fillmore was singing a Toby Keith song as he sped down the flat, smooth road of Interstate 70 as he headed east.

> *I said Dave!*
> *I ain't as good as I once was,*
> *My how the years have flown,*
> *But there was a time,*
> *Back in my prime,*
> *When I could really hold my own,*
> *But if you want a fight tonight,*
> *Guess those boys don't look all that tough,*
> *I ain't as good as I once was,*
> *But I'm as good once, as I ever was.*

He remembered when that song had come out a long time ago, and he'd liked it then, but only sang it when Edna wasn't around. His wife didn't approve of secular music,and she certainly didn't want him singing a bar-room brawl song. She said it was from the devil. And, maybe it was, Sparky didn't know for sure. But what he did know is that it took his mind off the pain in his lower back and the cramping in his ankles. He hadn't ridden a bike since he was a teenager, but there it was, leaning against the road sign with a note on it that said: "Take me - I'm yours!"

And so he had. For the past three days he'd pedaled the

bicycle across Kansas from west to east, watching the sunrise every morning, being scorched in the noontime heat, only to have the sun at his back in the afternoon. With the help of the bicycle, he was making amazingly good time. Already he could feel his old muscles beginning to tighten up and get back into shape. True, like the Toby Keith song said, he'd never be as good as he once was, but, still, perhaps he could be good enough just this one, last time. It certainly helped that he'd found some ibuprofen in an abandoned house the day before yesterday.

He had a two-quart milk jug that he filled with water on every occasion possible, which wasn't very often. Every time he passed an abandoned home or business, he went inside, found the hot water heater, and filled up his container to the top. Sometimes he'd find food as well. Yesterday he'd eaten a dead rabbit lying by the side of the highway. It wasn't road-kill, because there were no cars. He didn't know how it had died, but simply assumed it was from God. His new rule was: If it doesn't smell too bad, then go ahead and eat it.

And that's how Sparky survived on his way to testify God's Truth to General Rodney T. Branch.

August 11, Mission to Montana

"HAVE YOU HEARD ANYTHING FROM JACKIE AND HER team?" Dan Branch sat across the table from his Uncle Rodney. Jeremy was seated to the left of his Uncle.

"Nothing since last night. They reached Port-au-Prince okay and have started searching the resorts and hotels. We think he may be holed up there or in the surrounding country-side on a small ranch. I guess they call them plantations down there."

Rodney watched Dan's reaction for signs of stress and saw plenty. "But we don't expect to hear from her again until to-night."

Dan looked out the window, at a loss to say anything.

Jeremy spoke next. "It's okay, Dad. Donny is with her, and you know how good he is. He won't let anything happen to her. Donny is the best."

Uncle Rodney smiled sadly. "And don't underestimate her, son. You know how tough and smart that woman is."

Jeremy laughed out loud. "That's right, Dad. She can beat you in a game of Risk almost every time!"

Dan looked over the table to his son and couldn't help but smile weakly. "You still remember that night?"

Jeremy nodded. "Yup. And I'll cherish that moment for the rest of my life."

Dan laughed softly. "I think that's the night I began to fall in love with her."

"I think that's a story I need to hear, but not right now. We have something very urgent that needs my two best men. And it has to be done right away."

Dan forced himself back into military mode, and his face changed back to its prior sternness. Then he nodded to his uncle. "I'm listening."

Uncle Rodney leaned forward in the rickety, wooden chair as he spoke. "I need the two of you to lead a team out west, to Montana. There's something that has to be picked up and brought safely back to Iroquois."

When Uncle Rodney reached to his left, breast pocket for a nonexistent cigarette, Dan knew this was something big. He hadn't seen his uncle do that in weeks. Something about this made the general nervous, and that was saying something, because his Uncle Rodney seemed to always be in such firm control.

"What is it?"

Rodney paused, but then shifted in his chair to gaze out the window at the gray squirrel scampering about on the lawn. He didn't see a lot of gray squirrels in Iroquois. Most of them were the tan-shaded fox squirrels or the black squirrels. That's why he hadn't yet eaten this particular squirrel, though, sooner or later, if things got bad enough, he'd have to shoot this one as well. He turned back to his nephew.

"Twelve nuclear warheads."

August 12, Sammy Thurmond's Calling Card

Sᴛᴀꜰꜰ Sᴇʀɢᴇᴀɴᴛ Aᴅᴀᴍ Cᴇʀᴠᴀɴᴛᴇs sᴛᴏᴏᴅ ᴀᴛ ᴀᴛᴛᴇɴ-tion in front of General Branch. Colonel MacPherson was off to one side. standing at ease, but still rigid and alert. Mac was the first to speak.

"We found the staff sergeant duct taped to a tree about fifty yards inside the trees and just outside the perimeter. He had this sheet of paper taped to his chest." The colonel handed the note to General Branch who read it quietly to himself.

> *"I respectfully request to meet with you at a time and place of your choosing. We have much to discuss. As a token of good faith, I have chosen not to kill your staff sergeant.*

> *Respectfully, Samuel Thurmond*

Uncle Rodney smiled, and then lowered his head, shaking it from side to side. "Staff Sergeant Cervantes. Will you please explain to me how this man was able to duct tape you to a tree within one-hundred yards of my command post?"

Adam nervously bit his lower lip before answering. "I, I'm not sure, sir. Actually, sir, I have no idea."

Uncle Rodney cocked his head to the right just slightly and took an intimidating step forward.

"You have no idea?"

Adam did his best to maintain a position of attention, but it was a losing battle. He'd been thoroughly humiliated.

"That is correct, sir. I never saw him. I never heard him. The man was a ghost, sir."

The general nodded his head and then glanced over at Colonel MacPherson. Then he turned back to the staff sergeant before continuing. "I see. Well, staff sergeant, I don't believe in ghosts ... however, this man is probably about as close to that as they come." Then he glanced back over at the colonel. "Colonel MacPherson, this man is not to be punished. There is no shame in what happened to him. It could have happened to any of us." Then he paused, glancing back over to the colonel. "However, we cannot be caught unaware again. Please spread the word that the staff sergeant was subdued and duct-taped to a tree by a lone man. Everyone must be on high alert. and we can't afford for this to happen again."

The shoulders of Staff Sergeant Cervantes slumped involuntarily. He thought to himself, *I'll be the laughing stock of the unit.* And then an even more painful realization occurred to him: *What if Donny Brewster finds out? I'll never hear the end of it.*

And, unknown to Adam Cervantes, that is exactly what the general was counting on.

"That is all, staff sergeant. You are dismissed."

"Sir, yes sir!"

Adam did a perfect about face and strode out of the room. Once he was gone, Rodney turned to his friend.

"There's a storm comin' Mac. Can you feel it?"

The colonel let out a deep sigh, one filled with age and weariness. He nodded his head. "I suppose I do. For good or ill."

Rodney looked out the open window. It was hot, but a sudden breeze came into the room as if on cue. "Yes, for good or for ill." And then he turned to leave the room.

"Make the arrangements, colonel. It's time to meet Sammy Thurmond."

August 13, Sammy and Uncle Rodney

Uncle Rodney sat on the ground facing the granite headstone, listening to the birds in the white pine tree off to his left, watching the black squirrels scamper beneath the oak tree off in the distance. He heard another squirrel chatter in the big oak about ten feet behind him. His butt always got numb if he didn't shift back and forth from one cheek to the other, so he made the transition now to ward off the inevitable.

Rodney's eyes rested lightly on the granite rock in front of him, the words before him, etched in stone, left a permanence and a feeling of mortality that was disconcerting. You'd think Rodney would understand life and death by now, having witnessed so much of it over the last seventy years, but ... it was still largely a mystery to him. But seeing his last name on the headstone always seemed to unsettle him, to make him think twice, to question even the most basic ideas and the bedrock of his beliefs.

Six feet below him lie his brother, the little boy he'd grown up with, played with in the woods around him, splashed with in the Manistee river; they'd even played on many of these very headstones here in the cemetery a full sixty years prior.

It seemed like a lifetime ago.

And then Rodney laughed out loud at his silly thought, because, after all, it really had been a lifetime ago. His life was mostly gone now, all used up, with more thoughts behind him than in front, more deeds done than not. In many regards he felt like he was coasting now, just playing out the hand dealt to him, the last hand, but maybe the most important hand he'd ever played.

A cardinal, bright red in color landed on the tombstone in front of him. It always amazed him how quickly they could move. The cardinal was one of his favorite birds, perhaps because of their resilience. They stayed here in the winter, lending their bright red to the white snow, always staying, never giving up, always bright, lending color and contrast to the cold death of the north woods winter.

But now it was summer, and summer was the time for action. Rodney read the name in front of him "Ronald T. Branch." He'd been close to his brother, a twin in every regard, and that's why he'd retired early from the military to care for Dan when Ronny had died. There was a bond inside him that went deeper then mere blood. It was spiritual. A bond of the strongest kind - a bond of unseen blood. Yes, he and Ronny had always been close. and, indeed, always would be close, even in death.

But he hadn't come to his brother's grave to visit, at least not today. No, today was all business. He had come to meet his enemy, and, perhaps, just perhaps, the enemy of his enemy.

"You can come out now, Mr. Thurmond. I've been waiting for you."

The bushes on the west edge of the cemetery rustled just a bit, and then Sammy Thurmond stepped out, revealing himself for the first time. Rodney waited patiently as the man walked over. General Branch analyzed the man's walk; it was a gait of confidence with just a hint of military precision.

As he approached, General Branch moved doggedly to his feet and extended his right hand. Three feet away Sammy stopped and looked Rodney in the eyes. He hesitated, as if looking for something in particular. Then, appearing to find it, he reached out his right hand and clasped Rodney's in his own.

"Thank you for meeting with me, general."

For now, Rodney kept a stone face and simply nodded slightly. Sammy glanced down at the granite headstone in front of them. "Your twin brother. Died of an unfortunate accident at age 35. His wife had died a few years prior to that. You retired from the military, even though you had a great career ahead of you and you came home to Iroquois to finish raising your nephew, Dan, as your own son."

Uncle Rodney nodded and then motioned to the west. "Shall we walk, Mr. Thurmond?" Sammy didn't answer, but began slowly walking. Both men walked past one headstone after another. Rodney took note that Sammy fell in to his left and slightly abreast.

"You are a military man, Mr. Thurmond." It wasn't a question, and wasn't taken as such, so Sammy simply nodded. "The Blind Man is a civilian. I see nothing in him so far to indicate otherwise." Sammy nodded again before speaking.

"Yes, that is true. But he makes up for that lacking with an unusual understanding of human nature."

Rodney thought about this for a moment before continuing. "But the Blind Man has a weakness."

Sammy suddenly stopped. They were standing in front of a gravestone now in the older part of the cemetery. It was a larger stone, jutting up in a slab, with letters and numbers that were extremely worn and covered over with some moss. Rodney's old eyes could barely make out the words.

Pvt Jeremiah A. Cole
Born 1845 - Died 1864
13th Michigan Artillery

Sammy looked down at the head stone as well. "Apparently 13 wasn't his lucky number."And then he paused before continuing. "Yes, of course he does. Everyone has a weakness, General Branch." Sammy looked over at a grey squirrel ten yards in the distance. Rodney couldn't help but notice Sammy's fascination with the animal, as if it was the first time he'd ever seen one. There was a sudden childlike aura to the man that undergirded the extreme evil that showed on the surface.

"The Blind Man has many weaknesses. But ... he also has many strengths."

Rodney looked over at Sammy and began to walk again. The man quickly took his place to the left and slightly abreast. "Talk about the Blind Man."

Sammy wasted no time in answering him. "The Blind Man is highly organized. He likes everything just so, with nothing out of place, no loose ends, nothing that can come back on him. He is tidy and neat. He is a very polite man, and insists that others be courteous in his presence, even if they are about to die at his hand."

Rodney smiled. "That might be a bit too much to ask from a man."

Sammy's stone face hardened even more. "I never said he was reasonable. He is a hard man, unrelenting, inflexible, and pays great attention to detail. Much of his success is attributed to ruthlessness. He also prides himself on the amount of information he is able to gather on his enemies. He considers information to be power."

Rodney nodded. "So he knows his enemy well. How well does he know me?"

Sammy Thurmond stopped walking and turned to look at the general. Rodney also halted and turned. Both men locked eyes. "He knows every public detail about you plus many things private and considered unknown. He knows all save the most private thoughts of your heart that you have locked away for only yourself."

Rodney examined the man before him. He was a fascinating person, able to kill at a moment's notice, able to turn his emotions on and off as if flicking a switch inside him. Despite that, Rodney felt safe beside him, if, for no other reason than this: if Sammy wanted him dead, the deed would already be done, and they would not be talking right now.

"Mr. Thurmond, I assume, by virtue of our meeting, that there is something you wish to tell me, and that there is also something you wish to receive from me."

Uncle Rodney glanced around him at the head stones and chose the grave of Mary A. Redmond, born 1875, died 1917, the year Vladimir Lenin led the Bolsheviks in a successful revolution against the provisional government of Russia. He sat down atop the marble. He imagined the poor woman dying of influenza, reluctantly leaving her husband without a wife and her children without a mother.

Sammy Thurmond kneeled down beside a large, granite stone about five feet away. "What I want is quite simple, and, just by speaking with me you've already satisfied half my desires." He paused to let this sink in.

Rodney smiled. "So that tells me your weakness is curiosity?"

Sammy's face remained like a stone, but his eyes seemed to twinkle just a speck. Rodney noticed.

"But, General Branch, there is also something very important to me that I wish." Rodney waited patiently. "I would like to have dinner with your daughter-in-law."

Uncle Rodney was surprised, but he forced himself to remain unmoving. He simply nodded his head in understanding. He thought about it for a moment and then met Sammy's gaze once more. "Jackie is on assignment right now, and won't be back for a few days." Uncle Rodney hesitated a moment before going on. "Can you wait that long?"

"Yes."

Uncle Rodney was deep in thought, but he forced himself to focus on the hardened killer in front of him. "I will speak with her as soon as she returns, but I will not force her to comply."

Sammy answered right away. "If she was a woman who could be ordered, then she would be of no interest to me."

Uncle Rodney laughed spontaneously and honestly. "Yes, that's our Jackie. You know her well." And then he waited, but Sammy remained silent."So, Mr. Thurmond, what is it you'd like me to know?"

Sammy looked over to find the squirrel again, but he was already gone, probably high atop the maple tree. "I would like you to give this message to Special Agent Arnett."

The general gazed into Sammy's cold, green eyes and waited. *How did he know about Jeff Arnett?* But he didn't press it.

Sammy Thurmond leaned forward and extended his hand, palm down, and held it there, waiting for Rodney to meet him in the middle. General Branch leaned forward and placed his own palm below Sammy's. A small aluminum tube about an inch long and a half inch in diameter dropped down into Rodney's hand. Rodney withdrew his hand, as did Sammy.

The general rolled the simple metal tube between his fingers and examined it closely. It seemed to have a seam in the center, but Rodney did not attempt to open it. He simply placed it in the left breast pocket of his red, flannel shirt.

Both men, sensing that the meeting was over, stood simultaneously, and took one last look at each other.

"This has been ... interesting, General Branch."

Rodney smiled softly. "Same here, Mr. Thurmond. As soon as I talk to Jackie, I'll leave a note for you on my brother's gravestone with instructions on how to proceed."

Rodney turned to leave, but Sammy remained riveted in place. The general saw this and hesitated. "Was there something else, Mr. Thurmond?"

Sammy looked around, his eyes resting on several of the trees off in the distance on the edge of the cemetery. And then he asked an unusual question. "How many guns are trained on me right now?"

Rodney smiled and answered briefly. "Seven."

Sammy nodded. "Hmmm, I counted only six." And then he looked straight into Rodney's eyes. "It's always the one thing closest to you, the obvious thing, the thing that you don't see that gets you killed. Take a step back, general, and look for the obvious."

And then Sammy turned and walked away. Rodney watched after him, memorizing his gait, and every other detail he could find. Seven tiny, green laser dots licked hungrily across Sammy Thurmond's back, each dot wanting to reach out and touch him in a more intimate way. But Rodney didn't give the signal, and soon Sammy had escaped inside the trees.

A female cardinal, not near so brilliant as her mate, landed on a small bush ten feet away. Rodney looked over at it and smiled. Trusting an enemy had never been his strong suit. And then he walked away as well, leaving the dead to their own devices.

CHAPTER 9

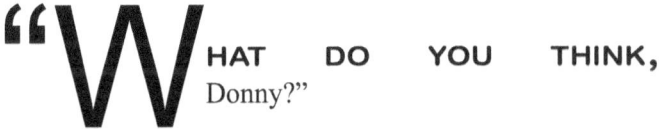

"**W**HAT DO YOU THINK, Donny?"

Donny Brewster took a step back and looked at the disheveled hotel room. At one time it had been a five-star resort, but now, without power for almost a year, it had fallen into intense disrepair, but that wasn't what bothered Jackie the most. Most disconcerting of all was the pool of blood on the floor, and the spray of dark red up onto the once-white drywall. It had been four days since Jackie had left Iroquois, but still, she was no closer to finding Joseph Donnelly, the Secretary of Veterans Affairs.

And now ... it looked as though he might be dead, indeed, may have been murdered in this very room. The country of Haiti had a lot of people in it, approximately ten million at the time of the collapse, though over half of those people had died due to starvation, waterborne illnesses and dysentery since then. The people who remained lived primarily in the surrounding rural countryside, somewhat insulated from the disease and violence so rampant in the city now. The upper class here in Haiti spoke French, while the commoners spoke Haitian Creole. The two were similar, and Jackie had a working grasp of both. That had made it possible for them to get around, but, still ... it was tough to communicate to the average Haitian as they were now very suspicious of foreign-ers, especially foreigners toting M4s and Squad Automatic Weapons.

Jackie looked out the window of the hotel suite. It stunk inside now, but just a year ago she wouldn't have been able to afford even one night in this once-elegant room. But this was definitely the type of hotel that Joseph Donnelly would have stayed in, and that's what had drawn Jackie and her team to this building. She looked down at the pool. There were still plush lawn chairs lined around the edge, but they were now tattered and rotted. The pool itself was filled with green algae, and she thought she even saw a rotting arm jutting up through the sludge.

She turned to Donny. "We have one more place we can go. I don't want to, but ... it seems we have no choice."

Donny cocked his head to one side, a bit puzzled. "Why not? What's wrong?"

Jackie shook her head back and forth, dismissing his ques-tion. "It doesn't matter. We just have to go there. This woman has been here a long time and knows a lot of people." She turned and strode out of the room. Donny, still puzzled, fol-lowed her. He activated his comm gear and ordered all to con-verge on the pick-up truck in front of the hotel.

Fifteen minutes later they were heading out of Port-au-Prince and into the surrounding villages.

Kenscoff, Haiti

It took Donny and Jackie almost ninety minutes to travel all the way up to Kenscoff. The road was still in place, but with lots of potholes, and a few places that had washed out recently. But, because they had four-wheel drive, they were able to make the trip without incident. When they got there, Donny was awestruck by the view.

"I can't believe this. We're looking down at the clouds."

Jackie nodded her head. She remembered the incredible

sight from two years ago when her and her first husband had been missionaries here. Looking now across the beautiful landscape and down the mountains, it was hard to believe that half the population had died and that the entire world had been thrown into chaos and darkness.

"The orphanage is just up ahead. Be careful not to scare the children with all the guns."

Donny nodded and issued orders to the four Shadow Militia soldiers in the bed of the pick-up truck. They quickly jumped out of the truck bed and formed a defensive perimeter around Jackie and Donny as they made their way down the hill.

A few minutes later they stood in the center of a worn-down playground. The swings were broken, and the merry-go-round remained deathly still. There was a silence about the place that chilled even Donny Brewster. Suddenly, a white woman stepped out from the door of the closest building with a shotgun leveled in their direction. She yelled out firmly in French.

"Pourquoi êtes-vous ici ?"

Jackie saw the woman and smiled. "Gena, it's me, Jackie."

The woman looked over and squinted her eyes, then she slowly lowered her shotgun and smiled weakly. "Lord God, Jackie, how can you be here?"

Jackie ran to the woman who lay down her gun and both embraced. Donny nodded to the four soldiers who quickly set up a defensive perimeter around the building.

Five minutes later they were inside, sitting around a bare, wooden table. The room looked like it used to be a cafeteria for the children.

"Gena, where are all the kids?"

The orphanage director looked down at the scarred, wooden table and cried unashamedly. "They are all gone. Taken."

Donny sat off to one side. watching the two women. They seemed as close as sisters. "Who took them, Gena?"

Gena paused long enough to wipe the tears from her eyes

before speaking. "There is a white man who seized control of the city just a few months ago. He appears to lead the local gangs from Port-au-Prince. I guess they had to move out of there because of all the diseases. They moved up here and came to get the children last week."

Jackie interrupted her. "But why would they want the children? All those mouths to feed."

Gena's eyes welled up again. "They are not good men, Jackie. Use your imagination."

Jackie remembered many of the children she used to love and play with here during her time with her first husband. She had fallen in love with them, and had been saddened when they'd left to return to the states.

Jackie lowered her head. "Oh, I see."

But then a fierceness came over her, filled her body like an adrenaline surge and heat emanated from her skin. "Where are they now, Gena?"

The missionary started to speak, but Jackie quickly shushed her. "Donny, get over here and take notes. I want those children back, and I want all the men who hurt them dead."

Sergeant Brewster looked at her strangely and then over at Gena. The woman was about five feet two inches tall, with unkempt, brunette hair. Her skin was a milky white, and her figure slim. It looked like she hadn't properly eaten in several days. Donny sat down at the table directly across from the two women. He took out a small, green, spiral notebook and black ink pen. As Gena talked, he listened and wrote down every pertinent detail.

Orders from Headquarters

Jackie listened intently as General Branch spoke to her regarding the situation there in Haiti.

"How many children are there?"

"Twenty-seven were kidnapped. But we don't know how many are still ... well ..., you know."

She paused and held the handset pressed tightly against her right ear.

"You understand, Jackie, that this isn't part of your mission, that getting involved in a bloody fight in a foreign country with a street gang could well get all of you killed?"

Jackie bit down lightly on her lower lip. "Yes, sir, I know."

Uncle Rodney took note of her use of the word 'sir.' He knew in his heart that what she wanted to do was the moral thing, but ... it could also jeopardize not just her mission, but also the entire future and stability of the United States. But he also knew that Jackie had the stubbornness of a Branch, and that, despite the fact she was asking permission, she might also disregard his orders should he refuse her. He sighed deeply, and Jackie could hear his struggle even across the thousands of miles. She played one last card.

"Uncle Rodney, we have no place else to look. And for all we know the Secretary of the VA could also be a prisoner along with the children." She paused, and when the general didn't answer right away, she spoke again. "It may lead us to another clue, general."

Uncle Rodney smiled but maintained a firm voice.

"Please put Sergeant Brewster on the line."

Jackie smiled and handed the handset to the sergeant who was standing beside her. Donny took the handset and pressed it to his right ear.

"Yes sir."

"Sergeant Brewster, I'd like you to reconnoiter the situation and get back to me as soon as possible. I want to know the feasibility of rescuing the children and preventing the hostiles from hurting any other innocent civilians. But it must be clean, and you are not to do anything that would risk the failure of your primary objective, which is to bring Joseph Donnelly back to CONUS. Do you understand, sergeant?"

Donny smiled slightly and then glanced over at Jackie. "Roger that, general. I will proceed immediately."

General Branch put down the handset to the SINCGARS radio. He shook his head from side to side and glanced over at Colonel MacPherson.

"She wants to rescue twenty-seven orphans from the evil clutches of a gang of monstrous killers."

Mac nodded his head. "That's not exactly mission-critical is it?"

Rodney didn't answer.

"Would you like some coffee, general?"

Rodney looked his friend in the eye. "You read my mind, Mac. Better make it black and extra strong. And the real stuff this time. Not those chickory weeds we've been drinking lately."

Colonel MacPherson nodded and went to the next room to make a cup of coffee. Uncle Rodney shook his head slowly from side to side. This was definitely not like the real army. But then ... he thought to himself. *That's what happens when you let the women do the fighting.*

Donny on Recon

THIS WAS NOT DONNY BREWSTER'S FIRST TIME IN A jungle. In fact, he'd seen lots of jungle during his time in the Corps, starting out with the army Jungle Operations Training Course in Hawaii. Since then he'd been deployed on covert operations all through Central America and the Caribbean, though this was his first time in Haiti and the Dominican Republic. But as far as Donny was concerned, jungle was jungle; they looked pretty on a post card but when you dropped down through the canopy you could pretty much plan on sweating, getting muddy, and getting rained on a lot.

This particular jungle was mountainous with one ravine and ridge leading to another. There was a lot of limestone and sandstone, which meant the ground beneath his feet could give way if he didn't watch where he was going.

At the moment he was seated on a piece of limestone, overlooking a cluster of large homes about two hundred feet below him. A large fern-type plant was growing right out of dirt lodged in a crack in the limestone, but it gave Donny ample concealment to watch the people below without being discovered. There was a small river beyond the houses, and this was obviously the rich part of town. The hostiles had set up house below him, apparent by the many trucks parked in a cluttered array across the lawn.

He slowly raised his binoculars up to his eyes and scanned the site below him. There were six men out front as well as roving patrols, seemingly without any hint of military precision or discipline. It reminded Donny of the horde of cut throats that had attacked Iroquois City just a few months ago. These men below were obviously experienced killers, but without military training, his men would have the edge in an all-out fight.

Donny made a sketch of the area on his notepad, then took several pictures on his cell phone. Most of the men walked with AK47s slung on their backs, but a few had only pistols, either in drop-leg holsters or simply shoved in the small of their backs.

Three hours later it was dark, and Donny took note of the changing of the guard. The foot traffic became much lighter, but the noise inside got much louder. Apparently, this gang had nothing to fear, because they partied with impunity, taking advantage of all the local residents, stealing their food, their property and also their women and children.

He made his way down off the ledge, traversing down the cliff from left to right, going slowly so as to not raise suspicion. The exterior was dimly lit with torches, and Donny was grateful that the power was out here as well. After reaching the bottom, Donny stayed off to one side of the dirt road, hidden in the bushes. He took out his night vision monocular and used it to scan the shadows in front of him. He saw no one and quickly scooted across the narrow road to the cover of an outbuilding.

There were three outbuildings that Donny was interested in, and he checked out the one he was leaning against first. He peered through the window screen but saw only darkness. It was then he heard the clucking of hens and realized it was just a chicken coop. He moved around to the door and stepped inside just to be sure. Donny thought to himself *Nothing but us chickens in here.*

He stepped back out and moved to the next building. It was further back into the shadows, making it easier for him to move around unseen. It appeared to be a garage with a cement floor. It was barren inside except for a folding chair in the middle. Tied to the chair was a naked man. Donny moved closer. Blood dripped down the man's bare back, and his head slumped down onto his chest.

The man appeared to be unconscious, so Donny moved in closer. Something about the man seemed familiar, but he couldn't quite place it. And then the man's eyes opened wide and he spoke.

"You're an American!"

Donny quickly hushed him. "Shh! Be quiet!"

Donny reached into his left, breast pocket and pulled out a picture wrapped in plastic. He looked at the man in front of him and then back down at the picture. And then Donny asked him. "What is your name?"

The man's voice was weak and raspy.

"My name is Joseph Donnelly. Please help me."

Donny stared back at him in disbelief. And then he thought to himself. *Jackie was right. Sometimes doing the right thing pays off even when it doesn't make sense.*

"How did you get here, Mr. Donnelly?"

The man lifted his chin off his chest. It seemed to take a lot of effort.

"They kidnapped me from my hotel in Port-au-Prince.

They were under the notion that I could be ransomed back to someone in the states."

Donny looked at the man in the darkness of the room. He was struggling with a moment of indecision. Normally, Donny knew exactly what to do, but this case presented special conditions. This man was his primary objective. He could take him now and declare his mission a success, but that would jeopardize the rescue of the twenty-seven children. Frankly, if the gang inside discovered Joseph Donnelly was missing, they would be alerted, then it might make a second rescue attempt impossible for the children.

The look of hesitancy in Donny's eyes caused a rush of fear to run through Joseph Donnelly's body. And then he said something that Donny hadn't expected.

"Aren't you going to save me?"

Donny smiled, showing his white, perfect teeth, then he pulled out a small k-bar knife and held it in front of the man's face. The fear on his face was quickly replaced with terror.

"Are you from the Blind Man?"

Donny moved his knife down to the man's bindings and quickly cut them away, causing the man to go limp and fall to the floor.

"Well, Mr. Donnelly. This is your lucky day. Now tell me. Where are they keeping the children?"

The Rescue

"THIS THIRD BUILDING IS WHERE THEY ARE KEEPING THE children. I saw only one guard and he is posted at the front door. It's a small building down by the river, maybe a boathouse or something, but it should be fairly easy to get them out. Then we'll float them down the river out of harm's way while we launch the assault on the compound."

Donny looked into the eyes of each of his four soldiers. "None are to be left alive. Do you understand?" The four men nodded and Donny jumped to his feet. "Okay then. Let's go kick some bad-guy ass!"

The Secretary of Veterans Affairs

"WHY ARE YOU LOOKING AT ME AS THOUGH YOU HATE me?"

Jackie Branch was staring at Joseph Donnelly without even realizing it. They had blundered into the completion of their mission not through skill or tact or even a well-thought-out plan. They had found the heir-apparent to the United States of America either by providence or by sheer, dumb luck. She was relieved by that, but right now she was more concerned with the pending rescue of the orphans more than Joseph Donnelly and his curiosity.

"Sorry, I don't hate you. Just worried about the children, that's all. I have a lot on my mind."

The man sitting across the table from her nodded slightly. He was about fifty years old, with black hair, and gray moving up from his temples toward the top of his head. "I understand. It's very noble of you and your friends to risk your lives for the orphans. Those men down there are animals and they need to be stopped."

Jackie didn't say anything. She didn't really feel like talking right now. The VA Secretary was quiet for a moment, until he could hold it in no longer. "Did the Blind Man send you?"

Jackie looked up in disbelief. "No. Of course not. We're fighting against the Blind Man. He's trying to take over America. We're fighting him to keep our lives and our freedom."

The man looked relieved. "But who are you? Forgive me, but ... you look like military, but not quite like conventional US military forces."

And then Jackie smiled. "We are the Shadow Militia."

The VA Secretary looked confused. "I've never heard of that one before. Please explain."

Jackie took a sip of the cup of water before her. "The

Shadow Militia is a group of highly trained US military veterans, mostly special forces types who were prepared for the collapse. We stood in the gap and prevented the Blind Man from taking total control."

The man reached down and took a drink of his water as well. "So, Jackie. May I call you Jackie?"

She nodded. "Jackie, what has become of the conventional US military? Where are they?"

Jackie hesitated, wondering how much she was authorized to tell him, but, in the end, decided that he'd have to be told sooner or later or all their effort was wasted.

"The Blind Man has some of it, but the bulk of Army, Navy, Air Force and Marines are holding out. Unfortunately, they are not unified. There is no one with constitutional authority left to command them."

Joseph nodded his head in understanding. "Yes, I know things are in a state of disarray. The president and vice president were killed along with most of Congress and part of the cabinet, but there must be someone who stood up and was sworn in to take over."

Jackie didn't say anything. She simply thought to herself. *He doesn't know.*

"That's the reason I fled the states. I have no security detail. They broke into my house and killed my whole family."

He stopped talking for a moment, and Jackie thought he might burst into tears, but he managed to choke them back.

"They were trying to kill me, but I got out before they succeeded." He lowered his head, as if in shame. "I should have died too." When he looked back up at Jackie, tears were in his eyes. "But I ran."

Jackie didn't say anything. She didn't know what to say that would make him feel any better. Nothing could bring back his family, nothing could turn the power back on or make all the death and destruction go away or give it any worthwhile meaning.

"I came down here because I thought it was the last place

they'd look for me. My wife and I used to come down to the Dominican Republic on short-term mission trips with our church to help build houses. I thought they'd never find me, but they did and I was forced to flee Santo Domingo, and I've been running for months now."

That information got Jackie's attention. "Who did you work with in the DR for your mission trip?"

The man hesitated. Then he softly smiled before continuing on.

"Praying Pelican Missions out of Minnesota. Do you know of them?"

Jackie's mood softened just a tad. "So you know John and Karen Stratten then."

"Absolutely. My wife and I have been to their house several times." And then the sadness returned to his eyes. "We had some good times with John and Karen."

Jackie suddenly had to admit she'd been judging the man, because he'd been investigated for possible fraud charges by the FBI way back prior to the collapse. And then she thought to herself *Who am I to judge? I cheated on my husband.*

But despite that, she still harbored an ill suspicion of the man. She didn't know exactly why, but for some reason she just didn't like this man, even though he appeared to be on the up-and-up.

"It's a shame when their son died last year. He was so young to have a heart attack."

VA Secretary Donnelly didn't hesitate to answer. "Yes, it was. A shame, a terrible shame."

Jackie nodded her head knowingly, but then the tone of her voice began to soften now. "Listen, Joseph. There's something you need to know." But then she hesitated before going on. "We are here to rescue you, but we have ulterior motives."

Joseph leaned involuntarily back just a bit. "Go on."

"Mr. Donnelly, you are the last remaining person who is authorized by the US constitution who can take over command of the country and its remaining military forces."

Jackie thought he was going to fall off his chair and onto the floor, but he managed to catch himself on the edge of the table with both hands. He sat back up straight and appeared to will himself back into control.

"I'm sorry. I guess I'm still weak from the torture."

And then he lowered his head again. "So ... my friends, my colleagues ... they are all dead?"

Jackie nodded. "Yes. You are the last one."

All Hell Breaks Loose, 4AM

Donny Brewster was positioned in overwatch high above on the same limestone ledge he'd used to do the recon earlier in the day. His four men were deployed all around the house, waiting for the go sign. Donny tapped his comm button. "Go! Go! Go!" And then all hell broke loose. Simultaneously, four white phosphorous grenades were tossed into the windows of the house and immediately began to burn anything within reach. The Willie Peter was followed closely by smoke grenades and flash bangs to create chaos. After that it was just a matter of shooting the rats as they abandoned the ship. First, Donny dropped the guard in front of the house with his .308 via a perfect head shot. Then two more ran out and paused on the porch. He dispatched them quickly with single shots to the sternum. Donny did his work quickly and methodically, void of all emotion, aside from a bit of excitement, but nothing that impeded his ability to kill.

He heard shots ring out at the back and sides of the house. hundreds of them. About two minutes into the fight, Donny heard the whine of a truck engine as it climbed up the driveway to the big home. Donny yelled into his microphone. "Get the SAW up front. I've got reinforcements coming in!"

When the truck arrived, Donny opened up with his .308 and managed to kill two men before the truck rolled to a stop. The other six men began to pile over the side, but didn't make it far before the SAW chimed in and cut them down like cordwood. Donny quickly dispatched the driver as he tried to escape on foot.

Donny heard a large explosion to the rear of the house."What was that? Somebody talk to me!"

"It was the propane tank cooking off. Not a problem."

"Angel Four, do you have the kids?"

There was no answer.

"All angels check in with sit rep."

"Angel one, all quiet on the west."

"Angel two, all quiet on the south."

"Angel three, still mopping up."

Donny was frustrated at Angel Four's silence.

"Angel Four, this is Archangel. Sit rep now!"

Nothing but silence.

"Angel one check out Angel Four and report back to me."

"Roger that, Archangel."

"Angel Two, slip over and help Angel Three with the cleanup."

"Roger that Archangel. Moving now."

Donny looked down, staring into the growing flames of the mansion below. It would no doubt destroy anyone inside, and soon leap to the houses closest to it. This whole block of rich people's homes would be black ash by morning, but Donny felt no remorse. The home owners were probably already dead anyway. Even so, this was Donny's purpose in life ... to kill people and break things. And Donny was very good at his job.

"Archangel, this is Angel One, over."

"Go with sit rep, Angel One."

"Angel Four's comm is down, but all children are secure, and floating down river."

Donny smiled. Gena had volunteered to extract the children. It was the obvious choice since she knew the river and would be able to calm the children and organize them quickly.

Donny and his men stayed another fifteen minutes just to make sure all hostiles were down. Three more were killed as they came in on a truck, but, after that, all was silent save for the crackling of the flames. Donny could feel the heat of the burning homes even two hundred feet above.

With great satisfaction, he withdrew his men, picked up the kids and beat feet back to the orphanage. With any luck, they'd be back in the states tomorrow night, and he couldn't wait to see his favorite nurse.

CHAPTER 10

August 16, I Smell a Rat!

Rodney Branch sat with his back to the maple tree about fifty yards from his home. He knew that he should be happy right now, that he should be celebrating with the others back at his house. The VA Secretary was recovered and safe, and, if all worked out, they would soon have a nuclear arsenal with which to battle the Blind Man, as well as portions of US air and naval forces. But ... something wasn't right, and he needed some distance, some time alone to think. It wasn't that his plan wasn't sound, because it was; it was a very good plan. At least as good as any he'd come up with and certainly the best he could hope for when his back was against the wall. The Blind Man had him outmanned, outgunned and, at least for right now, he was calling all the shots.

But things were going well. Jackie had found Joseph Donnelly, the VA Secretary, and he was in a secure location while he decided whether or not he'd like to be sworn in as the president. Even now they were busy trying to locate a federal judge in case they needed a swearing-in ceremony.

Justice Reed was working away at his better mousetrap, but Rodney suspected the old scientist was starting to get bored with the prospect, and that he might soon be ready to move on to something more potent. Of course, Justice Reed was just a back-up at this point. If the VA Secretary was sworn into office, then it would no longer be necessary for Dr. Reed to recommission the nukes.

Rodney looked up at the sky. It was a pretty blue up there today. A few wispy cirrus clouds were blowing by way up in the jet stream, so he watched them for a moment. Rodney thought out loud. "What are you doing Mr. Blind Man? What are you up to, and what are you going to do next?"

Jeff Arnett was furiously trying to decipher the password to open the files given to him by Sammy Thurmond, and that could be a game changer, depending on what was inside them.

Rodney thought about Sammy again. That man was an enigma. Strange. Very Strange. A deer fly buzzed around his head for a while, and Rodney kept swatting at it, trying to kill it, but it was just too fast. Every time he swatted, the fly buzzed away, and it was driving him crazy. If the fly would just sit still long enough, then he could kill it.

And then it occurred to him. The Shadow Militia was the deer fly, and they were driving the Blind Man out of his mind with frustration. But if they weren't fast enough, if they made even one tiny mistake, if they lingered in one place too long ... they'd get swatted and the game would be over.

Rodney took one last swat at the deer fly, pinning it to his scalp, where he rolled its body into death before flicking it off into the weeds. He looked after it and sighed.

"Let's not make any mistakes, general."

And then he thought long and hard about Sammy Thurmond's parting words to him.

> *"It's always the one thing closest to you, the obvious thing, the thing that you don't see that gets you killed. Take a step back, general, and look for the obvious."*

Rodney couldn't help but think that there was something he wasn't seeing, something obvious, but camouflaged so well, that it eluded him. He felt like he was walking into a trap.

And then there was the cryptic information on the tiny

slip of paper. inside the small aluminum tube given to Uncle Rodney by Sammy Thurmond back in the cemetery. He'd chosen to read it first before passing it on to Jeff Arnett as Sammy had instructed. Reading the contents of the capsule had rattled him to his core. At first he hadn't understood the clue, but after some research it had all come clear.

Uncle Rodney had been shocked and saddened, almost to the point of despair when he'd discovered the name of the traitor. When he'd realized his friend was the traitor, a wave of coldness and nausea had overcome him. There are some things a man never recovers from, like the horrors of war, but the loss of a lifelong friend, that you've trusted with your very life was even worse than that. When he'd first discovered the name, he'd wanted to disbelieve it, but ... he knew in his heart of hearts that the accusation was true. It made things clear.

But before jumping to conclusions, he first had to confirm the information from Sammy Thurmond. He needed proof. After that, the only practical question remaining was *How do I turn this to a tactical advantage?*

And then another question popped into his mind that saddened and terrified him even more. *What if he's not the only traitor among us? Who can I trust?*

But the answer to his question was not forthcoming. Uncle Rodney felt an extreme need for a cigarette right now as the weight of responsibility and his age beared down on him like gravity. And gravity always seemed to win. She was a tough taskmaster who never quit. And time was on her side.

The Blind Man's Lair

JARED HELD THE LONG-STEMMED GLASS OF PORT IN HIS left hand and swirled it just for fun before taking another sip. If this war didn't end soon, then his wine cellar would start to run low, and he certainly couldn't have that. In his right hand he held the handset close to his ear as he listened intently to all his operative had to say. Once the man on the other end stopped talking, Jared answered him politely but succinctly.

"Excellent. I appreciate the information. You will be hand-somely rewarded of course."

The man started to answer Jared, but the Blind Man quickly hung up, not out of rudeness, but more out of excitement than anything else. Jared suddenly lost his appetite for wine, and set the glass down on the table in front of him. His mind was busy trying to sort out all the details of what he'd just learned. This had real ramifications, and some heavy consequences if General Branch was able to pull it off.

"So ... you now have Joseph Donnelly. And you plan to swear him in as acting president of the United States?" Jared turned and walked toward the door.

"You are in for a big surprise, General Branch."

And then he focused his mind on the other important piece of information. "And you are trying to recover twelve nukes."

That little bit of information was most reassuring to Jared, as it confirmed that the Shadow Militia no longer had a nu-clear capability. And then he smiled and chuckled to himself.

"Sorry, general. No nukes for you!"

Pole Barn Headquarters

JEFF ARNETT SAT AT HIS DESK, CONTEMPLATING EVERY-thing that had been happening just in the past two months. Life was so unpredictable, so unpredictable and oh so fleeting.

General Branch sat down across from him in the simple. metal folding chair. He just didn't look like a general that Jeff had ever seen before, but still ... he commanded so much re-spect. It was as if all his people were lining up to die for him. Jeff didn't understand that fierceness of loyalty, at least not on an experiential level.

"We have a traitor in our midst, Mr. Arnett."

Jeff's hawkish nose tilted down, and his eyes narrowed their gaze. He hesitated for a moment and then leaned back in his chair before answering. "How do you know?"

Rodney leaned back in his chair as well. Then he reached into the left, breast pocket of his flannel shirt, where he used to keep his cigarettes and pulled out the aluminum tube that Sammy Thurmond had given him. "This was given to me by Sammy Thurmond along with a warning that someone in our inner circle is passing information on to Jared Thompson."

Jeff reached out to take the tube, opened it by twisting both ends. He looked inside and read the contents.

"This seems confusing. I don't know who any of these people are. Should I?"

Uncle Rodney smiled. "I didn't know at first either until I did some research, but then it all came clear to me."

So Uncle Rodney explained everything to him, and both reluctantly agreed they had a traitor in their midst. Jeff Arnett had an immediate plan to verify the identity of the culprit and General Branch instructed him to put it into action.

Rodney looked out the window of the pole barn. It was a small window, but he could still see outside, and it let in just enough light to see. "I hope that somehow, that we're wrong but ...."

Jeff Arnett frowned, trying to imagine how the general might feel right now."

"I'm sorry, general."

Rodney shrugged. "Thanks." And then he got up from his chair, a little more tired than he was before and turned to walk away.

"I'll let you know as soon as I get anything, general."

And then he called after Rodney.

"Wait, there's one more thing."

The general stopped and turned back around, waiting for Jeff to speak.

Jeff picked up a pen from his desk. It was blue, with a re-movable cap. He began to nervously pull off the cap and then replace it over and over as he talked. "

"I haven't been able to even make a dent in cracking the

password for the files Sammy Thurmond gave us." He paused, but General Branch didn't speak. The news had silenced him.

Jeff let his word trail off into the pole barn. It still smelled a bit like horses in here. He couldn't believe that he'd fallen so far, that he was now working in a pole barn that used to house horses and cattle.

"So what seems to be the hold-up? What can I do to help?"

After several seconds of quiet, Jeff Arnett finally spoke.

"A supercomputer would be nice. Do you have one?"

Uncle Rodney tried to smile, but it just wasn't in him today. "Sorry, Mr. Arnett. I was always more interested in tanks and grenade launchers than computers. Lack of foresight on my part, I suppose."

Jeff nodded and let out a sigh. "I just don't have the resources to do it here. Breaking a code like that usually takes a ton of processing power, and all we have here are laptops and desktop PCs with very limited software. It could take weeks to find the password, and even then ..." Jeff let his words trail off before continuing. "Even then we may not be able to crack it. I just wanted you to know that at this point in time, unless something changes, it's a long shot." He hesitated. "I just wanted you to know so you weren't planning on it."

Uncle Rodney's face grew stern and hard, then it seemed to relax into a thousand natural frowns, like leaves turning brown in the fall, just before they died and floated down to the earth. Gravity was a law that could not be denied.

"So, we can't open the files from Sammy Thurmond, the VA Secretary solution is a bit shaky, and we have a traitor in our midst. Any other good news, Mr. Arnett?"

Jeff Arnett lowered his head. "No, I think that about covers it, general. I'm sorry."

Uncle Rodney fumbled furiously for his left, breast pocket, but was quickly disappointed when no cigarettes were found.

"But what about the twelve nukes? Any problems there?"

Jeff nodded. "No problems there, sir. That option is still

in play, and plans are already underway to take delivery." He didn't take his eyes off Uncle Rodney as he spoke. It was like he was analyzing every action, even the most minute. "But those will be useless to us unless Justice Reed comes through." He paused a moment. "Is he still trying to build that stupid mouse trap?"

Rodney smiled nervously. "Yes, I'm afraid so." And then he looked off into the distance. "We may have to find another way to recommission them."

There was silence between the two men for almost a full minute. Finally, Jeff Arnett broke the silent stasis.

"General? Are you ... okay?"

Rodney let out a sigh, and then moved slowly and wearily to his feet. "Don't worry, Mr. Arnett. It's always darkest before the dawn." And then he cocked his head to one side as if in deep contemplation. "I wonder who said that?"

Jeff smiled slightly. "I think it was Thomas Fuller, sir."

Rodney hesitated. "Who?"

Jeff pushed his chair back and stood as well. "Thomas Fuller, back in 1650 or so. He was an English Theologian and historian."

Uncle Rodney laughed softly. "Of all the things to know." He turned to leave but mumbled back over his shoulder. "Well, let's hope the man knew what he was talking about."

The two men parted, unbeknownst to one another that both were beginning to doubt the other.

One Hour Later

THE BLIND MAN LOOKED OVER AT THE FRENCH Lieutenant standing before him at the position of attention. "It has been eleven days, lieutenant, and you still have yet to find Mr. Thurmond?"

The young lieutenant fought to maintain his military bearing, but the urge to squirm nervously was overwhelming him.

"That is correct, sir."

There was another man in the room beside them. This man was wearing a white lab coat and stood stock still, as if he didn't want to be noticed by the Blind Man. When the Blind Man glanced over at the scientist he didn't move or say anything. The scientist had learned long ago that if the Blind Man wasn't thinking about him, then he would probably live out the day.

The Blind Man turned his back on the lieutenant long enough to reach inside his front, right pocket and retrieve his pearl-handled .32 caliber handgun. He brought it up in one smooth motion and fired a round into the lieutenant's face. The shot was a bit to the left, and the French lieutenant went down but did not die. It was at that moment that Jared Thompson realized just how much he missed the efficiency of his former assistant, Sammy Thurmond. Sammy would have made a perfect shot to the ocular cavity, and the lieutenant would have died instantly with minimal mess. As it was, the lieutenant thrashed on the ground wildly, like an animal in his death throes. The scientist stepped back, but Jared heaved a deep sigh and moved in closer for the kill. He raised his gun and tried to aim at the man's head, but it was moving back and forth too quickly. Finally, because he couldn't get a good shot to the head, Jared aimed at the man's chest cavity and emptied the remaining five rounds into his body. He bled some more, spattering his blood on the floor and onto Jared's pant legs. The Blind Man looked on with disgust. The lieutenant's thrashing slowed before he quietly expired.

The scientist tried not to stare. He'd seen the Blind Man's barbarism before, but never by his own hand. Usually Sammy Thurmond would do his bidding. The Blind Man looked up from the dead body and made eye contact with the scientist. His eyes were ice blue, boring into him like cold death. The scientist tried to look away, but he couldn't.

"And now ... Dr. VanFleet ... let's talk about plan B."

Plan B, the Blind Man

WITH THE FRENCH LIEUTENANT'S BODY STILL BLEEDING onto the floor just a few feet away, Dr. VanFleet tried to compose himself long enough to give Jared an explanation.

"Well, you see, sir." He paused, sucked in some more air and tried to continue again. "It's not based on traditional RFID technology, but, rather on an advanced prototype of human-injectable tracking chip. The tracking is done via satellite, so we will know the subject's heading, course, and speed. It is accurate up to two meters."

The Blind Man turned away from the dead body and stepped over a widening pool of blood as he strode casually over to the couch. He sat down on the corinthian leather and leaned back as if fatigued. The unloaded gun was still in his hand. "And what will happen to Mr. Thurmond once you have activated this device which is already deep inside his body?"

The scientist glanced down at the dead body of the lieutenant before answering. "Well, the subject will begin to feel nausea and perhaps even experience a sense of disorientation. It will be mild at first, but eventually will increase, and within a few days will become debilitating."

The Blind Man frowned. "You are not to call him a subject. His name is Mr. Thurmond. He is twice the man you are." Jared reached down and picked up his wine glass from the mahogany table in front of him. "And how long will he live?"

Dr. VanFleet folded his hands together in front of his stomach. "A few days, sir. Perhaps as long as a week, but I doubt it. But the death will be very painful and discomfiting."

He took a small sip as if contemplating something deep. "What a shame. He was such a useful man." Then his blue eyes looked over at the scientist and made eye contact with him. "And he was so polite. So very polite. And incredibly efficient." He glanced down at the dead body on the floor. "Not at all like the French. I despise the French. They have no soul - so arrogant."

Dr. VanFleet took extra notice of the comment, and couldn't help but wonder *How does he feel about ... the Dutch?* `

August 17, A Dangerous Pick-up

"WHY ARE WE DOING THIS, DAD?"

Dan Branch looked over at his son just long enough to make brief eye contact. "Because Uncle Rodney asked us to."

Jeremy nodded his head. He glanced down at his M4 carbine and double-checked to make sure the selector switch was on safe. "Well, I know that, but ... what are we going to do with twelve nuclear bombs?"

Jeremy tipped his head back as if pointing with his eyes to the semi-trailer they were hauling. "I'm not sure I like being in the same truck with that much firepower. How do we know it's safe?"

Dan nodded his head as he drove down I-80 just west of Davenport, Iowa. They were over halfway home. "They're not activated, son. They are perfectly safe. In fact, it would be impossible for them to go off even if we were to shoot them."

Jeremy glanced out the window to his right. There was an incredible lack of corn in Iowa these days. Normally the fields would be a sea of green stalks reaching up ten to fourteen feet in the air. Some people joked that the corn grew so tall in Iowa that you could hang a treestand on a stalk to hunt deer. But that was before the collapse. Now there was very little diesel fuel available for the farm machinery, so the fields had not been planted this year. In fact, most of America, the bread basket for the world, was now lying impotent and fallow.

"Still makes me nervous, Dad. Can the radiation leak out and kill us?"

"Probably not."

Jeremy's head jerked back to his left. "Probably not!" His eyes got big with fear. "Are you telling me we could die hauling these things halfway across the country?"

Dan smiled lightly. "Don't overreact, son. When we took the radiation readings back in Montana, everything checked out fine. And the soldiers in back are all wearing dosimeters, so if it starts leaking then we'll know about it."

Jeremy rubbed the top of his head with his left hand before answering. "Okay, yeah, but ... doesn't radiation make men sterile?"

Dan Branch laughed out loud. "You mean to tell me, son, that we're carrying twelve nuclear warheads just a few yards behind us, and your biggest fear is future sterility?"

Jeremy suppressed a smile of his own. "I know, Dad. That probably sounds weird, but I'm still young, ya know. I mean, There could be a woman and kids in my future still."

The father reached over with his right hand and patted his son's knee. "Don't worry, son. I would never jeopardize the existence of my future grandkids. I plan on living to a ripe, old age myself."

"You've already lived to a ripe, old age."

Dan's face took on a mock sternness. "Hey! Watch yer mouth, son."

Jeremy laughed again. "Don't get mad at me. It's not my fault yer so old!"

And then Jeremy took on a serious air. He leaned his head over and pressed the right side of his forehead against the window glass. "Dad ... it occurred to me the other day, that ... well ... maybe I've already lived to a ripe, old age. Ya know what I mean?"

Dan let out a sigh as he pondered his son's statement. "Yeah, I know what you mean. The average life expectancy of a man these days doesn't seem to be as long as it used to be. Life is pretty tenuous when you stop to think about it. It always was. We just didn't realize it while life was so easy back before the Fall."

Jeremy looked out the window again. The fields were full of weeds taller than a man. The farms were already returning to prairie. "What do you think Tonya is doing right now?"

Dan squinted with his eyes at the question. "Our old neighbor back in Menomonie?"

"She wasn't that old ... younger than me."

Dan smiled. "So you still think about her huh?"

Jeremy got a faraway look in his eyes. "She's the only woman I ever ... well ... you know." He paused. "And it's not like I didn't have any feelings for her ya know."

Dan didn't answer. He didn't quite know what to say. "Dad, do you think she's still alive? I mean ... it was getting pretty rough there when we left."

Dan nodded. "It's possible, son. I think for most people, if they survived the first winter, then they'll be okay."

His son stared up ahead at the almost-empty interstate. "I suppose I'll never see her again though. Things are so screwed up out there."

The two men were suddenly silent together. Dan changed the subject. "What mile marker is that truck stop at again?"

Jeremy snapped back to reality and took the folded map off the console between them. He opened it up and looked for the spot.

"It's the Flying J, just two exits down on the right I think."

Dan nodded and they rode the next few miles in silence. When they reached the exit ramp, Dan pulled off the highway and drove into the parking lot. There were several other semi trucks there, but they appeared to be abandoned, and one had been set on fire.

"Keep a sharp eye out, Jeremy. It's a bit risky pulling over here."

"Then why are we doing it, Dad?"

Dan looked around cautiously while the Shadow Militia soldiers piled out the back and set up a defensive perimeter around them.

"Because I need to go to the bathroom really bad, and it's the kind I can't do while driving. I recommend you do the same thing."

Jeremy smiled and looked around for a place to go. They'd

already learned that every truck stop or gas station had already been looted, and sometimes had someone living in the abandoned buildings. The toilets didn't work, but that hadn't stopped people from using them; they were always clogged to the brim and incredibly stinky. Dan had learned to just find a bush with some cover and let nature take its course.

After both men had gone, they sat off to one side of the truck under a tree. Dan fired up the radio and contacted his Uncle Rodney. He'd been ordered to phone in his progress every four hours.

"Dad? Do you hear that sound?"

Dan dropped the handset. "Yeah. I think it's a helicopter."

Dan yelled over to the Shadow Militia team, but they were already deploying behind cement embankments and any other cover they could find.

"Get down inside that drainage ditch, Jeremy!"

His son followed him down the ditch and into the concrete tunnel about three feet high. It was dry now, but in the spring and fall it would funnel water under the drive and away from the parking lot.

The Apache attack helicopter came in low from the south, just above the buildings and treetops. It took only one pass to blow the semi-trailer to pieces and set it on fire. Dan and Jeremy cringed under the safety of concrete and dirt as they listened to the thirty millimeter M230 chain gun rip their ride to shreds. Then they heard the Hydra 70 rockets firing and reaching out to the semi-truck just a hundred yards away. There were several explosions as the two point seven five inch rockets found their mark. Dan involuntarily covered his head with his hands and waited for the radiation to consume him.

CHAPTER 11

August 17 - Sparky Sees Action

"**H**OLY MOLEY LORD GOD AL-mighty! Would you look at that!"

Sparky let his bike coast slowly to a stop as the explosions to the east of him rocked the Flying J parking lot. He'd been dutifully pedalling his bicycle every day now since leaving Western Kansas without so much as a single day off. Every morning he woke up at daybreak and had a meager breakfast, and would peddle from sunrise to sunset. Sometimes he would eat something he'd scavenged from an abandoned house. There were many of them around as so many people had died, either from disease or a myriad of unnatural causes. Once he'd found a box of Twinkies and was amazed at their freshness. They still tasted just like they had before the collapse.

At other times he met good, Christian people who were willing to feed him a meal, plus give him something to take with him. Whenever he ran across an empty vehicle, he always stopped and searched it thoroughly. It was amazing what one could find in glove boxes and beneath the seats of old cars. Half-eaten granola bars, chewed-up teething biscuits stuffed down under a child car seat, even a few packets of melted gummy bears. Sparky didn't complain, simply because he had come to the realization that he was on a mission from God. He

113

just wished he knew more of what the mission was and why he was doing it.

But at times when he started to doubt, the old man simply quoted one of his favorite Bible verses.

Romans 1:17 King James Version (KJV)

17 For therein is the righteousness of God revealed from faith to faith: as it is written, The just shall live by faith.

So many stories in the Bible were becoming more than just stories, because he was living them out in his daily life. He found himself understanding in an experiential way how the Israelites may have felt as they followed Moses across the desert for forty years. So the Jews had manna from heaven, and Sparky had Twinkies from Hostess.

Sparky looked at the growing plume of black smoke rising up above the truck stop as he decided what to do. This was indeed unusual as he hadn't seen anything like this on his trip. In his experience most of these truckstops were abandoned, and he'd avoided the ones that weren't.

He hopped up onto the seat of his bike again and began to pedal toward the smoke, singing all the way, sure in every way that God would protect him against any danger that might be out there. After all - why not? He had so far.

I ain't as good as I once was,
But I'm as good once, as I ever was.

Dan Calls Home

"THAT'S AFFIRMATIVE STONEPIT. WE ARE WITHOUT A ride and our payload has been destroyed by hostile fire."

Colonel Branch stood beside the pavement on interstate 80 and waited for Colonel MacPherson's reply. As he listened he glanced down to the west and watched a tiny speck moving on the horizon. It was moving slowly but steadily in their direction. Dan pointed it out to Jeremy and the other Shadow Militia soldiers who quickly redeployed to meet the potential threat. Dan moved a few feet to the south down into the ditch where he couldn't be seen.

"Yes, sir. That is correct."

Jeremy looked over at his father, wondering what was going on. *Why had they been attacked? How were they going to get home. and. foremost on his mind, were they going to die of radiation poisoning?* Jeremy looked back to the west at the approaching person. He appeared to be on a bicycle.

"We sustained zero casualties, sir." A pause. "Yes, sir we remain battle ready."

When the bike rider was within fifty yards of Dan, the Shadow Militia soldiers moved out of cover and quickly apprehended the rider. Dan watched with interest as they quickly and efficiently frisked the old man, spoke to him briefly and then brought him forward to Dan.

"Yes, sir. We will head east and await further orders."

Dan replaced the handset in the SINCGARS radio pack, and then turned to his soldiers under his immediate command.

"What's going on, sergeant?"

The sergeant moved forward with the old man while the others deployed back into their defensive perimeter.

"He's unarmed, sir."

Dan reached his right hand forward to shake the old man's hand.

"Sorry about the rough greeting. We were just attacked and can't be too careful. I hope you understand."

The old man nodded. "Sure. No problem. My name is Sparky Fillmore." He accepted Dan's grasp.

"Colonel Dan Branch, Shadow Militia."

Sparky retrieved his hand and let it drop at his side.

"Really?"

Dan smiled. "Yes."

Sparky laughed out loud and Dan's smile faded.

"Why is that so funny?"

The old man turned his head as his laughter faded before answering. "I'm on my way to Michigan to meet with General Rodney T. Branch, commanding general of the Shadow Militia. You wouldn't by any chance know him would you?"

Dan's face grew stern. "I see. That seems like quite a co-incidence."

Sparky turned to watch the smoke, still rising up from the Flying J. "There are no coincidences in the Lord's work, Colonel Branch."

Dan scrutinized the old man closely, looking deep into his eyes, but he saw nothing but peace and kindness, certainly nothing his men should fear.

"So, tell me, Sparky, is the general expecting you?"

The old man smiled and shook his head from side to side. "Well, I would hope not. We've never met before. Although I wouldn't put it past the Almighty to give him forewarning."

Colonel Branch cocked his head to one side before answering. By now Jeremy had moved up and was standing beside Sparky and his dad. But Jeremy stayed quiet in deference to his father and his rank.

"Where are you coming from?"

"West of Hays, Kansas."

Dan folded his arms across his chest. Jeremy lowered his M4. "You rode on a bike all the way from west Kansas?"

Sparky shook his head and smiled yet again. Sparky loved to smile, and, when he did, it seemed to magically take ten years off his age. "No, not all the way. I started out walking, but God provided me this nice bicycle before I'd gone too far. The Lord always provides - does he not?"

Dan reached up with his right hand to stroke his bare chin. He'd just shaved before leaving Montana.

"In answer to your first question, we know the general."

Sparky smiled again. "Well, okay then." And then he

raised his hands up as if in mock surrender. "Take me to your leader!"

Jeremy laughed out loud. "This guy's cool, dad. I like him."

Dan's face grew serious again. He yelled to the Shadow Militia soldiers. "Let's go men! We need to put some distance between us and that burning radiation pile. Form up and double time."

The men formed up on either side of the highway and jogged to the east. Sparky Fillmore fell in to the west of them and followed casually behind on his bike. And he couldn't help but wonder *What does God have in store for me now.* And also *I wonder what my wife, Edna, is having for dinner tonight. Probably not Twinkies.*

A Cryptic Message

SPECIAL AGENT JEFF ARNETT LEANED BACK IN HIS OF-fice chair. There were three other people around him working at computers, trying desperately to hack into the Blind Man's network and to discover the ever-elusive password they need-ed to open the files given to them by Sammy Thurmond. But so far they'd been unsuccessful. Try as they might, they could not break into the Blind Man's system or open the files they so desperately needed to defeat the Blind Man. Jeff was starting to wonder if he'd signed up with the wrong team.

Jeff pulled open the pencil drawer in front of him and looked down at the jumble of pens, pencils and paper clips. There, nestled among them all was a small aluminum tube about an inch long and a half inch in diameter. The tall man looked cautiously around him, making sure that no one was looking. Finally, he reached down and lifted the silver capsule out of the drawer and held it in his right hand above his lap. He rolled it back and forth in his fingers.

Why had Sammy Thurmond given this to General Branch to deliver to him? Why was the former right-hand man to the

117

Blind Man now trying to help them, if indeed he was. For all Jeff knew, this could be part of the Blind Man's plan. In Jeff's line of work, trust was a rare commodity.

The Blind Man was a formidable adversary and not one to be trifled with, and Sammy Thurmond was his right-hand man, or at least he had been until recently. Jeff pondered it for a moment. Had Sammy Thurmond really abandoned his old boss? And if so ... why? In Jeff's mind, the best course of action was to just kill Thurmond at the first opportunity, just to be safe. He doubted they'd get anything useful out of him. The man was crazy, a total lunatic, but General Branch seemed to believe there was something useful about him. His mind drifted off to a list of possible outcomes, none of them desirable to him. Sammy Thurmond was an impossible mystery with no resolution in sight.

Jeff moved the aluminum capsule to the thumb and forefinger of his right hand. He placed his left thumb and forefinger on the left side of the capsule and twisted. It turned with moderate pressure and Jeff pulled it apart. The tiny slip of paper dropped out onto his lap. Jeff picked it up and held it out to the light before reading it again for the umpteenth time:

Keith Allen
Roger Rees
Alan Wheatley

At first he'd thought the names were a list of people who were disloyal to the Shadow Militia, but it hadn't been that easy. General Branch had told him that Roger Rees had been a British actor that had been in the movie *Robin Hood Men in Tights*.

Apparently all these men had something very important and unusual in common. They were all actors, and they had all played characters in some production of *Robin Hood*. They had all played the part of the Sheriff of Nottingham. And that had troubled Special Agent Arnett. Suddenly, he began to wonder if Rodney Branch was still able to lead the fight. He'd seemed discouraged lately, and many of his plans were coming unraveled.

Jeff put the paper back inside the capsule and tightened it down again. He slipped it into his left, breast pocket and leaned forward, resting his elbows on the desk in front of him. Jeff folded his hands together and placed them under his chin as he contemplated the far-reaching ramifications of having a spy in their inner circle. *The Blind Man could know everything.* And, if he did, then none of them were safe and it was only a matter of time before they were all killed and the Blind Man won.

Jeff thought back onto his last meeting with General Branch. Rodney had seemed so sad, so ... discouraged, maybe even resigned. That had to mean something. But despite that, Jeff determined that the old man wasn't about to give up. Or was he? And then another thought occurred to him. *Why was Uncle Rodney always one step ahead of him?*

Special Agent Arnett had enacted his plan to confirm the identity of the spy, and soon, very soon they would be able to flush him out, but, in the meantime, they would use the spy to their advantage.

The Inner Circle

"WHO DO I TRUST, JACKIE? WHO?"

Jackie Branch leaned back in the folding chair and sighed. Baby Donna was on her lap, reaching up with her soft, baby hands and trying to grab onto her mother's lips as she spoke.

"I don't know Uncle Rodney. Why are you asking me?"

Uncle Rodney smiled softly, almost humbly. "I ask you because you're a woman."

Jackie looked up from her baby and laughed. "Uncle Rodney, I'm pregnant, full of unstable, racing hormones, and you're asking me for advice on life-and-death issues? I'm not sure that's wise. Besides, you've known me less than a year. For all you know I could be on the Blind Man's payroll."

Rodney lifted his right hand to stroke his chin. "Hmmm, I see your point." And then he laughed again, but quickly grew serious. "Jackie, I need your help. I need a woman's intuition. That's one thing I've always trusted is that magical, unseen insight that only women seem to possess."

Jackie reached down and held her baby with both arms. "Uncle Rodney, you're starting to scare me. Why are you talking like this?"

Rodney picked up his chickory drink and took a sip. "What do you mean?"

Suddenly baby Donna let out a loud, unabashed baby fart, and it seemed to break the tension in the room. "I mean where is your confidence? You always seem so sure of yourself. You exude confidence, so much so that it infects everyone around you and makes them believe in you as well. Uncle Rodney you have the unique, almost mysterious ability to lead nervous people in a crisis, to give them hope and help them believe that they can win even when there appears to be no rational reason to have faith."

Jackie held her baby closer. "Uncle Rodney, you can't start to doubt yourself, because if you do then everyone around you will begin to doubt as well. And then ... the Blind Man will win."

Rodney set his coffee mug down on the desk in front of him. "I know you're right. But here's the deal, Jackie." And then he hesitated as if girding up his loins before battle. "One of us inside our circle of trust is a spy. Someone is feeding information to the Blind Man. That's how he knew exactly where Dan and Jeremy would be with the nuclear warheads. We lost all the nukes, Jackie. We lost them all, and we almost lost Dan and Jeremy."

Jackie frowned and nodded in agreement. "I know. Would you mind holding baby Donna for a minute?"

Rodney seemed put out by the request, but he reached his arms out and scooped up the baby, before setting her on his lap. Baby Donna immediately reached over her head and grabbed onto Rodney's cheeks and squeezed as hard as she could. Rodney bent his head down and kissed the baby on top of her head. Jackie smiled and leaned back in her chair.

Uncle Rodney, there's something I haven't told you yet, something that might be important, but which I don't have any proof. But, if I'm right, and this is just a hunch, women's intuition as you say, then it could mean the death of us all."

Rodney cocked his head to one side and then held the baby closer to his chest. "So why didn't you tell me this sooner?"

Jackie shrugged. "I needed to think about it first, get it straight in my own mind before I passed it on to someone else. But, after thinking about it for a few days, I still can't shake the feeling that I don't trust him, even though I have no tangible proof to the contrary."

Uncle Rodney moved baby Donna over to his left knee and held her there so he could get a better look at Jackie's face. The question kept lingering in his mind, like a splinter that had festered and swollen. "Okay then. let's have it. Who is this person you don't trust?"

"It's Joseph Donnelly."

Uncle Rodney didn't say anything at first. He just sat there as if not wanting to hear what she was saying.

"And what lead you to distrust him?"

Jackie told him of her conversation with the VA Secretary in as much detail as possible. Uncle Rodney took it all in, storing it away and comparing it with information he'd already received from other people. In the end, he agreed that Jackie was right to distrust him. But that didn't soften the emotional blow. If she was right about this one thing, then they were in worse shape than they were before they found Joseph Donnelly, and he didn't see much hope on the horizon.

Jackie saw the despair sinking in, threatening to destroy her general, so she quickly changed the subject, lest he give in to the gravity of the situation.

"I think we should make a list of everyone close to us, everyone who had knowledge of the nuke delivery, then and only then will we be able to have a chance at knowing for sure who the bad guy is."

Jackie reached past Uncle Rodney and scooped up a notebook and pen from his desk. Then she sat back down and began to write.

"What about baby Donna. Do we trust her?"

Rodney and Jackie laughed out loud, and baby Donna quickly followed suit. Thirty minutes later, they felt more positive and light-hearted about the whole situation. Rodney left the room feeling more confident than he had in days, and Jackie's faith in Rodney was bolstered as well.

Sparky Meets the General

"COLONEL BRANCH, WILL YOU PLEASE TELL ME HOW IN god's name the Blind Man knew exactly where and when you would be in Davenport, Iowa?"

Even though he knew it was just his Uncle Rodney, still, being chewed out by the old man was definitely a sight to behold, but not one to be desired.

"I don't know, sir."

General Branch cocked his head to one side and looked at his nephew with shock in his eyes. Everything inside him wanted to yell and scream, but he knew that it would accomplish nothing, that it would simply demoralize his colonel and damage their personal relationship. Besides, he knew in his heart of hearts that Dan was not to blame. It's just ... he was counting on those nukes to defeat the Blind Man.

"May I remind the general that patience is indeed a virtue and one of the sought-after fruits of the spirit as outlined in the book of Galatians, chapter 5 and verses 22 and 23."

General Rodney T. Branch looked over at Sparky Fillmore, a man he'd never met before today, and when he looked at him, he couldn't believe his ears. He'd just lost eight nukes, and now a total stranger was quoting scripture and rebuking him for his lack of self control. Rodney fought for patience.

"And who the hell is this man?"

Dan started to speak, but Sparky beat him to it. He moved forward quickly and thrust his right hand out to shake the general's hand. "My name is Sparky Fillmore, from western Kansas and I was sent here by God to give you a message."

Uncle Rodney put his fists on his hips and looked incredulously at the man before him. He started to talk, but slowly regained control of his anger. Finally, he reached out and shook Sparky's hand. "There now, General Branch, now doesn't that feel so much better to be in control of yourself? I can already feel the tension lifting."

Sparky looked over at Jeff Arnett, then at Colonel MacPherson, then to his nephew Dan. Jeremy Branch was the only one smiling in the room. He alone appeared to be having a good time. Finally, after mastering his emotions, the general spoke.

"Okay, Mr. Fillmore, I'm not above help from God, so why don't you go ahead and give me the message. What exactly does God want you to tell me?"

Sparky laughed out loud and starting shaking his head from side to side. "I have no idea, general! And isn't that just like God to do something like that? All I know is that God came to me while I was milking my cow one morning and told me to travel to Michigan in search of Rodney T. Branch, the commanding general of the Shadow Militia. He didn't tell me why or what message to give you. I'm still waiting for that part."

Uncle Rodney's head sagged down, almost far enough to rest on his chest. He was discouraged. After several seconds, he looked over at the maple tree to his left and saw the bright, red cardinal perched there on a small branch. Rodney watched the bird for several seconds, until it flew away into the woods. Before speaking, he let out a huge, audible sigh.

"Well, in that case, Mr. Fillmore, I'd like to thank you for traveling so far at your own expense and inconvenience to give me this message that hasn't quite come to you yet." He looked into Sparky's face and tried to smile. "Welcome to Michigan, Mr. Fillmore."

Jeremy Branch moved forward and slapped the old man from Kansas on the back. "He can bunk in my room. I'll sleep on the floor. I like this little guy."

Sparky smiled and turned toward his new, young friend. "Why thank you, young man. I really appreciate that. But I can sleep on the floor. Not a problem."

General Branch ignored the rest of their conversation as he turned back to his nephew. "Dan, I need to speak to you about a very important matter. Meet me in my kitchen at twenty-two hundred hours."

Colonel Branch snapped to attention and saluted. Rodney returned the gesture and strode away into the woods to finish cooling off. He needed some time to think and sort things out. So much was happening, so quickly.

CHAPTER 12

<u>*August 17, The Great Debate*</u>

"**A**BSOLUTELY NOT! THERE'S NO way in hell I'm letting you have dinner with that man!"

Dan Branch was fit to be tied as he paced back and forth in Uncle Rodney's dining room. Colonel MacPherson and General Branch were seated at the kitchen table, both with their hands folded atop the Formica. Jeremy and Donny were off to one side, leaning against the wall. Jeremy seemed entertained. Joe Leif stood beside the kitchen sink with a cup of coffee in his hand and had a concerned look on his face.

"Why not, Dad. It sounds like fun to me."

Dan Branch shot a piercing stare into his son, quickly silencing him for the duration of the conversation. Jackie was seated at the table across from Uncle Rodney.

"Now Dan, just calm down. I didn't say I was going to do it."

Dan walked to the far wall, turned around and came back again. "I can't believe he's even asking you to do it. First he sends you into a saracen camp of twenty-thousand men, and then he flies you down to Haiti, and now he wants you to have dinner with the most dangerous killer on the planet!"

Dan stopped and pointed his finger out at his uncle. "This is too much! You've just crossed the line! I will not allow this to happen."

Baby Donna curled her lower lip and began to whimper in Jackie's arms. "Please, Dan. You're scaring the baby."

Dan saw his daughter's fear and tried to calm himself down. He took a deep breath and tried to maintain more control as he addressed his uncle.

"Why are we doing this?"

Uncle Rodney sighed and looked up at his nephew. He thought about it for a moment before speaking. "Well, Dan. We're doing it because this man has information we need to defeat the Blind Man. In fact, he has intimate knowledge of every aspect of Jared Thompson's capabilities and I believe a small part of him wants to help us."

Dan crossed his arms over his chest and stood defiantly. "And just what makes you think he wants to help us?"

General Branch remained calm and stone-faced. "Because he abandoned the Blind Man at risk of his own life. He came to us and has already given us valuable information. And now that he's committed himself he has nowhere else to go. If he returns to the Blind Man he'll be tortured and killed."

Dan, normally a calm and rational man, was anything but rational when it came to the safety of the woman he loved. He turned to stare out the kitchen window, trying desperately to make this topic go away. Then he looked back at Uncle Rodney with pleading eyes. "But what if he kills her?"

General Branch opened his mouth to answer, but Jackie cut him off. "Dan, please. Calm down. You don't know this guy like I do. He could kill any of us at any time he pleases. He doesn't need to set up a time and place where we have control in order to do it." She stood up and handed the baby to Jeremy before turning toward her husband. "Besides, if he was going to kill me he would have done it when I was in the saracen army camp." She moved to Dan and placed her hands on each side of his face. "But he didn't do that. Instead, he let me go and gave me information that might defeat the Blind Man to boot."

Dan saw an opening and interrupted. "None of that information has helped because we haven't been able to access the files. He's given us nothing!"

Uncle Rodney stood to his feet, followed by Colonel MacPherson. Joe Leif was still sipping his coffee and trying to stay out of the line of fire.

"Jackie, why don't you and Dan take a walk and try to figure it out as a couple. All I can tell you is I won't order you to do it, and whatever you two decide is what we'll live with."

Dan looked over to his uncle, but then returned his gaze to his wife. He looked into her dark eyes. "Honey, do you have any idea how many people this man has killed?"

Jackie lay her head on his chest, her long, black Lebanese hair cascading down around her. Then she looked up into Dan's face and smiled. "Honey, I hear what you're saying, and I love you for it. But ..." She hesitated. "But honey, I doubt very much this terrible man has killed any more men than I have."

Dan's face tightened. She'd just said something that he'd never considered before. And it was true. In the last battle alone before being captured in the saracen camp, she'd killed over eight thousand people using poison hemlock and then a biological agent. His wife, however sweet and loving to her family, was a seasoned and proficient killer. He opened his mouth to speak, but all that came out was empty air.

August 18, A Touch Under the Weather

Sammy Thurmond was not feeling well these days. In fact, he hadn't been feeling well for almost a week now. He looked around the abandoned house he'd been staying in and felt a bit of a chill, despite the eighty-two degrees all around him.

Sammy slowly rolled off the bed, and his shaky legs hit the floor with a thud. A sudden wave of nausea spread over him, but he choked it down and stood upright. He was a little dizzy, but it seemed to pass as he walked out of the bedroom, down the stairway and into the bright sunshine. The strength returned to his legs and he made it the rest of the way to the cemetery with no more ill effects.

The nausea had begun a few days ago, and now he was feeling disoriented, and finding it very difficult to focus on things he needed to do. This was a disconcerting feeling to Sammy, as he'd always been in full control of his faculties as well as his body. It was frustrating to lose control of himself when he was accustomed to controlling not only himself but most others around him. Something was wrong, but he didn't know what it was.

Pausing at the edge of the cemetery, Sammy watched the trees at the far edge of the cemetery. After fifteen minutes, he caught the movement, however slight, and then brought his binoculars up to his eyes to focus in. They were cheap binoculars, a pair he'd found in the garage in a chest full of old bowhunting gear at the house where he was staying, but they were enough for him to identify the man in the ghillie suit keeping watch over the grave of Ronald T. Branch.

Sammy watched for another half hour, seeking out any other soldiers, but saw none. In Sammy's mind, one soldier would be there simply to observe and report, but a squad of soldiers would be a kill team. Not that it mattered. If General Branch wanted him dead, he could certainly have killed him on their last meeting. But he hadn't done so. Sammy and the general had achieved a delicate detente of sorts which allowed them both to live and breathe and meet. Sammy knew that it was temporary, that it had to be, and that it was based solely on a personal one-on-one principle of mutual assured destruction. They both had something the other wanted, and, as long as that situation existed, as long as both believed the other could kill on demand, then both men could rest easy. But for now, the tenuous truce was in force and Sammy had nothing to fear. Despite that, he approached from the east side of the cemetery instead of the west as he'd done before. Sammy would never be good at trust.

He stood up and walked briskly toward the granite head-stone. When he got closer, he saw the piece of white paper sitting atop the stone inside a plastic bag. He looked at it for a moment as if searching for some form of treachery. At last, he reached down and picked it up. As he was opening the bag, Sammy sat down on the headstone across from Rodney's brother. He read the note and almost smiled inside ... but not quite.

> *"Tomorrow, 6PM, this location. Bring an appetite. It will be good to see you again, Mr. Thurmond.*
>
> *Respectfully,*
> *Jackie Branch*

Before he realized his actions, Sammy lifted the paper to his nose and sniffed it. He could still smell her.

Then he folded the paper back up and placed it neatly inside the plastic before putting it inside his front jeans pocket. He would need to take a bath and comb his hair.

DONNY BREWSTER WATCHED IN HIS RIFLE SCOPE AS Sammy Thurmond walked toward the woods as he departed the cemetery. It would take but a pound of trigger pull to kill this man, but his orders had been specific: do not engage under any circumstances. Simply observe and report. And that's exactly what he'd done. Donny was confident that he hadn't been seen, so now he watched just long enough to seal the deal and complete the mission.

But then the man hesitated and slowly turned back toward the cemetery. Donny was a hundred yards away, but the man looked up, into Donny's tree, and seemed to be looking directly at him. Donny frowned and zeroed in on the man's head via the scope. He could see the man's face perfectly now, his cold, green eyes, the chiseled, stone-like features of his jaw and face. And then the man smiled slightly and turned to walk away.

Donny was dumbfounded. And then he whispered out loud. "Well I'll be buggered." And then he couldn't help but smile respectfully. "Amazing."

August 19, Dinner Date with Death

THE NEXT DAY, JACKIE BRANCH STOOD BESIDE THE PLAS-tic folding table at the grave of Ronald T. Branch. The table was eight feet long and there were two comfortable folding chairs set up across from one another. At the center of the table was a candle. Jackie struck a wooden match and lit the wick. The candle burned, flickered, and then burned brighter. The air was a dead calm, the sun leaning down toward the treeline which lengthened the shadows and lent a coolness to the late summer air.

Sensing movement to her right, she glanced over and saw Sammy Thurmond walking toward her across the grass. Normally, the grass of any cemetery was short, thick and well kempt, but now the grass was almost knee high and already starting to turn brown from the unrelenting heat of an entire summer. She was nervous inside, but kept her jitters hidden as she forced a smile onto her face. She bowed her head slightly as Sammy stopped at the table across from her.

"Good evening, Mr. Thurmond. I'm glad you could make it."

Sammy nodded his head and stood in front of the chair for several seconds with an awkwardness uncharacteristic of his usual demeanor. Finally, he bowed his head slightly and then walked around and held the chair back so Jackie could sit down.

"Thank you, sir."

He then moved back around and seated himself. At first he said nothing, but Jackie didn't rush him. A tiny breeze kicked up and the candle flickered slightly, but then burned bright again as the air died down.

"I am happy to see that you are still pregnant, Mrs. Branch."

Jackie smiled softly and answered politely. "Why thank you Sammy. I've just started my second trimester, and it's starting to get a bit uncomfortable with all this heat." She hesitated, but he didn't join in, so she continued on. "But in another month it will cool off again and things will get better."

Sammy looked across the table past the candle and deeply into her eyes. Two months ago the intensity of his gaze would have rattled her to her core, but now ... it was different. She was different. She met his stare and returned it.

"General Branch says you just returned from an assignment." He paused. "I hope it went well."

Jackie nodded. "Yes, it did. It went very well." She couldn't help but be reminded of a husband and wife, talking about their day at the office over a romantic dinner. Oddly enough, she found it intriguing, two deadly assassins, both having killed thousands of people, talking over dinner as if they were normal.

"I was in Haiti on a special assignment."

Sammy broke eye contact and looked away. When he turned back, Jackie thought she saw a bit of compassion in his eyes. "Was it hard for you to go back there?"

She kept the smile pasted on her face, but her eyes were frowning now. She simply said "Yes. Hard. Very hard."

"And did you find what you were looking for?"

Jackie hesitated, wondering how much he already knew and how much she should tell him. Then she recalled the last dinner she'd had with him and how well it had gone. She had been very open and candid with him, so she decided to do the same today. Instinctively she knew that any information she withheld would carry the same weight as a lie.

"Yes, we rescued the Secretary of Veteran Affairs from a gang. He'd been kidnapped."

Sammy nodded with renewed interest. "We had located him in the Dominican, but he slipped through our grasp several times. The Blind Man was very disappointed."

And then Sammy looked away from the table and scanned the trees and the edges of the cemetery. "How many people are watching us right now?"

Jackie didn't hesitate. She was totally committed to her role. "I'm not sure. I didn't count them. But at least twelve I think."

Sammy's face brightened a bit. "That's good. I like to be taken seriously, anything less than ten would have been an insult."

Jackie laughed softly. "Mr. Thurmond, is that humor?"

Sammy nodded. "I hope so. It's been a long time though, so please do me the honor of chuckling regardless."

She laughed again, this time with a more genuine tone. "A sense of humor is like riding a bike I suppose."

"So, General Branch is going to place Joseph Donnelly as the acting president, take control of the remaining US military forces and attempt to defeat the Blind Man?"

Jackie paused and then nodded. "Yes, I believe that is the plan. At least most of it. Uncle Rodney would never usurp power though. Once the Blind Man is defeated and constitutional control is once again secure, then all of us will quietly bow out and return to our normal lives."

Sammy cocked his head to one side and looked at her as if she'd just said something very surprising. "General Branch is going to willingly give up power?"

Jackie nodded. "Yes, of course. Anything less would be dishonorable."

And then Sammy looked off over Jackie's shoulder, as if remembering a Truth that had somehow been forgotten long, long ago. "Hmmm, that is highly irregular, to give up power I mean." Jackie said nothing in response.

"The Blind Man will not see that coming."

He turned his head back to Jackie and stared into her eyes.

"But you must understand that he will not allow the general to follow through with his plan. He will have to counter."

Jackie moved her hands up on the table top and clasped them together lightly. "By that you mean he will try to kill Mr. Donnelly?"

He looked into the flame of the candle burning on the table. The flame flickered in the center of his eyes. "Be careful with him, Jackie Branch. Skim milk masquerades as cream."

Sammy smiled, and his icy green eyes made the hairs on Jackie's neck stand up. "I doubt you'll anticipate what the Blind Man has already planned." He looked at the dishes on the table. "If The Blind Man wishes the secretary to be dead, then he will soon be dead. If he wishes to use him in some other way, then ..." Sammy let his last statement trail off into the woods beyond the cemetery. Jackie took note of it and stored that information away for later analysis.

"Enough shop talk for now, Mr. Thurmond." Jackie lifted the cover off the cast iron kettle to her right as she changed the subject. "I hope you are a meat and potatoes man. I made beef pot roast. It's one of my specialties."

The man moved his hands back down to the table top and his smile softened. She seldom knew when he was playing games and when he was deadly serious.

"Mrs. Branch, I'm guessing that you already know how much I love pot roast. If you don't, then it would be impossible for me to respect General Branch if his intelligence gathering were so shoddy."

"You grew up in Iowa, Sammy. I would be very surprised if you didn't appreciate a good roast served with corn on the cob, butter and mashed potatoes and gravy."

Sammy laughed out loud, but this time it didn't sound creepy. Jackie asked for his plate and quickly cut him a generous slab of pot roast, then some corn on the cob and mashed potatoes. Last, she ladled on some beef gravy.

"I hope you brought your Iowa farm-boy appetite with you today."

Sammy didn't say anything. The smell of the roast wafted up and into his nostrils, causing the nausea to rise up as bile in his throat. It came over him quickly, but he mastered it almost immediately. Jackie noticed a slight change in his face, but then it was gone, almost as quickly as it had come.

"Are you alright, Mr. Thurmond?"

Sammy nodded and smiled slightly. He reached over to accept the full plate from her. Then he slowly picked up his fork to eat, but Jackie quickly admonished him.

"Not yet, Sammy. First we give thanks."

The stone-cold killer across from her hesitated, as if making a decision that didn't quickly compute, and then he closed his eyes and folded his hands on the table in front of him. Jackie did the same and then began to pray.

"Dear Lord, we thank you for this food. We thank you for this wonderful day and for all the ones who love us. Amen."

While Sammy ate, Jackie made a plate for herself.

"So, Sammy, what do you think?"

Sammy waited to finish the bite in his mouth before answering. "It's absolutely wonderful, Mrs. Branch. I expected no less."

Both of them ate in silence for the next ten minutes. Jackie pondered the craziness of the situation she was in, eating a civilized dinner with a pathological murderer, a man who could kill on command without batting an eye or feeling an emotion. It was a job to him. And then she wondered ... how much of a difference was there between Sammy and Uncle Rodney, or Sammy and Donny Brewster? All three of those men could kill, in great numbers, skillfully, had indeed studied the art and science of killing and had mastered it like a craft, like a painter or a concert pianist.

And then she wondered ... *how many people have I killed?* And, more importantly, *am I any different than Sammy? If I continue killing, will I become unrecognizable, like the creature, Gollum, in Lord of the Rings? What would distinguish me from the man sitting across the table?*

Sammy finished his food and gently dabbed his mouth with the white, linen napkin. Jackie quickly finished her last few bites and did the same.

"Well, Mrs. Branch, I want to thank you most profusely for the conversation and the meal. It was most enjoyable."

Sensing that he was about to leave, Jackie was tempted to ask him questions, to get information that would help them defeat the Blind Man. She knew that's what Uncle Rodney would want, but ... somehow, she sensed that pushing him would be the wrong move. But if he told them nothing, then why was she going through all this trouble? Jackie bit her tongue and responded politely.

"It was no trouble at all, Sammy. I'm glad we had our talk. It's my way of returning the favor you gave to me." She looked him directly in the eyes now, and what she said next was neither forced nor contrived. "You saved my life, Sammy. I know that, and I'm grateful."

Sammy smiled so genuinely, that Jackie found it hard to remember that he was a heinous killer. He could be very charming when he wanted to. He slid his chair back roughly in the grass and then stood to his feet. Jackie saw him hesitate halfway up, and Jackie wondered what that was all about, but he straightened and then nodded politely to her.

Jackie extended her hand, and Sammy reached down and gently touched her, lifted her hand to his lips and pressed them together in gentlemanly fashion.

"Chivalry is not dead, madame, especially in Iowa. I want to thank you for this warm and wonderful down-home, Iowa dinner. As always, you've been a splendid hostess, and I want you to know that this one meeting, coupled with my conversation with General Branch, made all the sacrifice worthwhile. Thank you so much."

Jackie smiled and nodded as he released her hand. She was confused by his warmth and gentleness, and by his words. *Sacrifice? What did he mean by that.* As she looked into his stone-green eyes, she thought she saw a hint of compassion, but it was fleeting, there for just a moment, like a vapor, and then it rose up and was gone. In her heart of hearts, she knew that Sammy Thurmond was a huge tome of secrets, that it might take a lifetime to figure him out, but still ... she forced herself not to push him. He would share when he was ready, and, somehow, she sensed that they would be having dinner again soon.

And then Sammy Thurmond turned and walked away, slowly at first, with the subtle hint of a military stride, and then he gradually slowed. Jackie watched as he walked, not knowing what to expect, thinking, *is this all there is?*

And that's when Sammy Thurmond fell to the ground and ceased to move.

CHAPTER 13

Life and Death

"**S**AMMY THURMOND! SAMMY! Wake up!" Jackie Branch kneeled down on the cemetery grass beside her dinner partner. There was a sudsy, white foam coming from his mouth now, and Jackie wiped it away with her linen napkin. There was a chalky pallor to his face that seemed eerie in the failing light of the graveyard. And then he began to shake. At first, Jackie grabbed his arms and tried to hold him still, but he was much too strong for that.

"Sammy! Are you okay?"

But Sammy didn't answer. His body continued to convulse, and then his eyelids snapped open wide. Just for a moment, Jackie looked into the icy, green stare, but slowly, ever so slowly, the green of his irises rolled up into his head and only the whites showed. The shaking continued for almost a minute, and then it stopped as quickly as it had started. Sammy lay there in Jackie's arms, exhausted and motionless on the ground, with the tall, brown sedge grass rising up around his head.

He opened his eyes and looked up at Jackie. Then he spoke weakly. "You are such a beautiful woman."

Jackie laughed out loud nervously, but relieved that he was still alive. She could hear people running up behind her and knew her protection detail would be there soon. She sensed that things were coming to a climax, or perhaps even a hasty close. She didn't know what to say, so she just spoke from her heart.

"Why thank you, Mr. Thurmond. I hope my pot roast had nothing to do with your present condition."

Sammy chuckled softly with all the energy he could muster. "No, my lady." Sammy looked up at Jackie's face, a silhouette against the darkening sky. He smelled the dead and dying sedge grass around him and knew he was standing on a new precipice. "This one is courtesy of the Blind Man." His words were becoming forced now. "Not altogether unexpected. I wondered what surprise he had for me." Sammy's eyes looked up into the sky beyond Jackie's head. "The Blind Man seldom disappoints."

Jackie smiled down compassionately. "Is there anything we can do to stop it?"

Sammy tried to shake his head from side to side, but the motion served only to heighten his vertigo. "No. The Blind Man has always been ... thorough. Do not under estimate him or you'll suffer my fate."

The whites of Sammy's eyes started to pool up with blood at the corners, and then worked its way into the irises toward his pupils. The mixture of red and icy green was horrifying to Jackie, but she pretended not to notice. And then Sammy's skin took on a flushed, pink color, and his very blood began to seep gently out through the skin of his face and arms.

Jackie steeled her will and continued to make eye contact with him. Right now she was feeling so many conflicting emotions for this man, this cold-blooded killer, this chivalrous hero who'd saved her life and treated her with kindness as he'd murdered so many others. "What can I do for you, Sammy?"

Just then Donny Brewster arrived. Jackie held him back with a wave of her uplifted hand, causing him to just hover in the background and Sammy whispered his last.

"Come close, my lady."

Jackie hesitated just a second, but then moved her face down closer to his own. "I have a message for General Branch."

She was confused, but nodded her head.

"Remember."

Jackie moved just a bit closer.

"h, 4, 8, b, 5, a, t, plus, k, w, l, s, minus, 8, y, h, 4, g, u, q."

Sammy closed his eyes for a few seconds, then opened them back up again. The edges of his eyesight were failing now, and he knew the end was near. He thought back to so many other countless men that he'd killed. At the time he'd given no thought to his own death, but ... he wondered. *Had it been like this for them as well?*

Jackie looked up at Donny. "I need a paper and pen! Quickly!" But she saw that Donny was already writing down the characters in his sniper notebook.

Sammy repeated the sequence again, this time softer and harder to hear. And then he was quiet for a few seconds before looking back up into Jackie's face. So many he'd killed ... with knives up close, cold and impersonal at one-thousand yards, bullets in the ear, the back of the head, sometimes in the guts just to watch them suffer.

So many of the deaths did not bother him, but he still re-membered his first. It had been the hardest, and it weighed on him now, like an anchor that threatened to drown his soul in a sea of lifelessness. And then the name Steven Maxwell came to his mind ... the man who had unwittingly started it all, the man who'd injected the god virus into the heart of America. He still remembered Steven by name, as a pitiful man, a geek with no future outside a computer screen. If memory served him correctly, he'd shot that man in the eye, the left eye. And then he thought out loud, his words confusing Jackie. "It wasn't such a bad death."

Sammy Thurmond came out of his musings and tried to

reach up to Jackie, but he didn't have the strength. Jackie reached over and grabbed onto his right hand with her left. She felt the wet, slippery blood, seeping through his skin, but felt no compunction to pull away from him. No man, even a killer, deserved to die alone.

"I'm here, Sammy. I'm here for you."

The sight around the edges of his vision began to close in on his pupils even more, like a tunnel of light, surrounded by an ever-growing and unstoppable darkness.

"Sammy! Stay with me! What can I do?"

The man's voice opened and a small puff of air came out, trying to form words. Jackie didn't understand, so she moved down closer to just a few inches away from his mouth.

"Pur ... pose."

There were tears flowing down Jackie's cheeks now.

"Get ... him."

The last thing Sammy Thurmond saw was Jackie's black hair covering his face. The last he felt was her tears falling lightly on his cheek. The last he heard was the whimper of a woman who cared about him. And then his senses failed him, all save one ... the light smell of olive oil, scented with lilac. And then his final thought on earth ...

It's more than I deserve.

Jackie felt his hand go slack, and she collapsed onto his chest and wept.

GENERAL BRANCH STOOD OVER THE GRAVE OF SAMMY Thurmond, a hardened criminal, a killer, and only God and the Blind Man knew what else. But Jackie had insisted on a proper burial, and Uncle Rodney had agreed with her. Whatever else Sammy Thurmond had been at his death, it had not always been so. At one time he'd served his country with distinction and honor. And it could be argued that his country had used him and helped to make him what he was at his death. Regardless, Rodney gave him a military funeral with full honors and a military honor guard. Their new and mysterious friend from Kansas, being a religious man, had presided in the burial service. Now, Sparky Fillmore had moved to the back to give Uncle Rodney center stage.

General Branch stepped forward and rendered one, final salute. The others in the group, Colonel Ranger MacPherson, Colonel Dan Branch, Sergeant Donny Brewster, and Corporal Jeremy Branch, along with the honor guard, all saluted as well, then cut away when Uncle Rodney lowered his hand.

Jackie cried off to one side until Dan pulled her in close and held her tight. He didn't fully understand the bond between her and the killer, but ... he forced himself to accept it and not ask questions. Four soldiers lowered the pine box down into the ground with ropes. They buried him pretty much where he and Jackie had enjoyed their dinner the day before. Uncle Rodney owned several plots near his brother, and determined it was only fitting.

Jeremy and Dan stepped forward with shovels and began to throw dirt into the hole. The others filtered off into the distance, some talking softly to one another, but, eventually, it was just Jeremy and Dan, alone in the cemetery. Jeremy was the first to speak.

"This brings back old memories."

His father thought about that a moment or two before making the connection.

"Yeah. It's amazing isn't it. A year ago I'd never dug a grave, but since then I've been digging a lot of them, sometimes for people I had to kill myself. It's amazing what a year of time and life can do to a man."

Jeremy's upper body had filled out since digging his first grave back in Wisconsin. The first had been for his own mother who'd committed suicide the day after the great fall. Both men thought quietly as they shoveled.

"Dad, do you still think about Mom sometimes?"

Dan stopped in mid-shovel and looked over at his son. Sometimes he forgot he was still a bit of a boy inside, in light of all the living, fighting and killing they'd both been forced to do in the past year.

"Yeah, sometimes. Though, I have to admit that with so much going on and so much we have to do just to survive, I don't have as much time for introspection as I would like."

Jeremy shrugged. "I suppose so. But ... ya know, Dad, us snipers have a lot of time to think. That's mostly what we do, just sit around making plans for the next battle or laying in a hidey hole just waiting for the next person we have to kill."

The words of his son spoke volumes, and Dan moved closer, dropped his shovel and embraced Jeremy. The boy had grown tall and strong and was physically now Dan's equal. Jeremy returned the embrace.

"I'm sorry I haven't been as accessible to you as I should be. There's just so much to do, son."

Dan had been surprised to hear his son identify himself as a sniper, as a killer, and it saddened him to his core. Jeremy moved back away from him and sat down on the edge of the hole. There was still about two feet of dirt that needed to be filled in.

"Do you remember what you told me last year when we were burying those three guys who attacked Jackie at her cabin in Wisconsin?"

Dan thought for a moment. "No, not really. What did I say?"

Dan then sat down on the edge of the hole across from his son.

"You told me that we bury good guys in single graves, and we pray over them, but the bad guys get one hole and no prayer?"

Dan looked over at his son, not really sure how to respond. "I really said that?"

"Yep."

"That sounds kind of callus doesn't it?"

Jeremy had the shovel in front of him, so he grasped the

wooden handle tightly in both hands.

"Yeah, I suppose. But Dad, in your defense, those were some pretty tough times. I mean ... think about it. We were burying guys left and right back then and it was still pretty new to us." And then he paused and leaned a bit forward until the left side of his face made contact with the wooden handle. He paused just long enough to form his thoughts. "I think it was pretty good advice, considering the circumstances."

Both men were silent for almost thirty seconds. "So why did this guy get prayed over and a salute and the whole honor guard thing? He was a pretty bad guy, right? He worked for the Blind Man and he must've killed a lot of innocent people."

Dan leaned forward on his shovel handle as well, thinking about the best way to answer his son. "Well, yeah, you can look at it that way I suppose, but ... I don't know, everything isn't as black and white as we'd like it to be, ya know. Talking about good guys and bad guys and like everything is black and white and easy to figure out." A bird flew over to a nearby headstone and landed lightly atop it. "People aren't all good or all bad. We're all a mix. Sammy did mostly bad things in his life, but ... at the end, maybe when it mattered the most, he did some pretty good things." The bird flew away, and Jeremy agreed with him.

"Yeah, I can see that. First he saved Mom's life. Then he gave us all those files, and then some kind of code to try and help us get back at the Blind Man."

Dan nodded. "Yeah, he did some good things at the end."

The two men stood back up and started filling in the hole again. Jeremy spoke again. "So, is this guy going to hell or to heaven?"

Dan dug his shovel into the sand pile and threw another heap into the hole. "I don't know, son. But the way I figure it, questions like that are way above my paygrade."

The two men smiled gently at one another as they shoveled. "Good point, Dad. So should I ask Uncle Rodney or Mom?"

Dan finally laughed out loud as he continued to shovel, and then he said. "Yes! Absolutely!"

When they were done, a small mound of sand lay before them. In another few weeks the fall rains would come, the days would shorten, and grass would start to grow up, as well as various kinds of weeds. And by this time next year, there would be no trace of the man buried below ground. His life, the sum total of his good and bad, would live on, but only in the lives of those he'd impacted, for good or for ill.

They both stood there, leaning against their shovels, wiping sweat from their brows in the early afternoon heat of August. By now everyone else had gone. Dan turned to Jeremy, put his right arm around his shoulder and they both walked away without looking back.

CHAPTER 14

JEFF **A**RNETT HAD BEEN UP ALL night long, struggling with the password given to Jackie by Sammy Thurmond. It looked like a twenty-character alphanumeric string, randomly generated by a computer. As such, that made it nearly unbreakable with just the laptops they had at their disposal. If he'd still been in Langley, then yes, by all means. He could put a supercomputer on it along with a full team of cryptologists, and they'd have it cracked in a matter of days. But now ... now he had what appeared to be the majority of the character string in tact. But when he typed it in, it didn't work.

In order to solve the mystery, he went on the assumption that Sammy Thurmond really did want them to access these files, so that meant that it was indeed possible. Jeff closed his eyes and tried to put himself in Sammy's shoes. He was in pain, semiconscious and convinced that he had but a few seconds to live. He would have to abbreviate, saying things as concisely as possible, even if they weren't one-hundred percent precise. On top of that, he would either be convinced that he'd just been poisoned by Jackie, or that the Blind Man was somehow killing him. Jeff guessed the latter simply because the Shadow Militia had no reason to kill him; it would be in their best interest to keep him alive for the information he might give them. Besides, Uncle Rodney could have had him killed after their first meeting, but he had not. On top of that, the Blind Man had motive. He certainly could not allow Sammy to live, because he possessed a mountain of information that could possibly bring the Blind Man to his knees. Certainly, it was in the Blind Man's best interest to kill Sammy Thurmond, and Sammy would definitely decipher that. After all, he knew Jared Thompson better than anyone else in the world.

Jeff studied the character-string again. *What was missing?*

There are no upper-case characters. A computer program designed to create a random, twenty-character password would definitely use at least two upper-case letters. What else? And then he smiled. Yes, the words 'plus' and 'minus' had to go. They should be replaced with mathematical characters. And then he looked at the '8' character just following the minus. A dying man, in Sammy Thurmond's condition, would find it very difficult to say the word 'asterisk.'

Jeff pulled up the software program he was using to try and crack the password. He opened the code and made a few changes, saved and then executed the program again. After two more hours of trial and error, Jeff got the message 'password accepted."

What Jeff saw in the directory amazed him. There were hundreds, maybe thousands of files at his disposal. He double-clicked on one and opened it up. Agent Arnett nearly fell off his chair. He had to call the general at once.

August 21, Pole Barn HQ

"SO HERE IS THE RAW ALPHANUMERIC SEQUENCE THAT we were given by Sammy Thurmond as he lay dying." Special Agent Jeff Arnett wrote the following characters on the white-board in front of him. They were in the pole barn he used as an operations center. They had minimal power, so the room was dimly lit, but they could still see just fine, especially dark characters on a white board.

h, 4, 8, b, 5, a, t, plus, k, w, l, s, minus, 8, y, h, 4, g, u, q

"So we go ahead and change the words 'plus' and 'minus' to numeric characters, then we change the first occurrence of '8' to an asterisk symbol, and then we have this:

h, 4, *, b, 5, a, t, +, k, w, l, s, -, 8, y, h, 4, g, u, q

"Any decent hacker knows that to make a near unbreakable password, you need twenty characters using a mixture of upper case and lower case with numbers and special characters as well. So I ran it through our code-breaking program, which took almost 25 hours, and came up with this password:

H4*b5at+kWls-8yh4Guq

Under normal circumstances, we could have eventually broken the password without his help, but things being as they are, with limited power and working without super computers, it's safe to say that we never would have broken the password without Mr. Thurmond's help."

Jeff Arnett turned away from the board and back to his audience. General Branch and Colonel MacPherson were seated in folding chairs while Dan, Jeremy and Jackie stood off to one side.

General Branch interrupted him impatiently. "So, are you saying that you broke the password, and you can now access the files he gave us?"

Jeff nodded his head. "Yes, General Branch, that's exactly what I'm telling you."

Uncle Rodney smiled widely. "Good job! Did you find any actionable intel?"

Jeff smiled uncharacteristically. "Only the location of the Blind Man's alternate headquarters as well as a list of his military assets and where they can be found, along with security details that will make it possible for us to launch a surprise attack on his forces and his supplies."

Uncle Rodney stood to his feet, the chair pushing back behind him, scraping loudly against the cement floor before falling over with a crash. "Thank God! Now we have a fighting chance!"

The general walked around the table and shook Jeff's hand, pumping it up and down vigorously. Colonel MacPherson breathed a sigh of relief and then folded his arms across his chest. Dan Branch looked nervously around at the others, wondering if anyone else was thinking what he was thinking. Jackie reached over and hugged her son with her left arm. After several seconds of congratulatory celebration, Dan spoke out loud.

"Mr. Arnett, how do we know this information is accurate?"

"Excuse me?" Jeff turned toward Dan Branch. "What do you mean?"

Dan took a deep breath. "Listen, I don't want to rain on anyone's parade here, but ... has it occurred to anyone that maybe Sammy is feeding us this information on purpose, and that maybe this is part of the Blind Man's plan? If we act on this intelligence without confirmation, we could be walking into a trap."

The room suddenly turned quiet. No one moved. The smiles faded and eventually disappeared altogether. Jeremy was the first to speak. "So, dad, why would he lie to us?"

Dan pivoted to face him. "Oh, I don't know. Maybe because he's a sociopath and he likes to play games with people's heads even if it is from beyond the grave."

"Dan has a point." Colonel MacPherson moved up to the white board and stood beside Uncle Rodney and Jeff. "The man is a lunatic, and we have to be very discriminatory about how we use any information from him."

Jeff Arnett nodded his head in agreement. "Absolutely. Every bit of information we get from these files should be verified before putting people in danger."

Uncle Rodney took a step back and leaned against the hot steel of the pole barn walls. The humidity was blistering hot today. It was almost like a steaming jungle both inside and out.

"Dan's right. We need to send people out to confirm every scrap of data we get from Sammy Thurmond. That just makes sense." And then he paused before looking over and making eye contact with Dan. "My gut tells me that we'll find everything Sammy gives us to be accurate."

Dan met his gaze, all the while knowing in his heart of hearts that what Uncle Rodney was saying was most likely true. He nodded without saying anything and Rodney smiled. Jeremy quickly broke into the conversation. "What makes you so sure that his intel is reliable?"

Rodney took a step forward again, and, as he did so, the sheet metal of the pole barn snapped back in with a small pop."It's obviously a matter of the heart, Jeremy." But his grandson looked confused. "Sammy's personality and actions are always consistent. When he was loyal to the Blind Man, then he was fiercely, loyal, even unto death." And then he paused. "But then he met Jackie and transferred his loyalty to her ... and everything changed."

Jackie's face flushed red and she looked down to hide her eyes. Dan looked over at her, but she refused to meet his gaze.

When she finally looked back up, there was hair in her eyes, so she brushed it back away with her long, slender fingers. "I ... I think he was ... in love with me."

All the color drained from Dan's face, but he said nothing. He was in a state of shock. Jeremy spoke first. "That does make a little bit of sense. After all, he did help her escape from the saracen army. And then he put his own life on the line when he abandoned the Blind Man and walked for weeks to get here to Iroquois. That sounds like the kind of thing a man will do when he's in love."

Dan lowered his head as Jeremy continued, not really knowing what to think. "And then when he arrived, he wanted to have a candlelight dinner with that same woman." Jeremy nodded his head up and down. "Yep, That makes sense to me."

Uncle Rodney nodded in agreement. "Sammy Thurmond didn't give us the information so that we could save ourselves or because he believed in our cause. He did it to save the woman he was in love with."

There was emotional tension in the room, and it made Ranger MacPherson uncomfortable. He looked down and then quickly back up again. "General, with your permission I'd like to get a copy of this data and begin examining it, assuming that it's verifiable, and then draw up plans for possible attacks."

"Absolutely. And Dan, I want you to make a plan for sending out recon teams to verify all this information. We need to know for sure that it can be trusted before we put people in harm's way, and we need it done as soon as possible."

Dan looked up and nodded, still wrestling with the concept of another man being in love with his wife. "Right away, sir."

General Branch, in a loud command voice started issuing orders, but Jeff Arnett quickly interrupted him.

"General Branch, there's something else you need to know."

Uncle Rodney stopped in mid-sentence, and everyone else turned to stare in his direction. "You mean there's more?"

Jeff nodded. "Yes, I'm afraid so, sir."

But Jeff didn't continue. He simply looked down at the bare concrete floor as if waiting for permission to continue.

"Okay, Mr. Arnett. What do I need to know?"

Jeff moved over to his desk off to the right. "Perhaps it's better if I show you, sir."

Jeff moved his mouse to awaken his screen, then he quickly clicked and launched a jpeg file. All the others in the room began to gather around Jeff's desk to get a closer look. After several seconds, the photo began to load from the top, until, finally, two men could be seen shaking hands. They appeared to be at a gas station after the collapse as the pumps were plainly visible. A handwritten sign was taped over the face of the pump saying 'NO GAS."

Jackie Branch sucked in her breath and placed her hand over her mouth. Dan gasped out loud but said nothing. Ranger MacPherson stiffened to attention, but also remained quiet. Jeremy started to say something, but his father raised his hand to stifle him.

Uncle Rodney's darkest and most frightening suspicions had just been confirmed. He stepped closer to the screen, placing both hands on the desk top as if needing the support to keep from falling.

The man on the right was Sammy Thurmond, but the man on the left was the one commanding all the attention. Uncle Rodney looked into the man's eyes, as his own face seemed to harden, taking on a stone-like visage.

Uncle Rodney began to shake his head involuntarily back and forth. "I ...was hoping it wasn't so."

Jeff Arnett took a step back from the screen before answering. "I'm sorry sir, but it's confirmed. The man we were counting on to save us ... is a traitor."

God Finally Speaks

"UNCLE RODNEY? SPARKY WANTS TO TALK TO YOU, AND I think it's important." Sparky and Jeremy had become quite good friends in the past few days of bunking together. Sparky served as a grandfather figure to the young man, and also had helped Jeremy to work through his feelings of guilt at having to kill so many people in the past year.

General Branch was looking at a laptop computer screen with Jeff Arnett inside his kitchen at the table. Uncle Rodney looked over at Jeff Arnett who seemed to smirk, just a bit. Jeff had already run as complete a background check as he could under the present grid-down scenario, and had found nothing to suggest that Sparky Fillmore was anything other than what he claimed to be: and old man from west Kansas who'd been sent by God to deliver a message. But Jeff didn't fully believe

151

it.

"Hold on a second, Jeff." Then he turned to Jeremy. "Show Mr. Fillmore in, please."

Jeremy left the room and Sparky walked in shortly after, with Jeremy close on his heels. "Thank you for seeing me, General Branch."

Uncle Rodney sat down in his chair and motioned for Sparky to do the same. "Would you like some tea or lemonade, Mr. Fillmore?"

Sparky's smile brightened even more. "You have lemonade? Really?"

The general laughed out loud. "Well, Mr. Fillmore, it's what we call lemonade, but it's really made out of staghorn sumac berries and sweetened up a bit with honey. And, of course, there are no ice cubes."

"I'd like to try that, general. It sounds very interesting to me."

Rodney motioned to Jeff. "Do you mind, Jeff?"

"Not at all, general." And then Jeff moved over to the sink and began pouring four cups of sumac lemonade into coffee mugs. He then brought them over two at a time and placed them on the table. Jeremy sat down to the right of Sparky.

"Okay, Mr. Fillmore. How can I help you?"

Sparky took a sip of his lemonade and his face seemed to glow with happiness. He'd been spending most of his time alone in his room the past few days, just fasting and praying, reading his Bible and seeking out any word from God.

"Oh my! This drink is delightful!" And then he looked up. "There's no alcohol in it, is there? Because I don't think Edna would approve of that. She's a bit of a teetotaler you know."

Rodney smiled patiently. "No alcohol, Mr. Fillmore. Now what is it you want to tell me?"

Sparky glanced over at Jeremy and smiled. Then he looked back over at Jeff who was now sitting down with the rest of them.

"Well, general, God spoke to me last night, and here is his message." Sparky paused, took a drink of his lemonade and then continued on. "First, God wants to encourage you and commend you for all your work. He thinks you're a lot like his servant Joshua." He chuckled to himself. "I think so too."

Rodney smiled slightly. "Go on, please."

"Also, he'd like you to know that your pending trip to Texas is a good idea, and that you will succeed, provided you rely on his strength instead of your own, and that you keep faith in Him."

Uncle Rodney almost dropped his coffee mug. He glanced over at Jeff Arnett, then back to Sparky. "And how did you know about our trip to Texas?"

Sparky ran his right forefinger around the rim of his coffee mug, trying to make it squeak, but it wouldn't work for him. "Well ... general, I just told you. God came to me and gave me the message."

Rodney looked over at Jeremy. "Son, did you tell Mr. Fillmore about this?"

But the young man shook his head from side to side. "I didn't know about it until just now. When are you going to Texas?"

Then Jeff Arnett spoke up. "General, only you and I and Colonel MacPherson knew of this plan. I've told no one else."

The general nodded. "I didn't even tell Dan about it. I haven't seen him since we made the plans to go." Then he looked over at Jeff. "I'll double-check with Mac to make sure he held confidence as well, but ... it would be unprecedented for him to break mission secrecy."

"Oh, and there's one more thing."

Rodney turned his head back to Sparky. "And that is?"

Sparky smiled eagerly. "God says I'm supposed to go with you."

The general's face screwed into a frown. "Excuse me?"

"God says the mission will fail if I don't go along. I don't know why."

Jeff interrupted. "General, that would be totally foolish. He's completely untrained. We don't know him. We don't trust him, and he certainly is not mission critical. He would be nothing more than an unknown liability."

Sparky laughed out loud. "Yes, I know. Isn't it the craziest thing you've ever heard?" And then his face got more serious. "But God has a history of picking people to serve him who are ungifted, who have little to offer, at least by the world's standards. David was a mere shepherd boy. Moses had a speech impediment. Gideon was a farmer." And then he looked deeply into the eyes of General Branch. "But despite their lack of talent and training, these men led God's people to victory."

General Branch pushed his coffee mug forward and stood to his feet. "Well, Mr. Fillmore, I want to thank you for delivering the message. I'll confer with my Chief of Intelligence before getting back to you on a final decision." And he quickly added. "And, of course, I'll be sure to consult the Lord about it as well."

Sparky's entire face beamed. "Now that's always a good idea, General Branch!" Sparky pushed his chair back and then quickly left the room, followed closely by his young protege.

Once they were gone, Jeff and Rodney looked at each other dumbly. Finally, Jeff broke the silence. "Okay then, general, do you want to pray first or should I?"

Uncle Rodney shook his head from side to side as he spoke. "This is the damnedest thing, Jeff. The damnedest thing I ever saw."

Secret Location - VA Secretary

JOSEPH DONNELLY LOOKED DOWN AT THE FOOD IN front of him. It was in a sealed, light-brown, waterproof, plastic bag, and he was seriously perturbed at the prospect of eating these things the military called food even one more time. He couldn't wait to get out of this hole and back into some semblance of civilization.

He was living temporarily in what appeared to be an old wooden barn. There was old straw on the floor, and a few animal stalls off to his left. The place smelled musty, like dried manure that had been reconstituted. Joseph picked the survival food pack off his lap and read the contents.

> Menu 23, Pizza Slice, Pepperoni
> MRE, Meal, Ready-to-eat, Individual
> Warfighter Recommended
> Warfighter Tested,
> Warfighter Approved

Joseph threw the food down on the barn floor in disgust. He was not a warfighter! The first thing he was going to do when sworn in as president of the United States was to outlaw MREs and hire himself a decent French Chef. Then he thought to himself *How did I get into this mess? I should have told them no when they'd first approached me*. Then he laughed softly. The truth is he hadn't had much of a choice. At least he was alive and was just waiting to be sworn in and take command of what used to be the most powerful country on the planet. Who knows, maybe it still was, but ... it didn't matter now. Even if America was still the most powerful country on earth, which he'd find out later after being sworn in, it still was only a shadow of its former self.

Hunger pangs growled up from the pit of his stomach, so he reluctantly swallowed his pride and reached down to the floor for the MRE packet. He tried to open the plastic, but the seal was too strong for him. He yelled over to one of the Shadow Militia soldiers in his protection detail.

"Hey soldier! Can you help me open this damn thing up, please?"

Sergeant Donny Brewster slung his M4 onto his back and walked over to where Joseph was sitting on an old, wooden potato crate. Donny stopped beside him and reached down to take the bag. Joseph was disgusted, and maybe even a little ashamed of himself when Donny opened the bag with ease and handed it back to him. Joseph grunted out loud.

"Okay, so I need to work out a bit. I'll do that later."

Donny smiled and returned to his post, watching the yard through the spaces between the wooden slats of the barn. He didn't like this assignment any more than Joseph Donnelly, and he found it disconcerting that the fate and freedom of the entire free world depended on the backbone of this weak and sniveling shell of a man. Donny didn't like him, but ... what could he do? Orders are orders, and he'd fight to the death to keep this man alive, at least until orders to the contrary came down the pike.

His mind drifted off to more desirable thoughts, more memories of a certain beautiful, blonde nurse, and he composed a list of things that he'd say to her, of chivalrous deeds, and gifts he'd present to her that no woman could resist. He was determined to win over the love of his life, but first ... they must defeat the Blind Man. And then he looked over at Joseph Donnelly, who was having trouble opening the interior plastic bag of his MRE, and he couldn't help but doubt the plan from General Branch. And then he thought to himself, *Maybe we're putting too much hope and stock into one man ... a man who can't even feed himself?*

But Donny Brewster was just a sergeant, and noncoms don't get paid to think; they get paid to obey orders, so that's what he would do. Donny Brewster would hurry up and wait, and then he would carry out his orders unflinchingly and to the letter. And, after that, when all the fighting was done. he'd head back home to win the girl of his dreams.

The Shadow Militia - out of the Shadows

"It's a pleasure to meet you, General MacDermid. This is my exec, Colonel MacPherson, and my Chief Intelligence Officer, Jeff Arnett."

Sparky Fillmore stood behind them, but Uncle Rodney

didn't mention him. The commanding general of Dyess Air Force Base in Texas looked skeptically at the man in front of him, claiming to be the military leader of some outfit called the Shadow Militia. General MacDermid had heard of the Shadow Militia, but only knew what his intel people were telling him: That they had engaged the Blind Man and were fighting to defeat him. He'd even heard intel suggesting that General Branch had a nuclear arsenal.

General MacDermid appeared to be about fifty-five years old with a cleanly shaven head. His most distinguishing characteristic was a large, bulbous nose. His eyes were set closely to one another, and were an intense brown color. General MacDermid had been the commanding general of Dyess Air Force Base in Texas for over a year now.

"Well, General Branch, or whoever the hell you think you are. The question foremost on my mind is how in god's name did four unauthorized civilians get past my security and into my office? For that matter, how did you even get through the front gate?"

General Branch glanced over at Jeff Arnett who immediately launched into an explanation. "Well, sir, we simply accessed government Top Secret files to learn everything possible about your installation's security measures. Then we created our own security badges, giving us access to everything at your command. It was quite simple, really."

The general was visibly perturbed and made no attempt to hide it. "And how the hell did you do that? You make it sound easier than ordering chinese take-out. Is my security that lax?"

Jeff smiled. "Everything's easy if you know how to do it, general. But you have nothing to be embarrassed of. I doubt anyone else would be able to do it, especially in this climate."

The general was standing now with his fists on his hips, taking turns glaring at each man in turn. "Mr. Branch, give me one good reason why I shouldn't yell to my sergeant out there and have you all arrested!"

"Because we have the president of the United States, and

we'd like to turn him over to you."

General MacDermid cocked his head to one side and lifted his left eyebrow. "What the ..."

And then he walked from the other side of the desk and stood before them. "The president, his staff, the VP and all the cabinet and most of congress are all dead. As far as we know, no one is in charge of the government right now."

Uncle Rodney started shaking his head from side to side and smiling. "No, that's not true. We've located the last remaining person in the presidential line of succession, then we found a federal judge and we are about to swear him in as president."

The general yelled to the aid outside his office, sitting at a desk. "Jenkins! Get in here!"

A man in a blue uniform rushed in and stood at position of attention. "Yes, sir."

"Call security and have an armed squad come to my office immediately!" He looked at General Branch and then over to Jeff Arnett. "Tell me how you learned to break into my system and forge security badges like that."

"I served for twenty-five years in the CIA, right up until the lights went out last year. The CIA was basically inoperative, so I offered my services to General Branch until the government got back up and running."

He turned to Ranger MacPherson. "And you? What's your story?"

The colonel remained stoic at the position of parade rest. "Forty years in the army, retired at the rank of Major General. Four tours in Vietnam and plenty of time playing in the sandbox earned me three purple hearts, the Distinguished Service Cross, two silver stars, two bronze stars, a bunch of other hardware, and, last but certainly not least, my Ranger tab."

And then Ranger MacPherson snapped to attention and crisply saluted before saying, "Rangers lead the way, sir, but it sure is nice of you fly boys to give us rides and air support from time to time."

The general didn't return the salute, so Colonel Macpherson cut his own salute and returned to parade rest. Uncle Rodney looked over at Mac and smiled. "Mac, is that a sense of humor you're growing? Hell, I've known you for over fifty years and I had no idea you could make jokes like that."

Mac smiled right back at him. "I've been waiting for the right moment, sir. Timing is everything in comedy."

Then General Branch looked back at General MacDermid. "So why don't you just call up Military Intelligence? MI can confirm all our stories. In fifteen minutes you can have our service records printed out and on your desk."

Just then a much older man in uniform walked through the door. He glanced over at the three strangers and then at his commanding general. He seemed to have a million stripes on his sleeve.

"I'm sorry, sir, I didn't realize you had visitors. I can come back another time." He turned to leave, but General MacDermid stopped him.

"Chief Master Sergeant McHenry!"

The man turned and faced his superior. "Yes, sir?"

"Before you transferred out of the army and into the air force, you served two tours in Vietnam did you not?"

"Yes, sir."

Then he pointed to Colonel MacPherson. "I'd like you to ask this gentleman some questions about that little ruckus that only a man with extensive combat experience would know about."

The Chief Master Sergeant looked over at Colonel MacPherson and the two men held eye contact for several seconds. And then his response shocked General MacDermid as well as the others in the room. He pushed past Colonel MacPherson and thrust his hand out to Sparky Fillmore.

"Sparky, is that you?"

Sparky smiled and took a step forward, shoving out his right hand. "It's good to see you again, Danny. It's been a long time."

And then the air force sergeant grabbed Sparky's hand and pumped it up and down happily. "My god, I haven't seen you since 1972! It's so good to see you again!"

General MacDermid looked over at his Chief Master Sergeant totally dumbfounded. "You know this man?"

Chief Master Sergeant McHenry forced himself to turn back to his commanding general. "Yes, sir. We served together in a grunt unit on my last tour in Vietnam."

As they were talking, a squad of uniformed military police stormed into the outer office. A lieutenant rushed in and stopped at position of attention in front of his general.

"Sir, you sent for a squad?"

The general looked over at his Chief Master Sergeant, then over to Rodney Branch who was trying not to smile.

"Damn it I hate surprises!"

Then he turned back to the lieutenant.

"Lieutenant, I'd like you to run an extensive background check on these four men, and then report back to me. I want it done within the hour. In the meantime, post two armed guards in the outer office here."

And then he turned back to General Branch. "Okay Mr. Branch. Have a seat and let's talk. I want to know everything, starting from the moment you popped yer ugly head out of yer momma's womb."

Rodney nodded and both he and Jeff Arnett moved to sit down on the couch up against the wall. The Chief Master Sergeant took Sparky Fillmore to the outer office where they got caught up on old times. General MacDermid yelled for an airman to bring them all coffee. And then Rodney Branch told the general everything he knew about the Blind Man, how the fall had happened, and how he'd located the presidential successor. After that he answered all the general's questions about the Shadow Militia.

Two hours later they shook hands.

CHAPTER 15

August 23, There is Another

JEFF ARNETT SAT ALONE AT HIS desk. Everyone else was taking a break, but Jeff, who refused to stop working, even for a moment, continued munching on the jalapeno cheese spread and crackers from inside his MRE. He knew it probably wasn't real cheese, just some hydrogenated soybean oil or some such thing, but he knew what he liked, and he loved this cheese spread. Sometimes, he even ate it without crackers, just sucked it right out of the foil package.

The door to his right opened and General Branch walked in with Jackie not far behind him. Uncle Rodney was wearing a red, flannel shirt, long-sleeved of course, and blue, denim jeans. Jackie held baby Donna on her right hip as she walked in. They both walked directly to Jeff's workstation.

Jeff smiled when he saw them, and leaned back in his chair with his hands interlaced behind his head. "Thanks for coming so quickly, general." Then he nodded at Jackie. "And it's always good to see you, my young, clandestine protege."

Jackie smiled back at him, but said nothing. Jeff had been the man who'd taught her how to spy prior to being inserted into the saracen camp. She couldn't help but notice that Special Agent Arnett was in an unusually good mood today. Uncle Rodney was the first to speak. "I hope you have some good news for us today."

Jeff nodded before picking up a file folder and placing it into Rodney's hands. "Read this. I think you'll like it."

Uncle Rodney sat down in the chair beside Jeff's desk, opened the folder and began reading. Every so often he looked up and over at Jeff, but quickly went back to reading the contents of the file without saying anything. Jackie sat down on the concrete floor and took some toys out of her diaper bag for Donna to play with. She wanted so much to know what was in the file folder, but she knew enough to let Uncle Rodney read in peace.

Finally, a half hour later, Uncle Rodney sighed and leaned back in the chair. "Holy mackerel!"

And then he gave the file over to Jackie, who immediately began to read to herself. "Did you verify any of this, Jeff?"

Jeff nodded curtly. "I did. Well, as much as anyone can in a grid-down scenario. But, I can safely say that I'm eighty percent certain that the US Secretary of Transportation is still alive and hiding out in an extremely well concealed location."

General Branch looked out through the closest window, staring out, deep in thought, analyzing the ramifications of what this new information meant to their cause. "This changes everything, Mr. Arnett. Where did you find it?"

The tall man with the hawkish nose looked over and nodded as he smiled. "I found it in one of the files that Sammy Thurmond provided to us. It's actionable intel, and I think we should get on with it." He paused. "Apparently, not even the Blind Man knows that he's still alive."

The general stood to his feet. "What is the Secretary of Transportation's name?"

"His name is Michael Townsend."

General Branch mulled this new information over in his mind before speaking. "I agree with you, Agent Arnett. We need to act decisively, but I want it done in a certain way. I'll coordinate it with Mac. If we do this right, it exponentially increases our chances of victory."

Baby Donna was on Jackie's lap, and now eating away at the corner of the file folder in her hands. As Jackie pulled the cardboard corner out of her daughter's mouth, she looked up. "I want to help, and please don't tell me he's in Haiti."

Jeff smiled and shook his head from side to side. "Not this time, Jackie. Think closer to home. Because the Secretary of Transportation has relatives right here in Michigan."

Uncle Rodney tore his gaze away from the window and looked Jeff full in the eyes. "Okay, I'm listening."

So Jeff Arnett then gave the outline of a plan he'd been forming over the last few days.

August 24, The Master Plan

ALL THE INNER CIRCLE OF GENERAL RODNEY T. BRANCH sat around the dining room table, listening to every word as if their very lives depended on it, because, of course, they did. Seated from left to right were: Colonel Ranger MacPherson, Colonel Dan Branch, Chief of Intelligence Jeff Arnett, Jackie Branch, Sheriff Joe Leif, and Jeremy Branch.

"Here's the situation." General Branch stood before them, the white board moved off to one side as he spoke to them earnestly and candidly.

"This has been kept secret and should not leave this room. Justice Reed, the scientist Sergeant Brewster and Colonel Branch recovered a short time ago, has agreed to recommission eight more nuclear devices for us. As you recall, the first arsenal of twelve were destroyed by the Blind Man. For the past two weeks Professor Reed has been working feverishly on making these eight nukes battle ready." He looked around the room solemnly. "I've just been informed that all eight nukes will be ready for deployment in just two days time."

Dan looked over at Jackie and smiled. Jeremy let out an adolescent shout, but the general quickly admonished them.

"Calm down everyone."

Dan Branch lifted a finger and the general acknowledged

163

him. "General, exactly where are these nukes being kept? Are you sure they're safe? We lost them once and I don't want it to happen again."

Rodney smiled and nodded. Then he looked over at Sheriff Leif. "I think you'll appreciate this one, Sheriff. Do you recall our little run-in with the Chief of Police at a town in Wisconsin?"

The sheriff looked up and squinted his eyes. ""You're kidding me. Eagle River? You're keeping eight nukes at Eagle River? How are you doing that? The last time we went there we were both almost killed by that maniac!"

Uncle Rodney's smile got even bigger. "Well, let's just say that there's been a major realignment of power in that city and that the good chief is no longer serving in a law enforcement capacity."

Sheriff Leif bowed his head and wagged it from side to side. "Rodney did you kill that man?"

The general raised his hands as if in mock surrender. "Of course not, Joe. Let's just call it an early retirement and leave it at that. We were able to make an agreement with the mayor and city council. In exchange for safety, we are now using the city and its small airport as a refueling base for our choppers. All we have to do is keep out the riffraff, and, in this case, that included the former Chief of Police. I insisted on that one personally."

The sheriff glanced over at Dan who was sitting beside him. "Can you believe this guy, Dan. He just took over a whole city in Wisconsin."

Dan smiled and looked down at the table. "Quite frankly, Joe, I like the idea of a little payback. If you'll recall one of his deputies beat me almost to death." And then he added as if in passing. "Besides, it's just a small city. Not a big deal."

Then General Branch interrupted them. "Let's move on, gentlemen. There's more." Uncle Rodney glanced over at Jackie for this one. "Jackie, after you rescued the VA Secretary from Haiti, we moved him to a small military base in Denver. The VA Secretary will be sworn in as president at noon day after tomorrow at that same base. Once that is done, we'll be flying the acting president to the USS Ronald Reagan, an aircraft carrier off the Gulf coast. At that time, the new president will commence consolidation of the remaining US armed forces and commence the destruction of the Blind Man and his military forces."

Everyone around the table began to chatter back and forth excitedly. Only General Branch and Colonel MacPherson maintained their silent military bearing. The two men made eye contact for a moment. then glanced around the room at the happy and long overdue celebration.

Fifteen minutes later, after a short question-and-answer period, all attendees were dismissed, leaving Mac and Rodney alone in his dining room.

"Well Mac, what do you think?" Colonel MacPherson shrugged and shook his head from side to side. Finally he answered curtly. "I don't know, general. Ask me again in two days and I'll tell you. Right now, I'm not sure I even know what to think. So many of our plans this time around have fallen apart."

Blind Man HQ, August 25

JARED THOMPSON LISTENED ASTUTELY TO THE VOICE on the other end of the line, analyzing every detail and committing it to memory. He paced back and forth as he held the handset to his right ear, every once in a while taking a tiny sip of wine from the goblet in his left hand.

Another thirty seconds passed before he finally spoke to the other man. "Very good. But you are certain of the accuracy of this intelligence?" He listened to the other man's response and smiled as he nodded his head.

"Why do you want to be extracted at this point? You are worth more to me embedded in your present location."

The Blind Man nodded. "I see. Yes, they will definitely know it was you. Your cover is blown. Meet us at midnight tonight at the predetermined extraction point. Don't be late."

Jared sipped his wine again. "Yes, correct. You and your family. You will never know strife or discomfort again. Get ready for a life of luxury and warm winters."

The Blind Man pressed a button and ended the conversation before calling for his aid. The man had learned long ago to be ready at Jared's beck and call. He immediately popped his head through the open doorway and Jared waved him in before seating himself in the recliner in front of the mahogany end table. He propped his Italian, leather shoes onto the glass top and took a tiny sip of his wine, savoring it in his mouth before swallowing. The aid waited patiently and nervously. He never knew what to expect from his boss. Finally, Jared looked up as if suddenly becoming aware of the other man's existence.

"Have you confirmed that Sammy Thurmond is no longer with us?"

The man nodded as he spoke. "Yes, sir. Dr. Van Fleet confirmed it. He is certain, sir."

Jared looked up at the oversized TV screen on the wall before him. "Hand me the satphone then."

Deep inside, the aid muttered in disgust. On the inside he wailed with protest and called the Blind Man a lazy beast! But on the outside, he complied as a dutiful and grateful servant, walking over and picking up the satphone, which was already within the Blind Man's easy reach and respectfully handed it to him.

"You may go."

While his aid left the room, Jared punched in the number and then placed the phone beside his right ear. As he waited for the connection to complete, he mulled over his predicament.

"Yes, General Holland. I have a fire mission for you."

He waited a few more moments before continuing.

"General, I'd like you to obliterate Eagle River, Wisconsin."

He nodded. "Yes, that's correct. I want it done at midnight tonight, and I'd like to watch it on the big screen as always."

Jared disconnected the call and tossed the satphone down onto the couch. He put his wine down on the table and then leaned back to savor the moment. General Branch just didn't know when to give up, but Jared found the challenge worthy and exciting, so long as he had the upper hand. And, so far, he definitely had the Shadow Militia outgunned and outmanned. They continued to give him problems in the south and in the east, but that would soon end. He had a surprise for the general, and his only regret was that he wouldn't be able to see the look on his enemy's face the moment he found out.

But, alas, we all had to make sacrifices in time of war. He yelled for his aid to bring him another bottle of port.

Justice Reed's Change of Heart.

"DOCTOR REED. IT'S GOOD TO SEE YOU AGAIN. I'VE been told you'd like to talk to me."

Justice Reed was sitting about ten feet away from his workbench on a wooden stool, and he had the look of a man who'd been humbled, but was not happy about it. His silver hair, what was left of it, stuck up at odd angles all around the circumference of his head. As usual, he was stark naked. Justice nodded. "Yes, general. I have some issues with the accommodations here. They are totally inadequate."

General Branch smiled slightly and nodded. "Yes, I can see that, professor. I'll talk to my men immediately about getting you some clothes. I apologize that it hasn't been done yet. We would never willingly make a man walk around without clothing."

But the old man waved him off impatiently. "No, no, no, general; that's not what I'm talking about. You already gave me clothes, but I don't wear them. They're over there on my workbench."

Uncle Rodney tilted his head to one side. "Okay. So, what exactly is it I can do for you, Doctor Reed?"

Justice crossed his left leg over his right and put his left hand to his whiskered chin while leaning his left elbow to his left knee. "It's my mousetrap, general. I just can't seem to get it to work."

Uncle Rodney was amused, but tried not to show it. He was having trouble focusing on the face of a totally naked old man, with legs like a chicken. "And what seems to be the problem, Doctor Reed. I thought you would have completed it by now. Are you not getting the supplies you need. I can help with that if it's the problem."

"No, that's not it. Your men have been great. It's just ... well ... my hypothesis didn't pan out the way I'd hoped and I fear I'm getting bored with it."

General Branch nodded slightly. "I see. So what's the problem?"

Justice threw up his hands and waved them about excitedly. "It's the damn gravity, general! It always seems to work down, and I can't get the trap to function properly. You see, general, my mousetrap is revolutionary. There's never been anything like it, but it seems to only work in a gravity-free environment."

Justice Reed looked at the general as if the problem was easily understood and elementary to even the most basic of unscientific minds. Rodney tried not to disappoint him with more questions. "I understand and I share your disappointment, Doctor Reed. It's truly a loss to all of humanity as there is a terrible shortage of mice in space." And then he paused. "I don't suppose I could tempt you with a project of my own ... one that might keep you occupied, at least until you solve the gravity problem ..."

General Branch waited for what seemed like hours, but in reality was only about ten seconds. Justice Reed brought his frail hands up to his chin and sighed thoughtfully. "Perhaps. Do you still need those twelve nuclear devices recommissioned? I could do that for you."

General Branch thought it was odd, that a man was referring to activating nuclear devices as if it was as simple as making toast or boiling an egg. "Well, doctor, that job is no longer available."

Justice looked offended. "You got someone else to do it? Who was it?"

Rodney threw up his hands and then let them fall back down to his sides. "It's not like that, Doctor Reed. You see ... it was the Blind Man. He destroyed them while in transit, and, as you know, nuclear explosive devices are not that easy to come by."

Doctor Reed looked crestfallen, downright shattered. But then a glint came to his eyes. "Well, okay. But do you still need them or not?"

Uncle Rodney nodded without speaking.

"Well okay then. I'll tell you where to get more, and then you can run out and pick them up for me. Sound good?"

The general raised one hand to his chin and held it there as he thought. Finally, he couldn't hold back his amusement any longer. "Doctor Reed, you make it sound as easy as sending me out to pick you up a pizza!" The general's eyes danced happily in their sockets. "But hey! What's your plan?"

The doctor smiled openly. "Let's just steal some from Jared. He's got lots of them, and I know where they all are."

Not wanting to sound too anxious, General Branch waited for a full five seconds before responding. "Okay, so let's say I'm open to the idea. Where are these nukes and how do we get them?"

The old scientist jumped nimbly off the stool as excited as ever. "It's easy, general! I used to be the Blind Man's weapons designer. Most of what he has, I built for him." And then Justice Reed squinted his brow as if confused. "Are we still in Michigan?"

Rodney tried not to let the eccentricity of the doctor discourage him as he thought to himself. *Okay, so he doesn't know where he is half the time and he refuses to wear clothes, but ... that doesn't mean he can't recommission a nuclear bomb. Right?*

"Doctor Reed, let me get Colonel MacPherson over here on the double, and we'll get this whole thing worked out."

The nuclear scientist sat back down on the stool and clapped his hands together excitedly. "Great! There's one more thing, general."

Uncle Rodney furled his brow and waited.

"Do you have any bourbon?"

The general cocked his head to one side reluctantly, but the old scientist pressed him further. "It's medicinal bourbon. You know, for my aching joints. It helps keep me limber while I work."

Rodney smiled and shook his head from side to side. "I'll see what I can do, Doctor Reed."

And the old scientist smiled from ear to ear.

August 25, Uncle Rodney Goes Shopping

"MAC, I WANT YOU TO LEAD THIS TEAM PERSONALLY." General Branch looked intently at his second in command. "Make sure you take Sergeant Brewster as an overwatch. That man is a helluva force multiplier. Doctor Reed obviously has to go, but our recon team suggests you'll need at least a platoon to breach the complex and still have enough time to recover the nukes and get out before the Blind Man can react."

Uncle Rodney looked at the men around him. There was Major Larry Jackson and Captain Danny Briel, both leaning against the wall of the pole barn. Lieutenant Jason Little was seated at the table beside Colonel Dan Branch and his son, Jeremy. One of the Apache attack helicopter pilots was seated beside Dan along with one of the Blackhawk pilots. General Branch had insisted that Dr. Reed at least wear boxer shorts for the meeting, and he sat to the left of the Blackhawk pilot. He was sipping away at a decanter filled with scotch. The general had quickly learned that Justice Reed worked much better when he was properly medicated, as partial inebriation steadied his nerves and even his hands and concentration. Jeff Arnett stood near the back of the room thinking about the oddity of taking a naked, drunk man on a military operation where heavy fighting was likely to occur. But, then again, if he'd been in charge instead of General Branch, they wouldn't be mounting a major operation based on unreliable intel from a hopeless drunk. However ... he had to admit, General Branch did it all the time, and, so far, he'd been right. The man seemed to have a very accurate gut-check.

"According to our best intel, there is a minimal defensive force at this storage facility. It seems General Masbruch and our forces in the south and east are keeping the Blind Man very busy these days, using hit-and-run guerilla tactics. General Masbruch has played hell with the enemy's supply lines, and they've had to spread themselves more and more thin in order to protect their supply convoys."

The general pressed a button on the remote control he held and the laptop projector displayed a picture of the facility. "This particular facility is located in Grand Rapids, Michigan to our south. It will be easy to get to and is located outside the most dangerous parts of the city. The area around the grounds is relatively rural, primarily corn and fruit orchards as well as some urban sprawl. There could be significant resistance from criminal gangs in the city."

He clicked the remote several times and went through a series of aerial photos of the buildings on the complex. General Branch continued another five minutes and then asked for questions. Dan Branch was the first to raise his hand.

"General Branch, why would this facility be so lightly guarded. I mean, after all, if there really are nukes there ... that doesn't make any sense."

General Branch pointed to the only half-naked scientist in

the room. "I'll let Dr. Reed field that question."

Justice Reed stood to his feet and turned to face the majority in the room. "Well, that's easy. Those nukes have been there for over fifteen years. You know. Just sitting there in cases, waiting for Jared to use them for whatever he wants." He started to sit down again, but then stopped. "Besides, why guard something that is best hidden in plain sight? As soon as you put a bunch of soldiers on the ground in a populated area then you draw attention. Those nukes have been safe there for almost two decades, so I doubt Jared would be worrying about them now. He didn't even bother guarding them until after the collapse."

Rodney then called on Major Jackson. "So what kind of nukes are we talking about here?"

The general nodded again to Dr. Reed, who was already starting to answer the question. "Oh hell, we got quite an assortment down there. A few of the bigger ones I made myself, but most are small, tactical nukes of five to twenty-kilotons each. But the big ones are about five megatons a piece. They're not real big by modern standards but certainly enough to get a man's attention."

Rodney gave the nod to Captain Briel.

"Dr. Reed, since they've been down there so long, how do we know they still work, or, for that matter, if they're even safe to transport?"

Dr. Reed laughed at him. "Of course they're not safe! They might even be leaking. These are nuclear weapons we're talking about here." And then he turned further around to look the captain square in the eyes. "Why do you think I drink so much? This is a dangerous job!"

General Branch broke in quickly. "The doctor has assured me that he can repair any damage and bring the nuclear devices to full operational capability, provided we can safely transport them to a secure location."

Jeremy Branch raised his hand high in the air, and the way he did it reminded Dan of a young schoolboy. "So, where are we going to take them?"

The scientist looked over to the general and smiled, waiting for him to give them the good news. But the general hesitated, so Dr. Reed blurted it out. "We're taking them to the Palisades Nuclear power plant near Covert, Michigan. It's about sixty miles southwest of Grand Rapids, just off the lakeshore." He waited for a positive response, but the soldiers in the room didn't seem to share his enthusiasm. "What's wrong? It's a perfect place for this. It'll have all the labs and equipment I'll need to recommission the nukes."

Major Jackson looked first at Captain Briel, and then over at the general before he addressed the elephant in the room. "So, General Branch, at the risk of seeming undedicated, is this nuclear power plant safe? I mean ... it's been unattended for over a year now."

The general smiled softly and pointed back at Dr. Reed, who immediately launched into a technical explanation. "Oh, heck yeah! It's really safe, well, as far as nuclear power plants go. I mean ..." He stopped long enough to take a drink of his scotch. "Sure, there is some minor leakage from the re-actor and a little from the spent fuel rods, but you have to expect that kind of thing when you just let a nuclear power plant go uncared for." He took another drink. "We flew over it just yesterday, and, based on our measurements, we project it to be much safer than Fukushima and a whole lot safer than Chernobyl." Dr. Reed looked around the room, just now fig-uring out that people were uncomfortable being exposed to large doses of nuclear radiation. "Oh, guys it's nothing, really. I've had a lot more radiation than that, and look at me!" No one said anything. Colonel Branch looked down and held his head in his hands. But the doctor wasn't finished reassuring them yet.

"Just think of it in terms of having a CT scan every day for a year, only you're doing it all in one day." And then he smiled before sitting down and drinking some more scotch.

Rodney looked around the room and then shook his head.

"Please forgive our eccentric friend. Let me fill in the blanks in layman's terms."

And then he turned back to the projector screen and advanced through the presentation. "We'll be wearing full radiation protection suits while on site. It will be clumsy and hot, but it's better to be uncomfortable than sterile or dying of cancer ten years from now."

Young Jeremy Branch looked at his father and reached down to cover his groin region. "I'm going to be sterile?"

Uncle Rodney looked at his relative impatiently. "No, son. You're not going to be sterile. You'll only be there for a few hours while you get the doctor set up in his lab and the nukes are unloaded. Almost all the risk will be taken by Doctor Reed."

Colonel Branch looked around the room and then rose to his feet. "Well, then, general, I have only two questions left. When do we leave, and how much of that scotch can you give us. Cuz I think we're going to need a drink."

Doctor Reed smiled and raised his decanter in salute. "General Branch, I've always liked that man."

CHAPTER 16

C OLONEL MACPHERSON PEERED out to the gypsum mining complex in Grand Rapids, Michigan, through his binoculars, looking for any sign of military security. He quickly noted the four men bunched together at the foot of the loading dock on the east side. They could easily get to the tree line and neutralize all of them in a matter of seconds with a coordinated sniper attack with suppressed rifles.

That particular fire team had been there since seven AM once they'd relieved the night watch. They appeared to have four men on the surface at all times, which meant three shifts of four, and there were at least twelve soldiers assigned to guard the complex. Mac guessed another ten or so below ground in support.

He looked over his shoulder at Sergeant Donny Brewster and Major Jackson. "Sergeant, I want you and your snipers to take out all four simultaneously. I want all four to go down and make it sound like one gunshot. Got it?"

Donny nodded. "Not a problem, sir. We'll suppress our rifles just in case."

"Major, you can take your platoon in through the main entrance there while Captain Briel takes his platoon down the freight elevator in back. That should give you overwhelming firepower to get the job done. You'll have Dr. Reed with you, and that should enable you to locate the devices fairly quickly. He claims to know where they are. There are a lot of shafts and tunnels down there, so we can't afford to get lost."

Major Jackson nodded. "Not a problem. Then as soon as we find the nukes we radio out for the transport team?"

"Affirmative, major. But, above all else, this has to be done quickly, before anyone inside can report the activity to the Blind Man. Eventually, he'll discover what we've done, but we'd like it to be later rather than sooner. Understood?"

Larry Jackson paused before answering. "Yes, sir. It'll be done. Should only take a few minutes to get down and take control. I'll radio up as soon as I'm ready."

The colonel looked out again at the facility, at the parking lot, the loading dock and then again at the four enemy soldiers shooting the breeze in the hot, August sun. They were probably happy to have such a low-risk job, but ... today that would end.

"Sergeant, we launch in fifteen minutes." He turned to Major Jackson and Captain Briel. "Get your men in place. You go as soon as you see the sentries go down."

Ranger MacPherson radioed to General Branch that all was well. Then he waited for everyone to get staged. At exactly fifteen minutes after eight AM, all four sentries crumpled down in a heap. One was inhaling a cigarette, another was urinating on a wall, while the other two were just talking together. All four shots to the cranium ensured that none of them had time to cry out for help. In fact, none of them saw the other fall; it happened that fast.

Mac watched as Major Jackson and his men entered through the loading dock door. So far there were no other gunshots.

Captain Briel radioed in his progress. "Cave Leader this is Caveman two, we are on our way down. No contact so far."

Larry Jackson called in as well.

"Cave Leader this is Caveman One. No resistance. We are on our way down to lower levels."

Colonel MacPherson smiled to himself. There was no one with him except his protective detail of eight men who had formed a protective perimeter around him. So far no resistance. That was good, Surprising ... but good.

"Cave Leader, this is Caveman One. We are at the lower level, on our way to the target. Have linked up with Caveman Two and he has our back."

Captain Briel deployed his twenty-five men around him and at each tunnel entrance. He was surprised to encounter no resistance. So far not a single shot had been fired by his men. He looked around at the tunnels branching off in four different directions. They appeared to be used as storage for computer media and even some paper files. Apparently the gypsum mine hadn't been producing product for many years now, and had simply rented out the storage space to local corporations. The tunnels were no longer dirty and filled with loose rock. The floors had been cemented over and load-bearing columns had been added to shore up the ceilings.

Captain Briel began to get nervous. He always worried when things went too smoothly. He made the rounds, checking in with his sergeants, but everything appeared secure. So now all he could do was wait for Major Jackson to find the nukes.

Major Jackson looked around at the tunnels surrounding them. Justice Reed seemed to be confused.

"Come on, Doc. We don't have all day. Let's just find these nukes and get the hell outta here!"

Dr. Reed stopped walking and pointed down the tunnel to the left. "I think it's down there."

Major Jackson sent a fire team down the tunnel with a wave of his hand. They quickly ran down the tunnel, with flashlights groping out like long, shiny talons. But Five minutes later they came back. "Sorry, major. Nothing down there but old mushroom-growing pallets. Just a bunch of old compost and dirt down there."

Larry looked back at the doctor. "Come on, Doc. Now's the time when you come through. You can either be the hero or the goat. And if you're the goat, then I'm gonna shoot yer sorry ass! Got it?"

Justice Reed nodded and started to sweat. "I need a drink."

Larry laughed out loud. "You can have a drink as soon as you find the nukes we need, and not a moment sooner!"

This seemed to motivate Justice Reed even more. He stopped to think, as if remembering something he'd forgotten all along. "Oh, I remember now! We're not supposed to go east. We need to go south!" And then he started running off ahead of Major Jackson. Larry looked on and shook his head from side to side. He thought to himself, *This is ridiculous, following a drunk down into a mushroom cave in search of nuclear bombs.* He reported in to the colonel.

"Cave Leader this is Caveman One. We've got nothing so far. We may need Caveman Two to assist in a random search of all tunnels."

"This is Cave Leader. What is the hold-up?"

"Our bird dog seems to be inebriated, sir."

Ranger MacPherson turned his head to one side and spit on the wooded floor beside him. *Damn that old man! He was drunk more often than not.*

"Caveman Two, this is Cave Leader. Leave a few men for flank security and begin a systematic search of all tunnels."

"This is Caveman Two, roger that. Commencing search pattern now."

Blind Man HQ

At the same time Major Jackson and Captain Briel were searching for the nuclear devices hundreds of feet underground, Jared Thompson was watching them on camera in his office. He sipped a crystal glass of cognac as he flipped from one camera angle to another. He watched the teams searching underground for several minutes until he caught sight of Justice Reed. Then he said out loud. "You should have stayed in your mountain cabin, Dr. Reed. I was content to leave you there until I needed you. But now ..." He shook his head from side to side and switched the camera feed to the drone circling high over the gypsum facility.

He picked up his satphone and was soon talking to General Holland. "General, you will proceed on my command. I'll count down from five." He took another sip of his cognac and then placed it on the glass table in front of him.

"Five, four, three, two ..."

He looked up and focused on the television screen on the wall, smiling with all his heart.

"One."

COLONEL MACPHERSON NOT ONLY HEARD THE BLAST, but he felt it as he was lifted off the ground and thrown twenty feet in the air. He landed against the trunk of a sapling. It bent and cushioned his fall. Dust and sand rained down around him along with pieces of rock, cement and wood. He lowered his head and covered it with his hands until the debris shower subsided.

Mac raised his head and then crawled over to the edge of the embankment. When he looked at the facility, his heart sank. A tremendous cloud of gypsum dust had billowed up from the ground and was now settling back down into a giant crater.

He crawled over to his radio and keyed the microphone. "Caveman One, this is Cave Leader. Come in, over." But there was nothing but silence except for the sound of falling dust on the August leaves around him.

"Caveman Two, this is Cave Leader. Come in, over."

Mac wiped the gypsum dust from his eyes before trying once more. "Overwatch, this is Cave Leader. Come in, over."

Donny Brewster responded at once. "Cave Leader, this is Overwatch."

"Overwatch, do you see any survivors?"

There was silence for almost a minute. Colonel MacPherson forced himself to wait patiently. Finally, Sergeant Brewster responded. "Cave Leader, this is Overwatch ..." And then a pause. "I see no signs of life."

Mac dropped the handset and rested his head in his hands. Part of his protection detail tugged on his sleeve. "Sir, are you alright?"

Mac turned around but didn't answer right away. "Sir, what are your orders?"

Colonel MacPherson looked around him, then off into the settling cloud of dust and the massive crater in front of him. Finally he responded.

"Prepare to move out, sergeant."

August 26, 11:30PM - Catching a Rat

Sheriff Joe Leif and his wife and son built a large bonfire in the clearing below the ridge. The sheriff was waiting for a helicopter from the Blind Man to come and take him to a retirement home in Florida. Joe loved this town, but his wife, Marge, did not. She never had, though she'd always put up a good front in public. And then so much had happened after the lights had gone out, so much that had made living here for her even more unbearable. But he'd been told that there were parts of the country with power and near-modern living conditions, and, quite frankly, he and Uncle Rodney had never quite seen eye to eye on how many things should be run.

Even with all that, it had been a difficult decision for Joe to make when the Blind Man had contacted him. In his own way, he loved Uncle Rodney and the town of Iroquois, though not much was left of it anymore. The sheriff had wrestled with the problem for days, but finally capitulated when it had been made clear that he really had no alternative. Either throw in his lot with the Blind Man, or his wife and child would suffer in darkness and possibly even death at the hands of Jared Thompson and his forces. He knew, indeed, had always known, that General Rodney T. Branch didn't stand a chance against the Blind Man, but the sheriff had kept his silence.

That, and he just didn't like Rodney's methods. He'd tortured a prisoner in his own jail by stabbing him with a knife, and even before the collapse he'd purchased illegal guns and all manner of military weaponry against state and federal laws.

No, Joe couldn't live like that. He needed the rule of law. He needed a sense of purpose and a hope that things would return to the way they were. The sheriff wouldn't admit this to himself, but, perhaps even more than anything else ... he needed electricity and refrigeration; he needed clean clothes and a shower everyday and a hot cup of coffee ... not that artificial stuff Uncle Rodney made out of chickory and lawn clippings, but the real stuff - with real caffeine!

The fire was blazing high now, and they had to back up a few feet to keep the heat from hurting their faces. Marge moved in closer to Joe while his son picked up a long stick to stab into the fire.

"We're doing the right thing, Joe." His wife put her arm around him in an attempt to console him, but it did no good. "We have no future here. With Jared we'll be in warmer weather during the winter. We'll have electricity again. Someday the country will rebuild, and, when it does, our son can have a real place in it." She squeezed Joe tighter. "Things can go back to normal for us."

Sheriff Leif just looked out into the night without saying anything. He wasn't sure of that, but ... none of that mattered anymore. He'd done the deed. He'd betrayed his friends, and now ... now he'd have to live with that ... for the rest of his life.

Suddenly, they heard the sound of a helicopter off in the distance, the thrumming of the rotors, slowly getting closer and closer. They were early. In a few minutes they would be off and away, never to return, beginning a new and exciting life. Joe Leif allowed the guilt he felt to slowly wash away. He was doing this for his family. Joe stepped away from the fire and out into the clearing. He raised the flare gun and fired it over his head high and into the air, according to the instructions he'd been given.

He could see the aircraft now and it adjusted its course and was soon hovering overhead. Joe watched the helicopter land in the clearing, the adrenaline rushing through his body as he felt the wind from the rotors push against his face.

A man stepped out of the Blackhawk helicopter and walked over to the sheriff and his family.

"Sheriff Leif?"

Joe thought he heard a foreign accent in the man's voice, and this surprised him.

"Yes. I'm Joe Leif, this is my wife, Marge, and my son."

Just then, Joe was surprised to see three soldiers in digital camo jump out of the chopper and rush over, quickly surrounding Joe and his family on three sides. The officer who'd first approached him took a few steps back, and then raised his right arm high over his head.

"I have a message from the Blind Man. He wishes to thank you for your service, but regrets to inform you that your request for political asylum has been denied."

Marge moved closer to Joe, grabbing her son as she did and pulling him up against her. The little boy shook with fear. Joe could hardly speak, knowing that he would soon die, that his family would die, and that ... he was the one who'd killed them. He was to blame.

"But ... but ... that wasn't the deal. I ..."

And then the gun shots rang out into the night. They fired again and again until all three figures fell to the ground. When it was finished, the officer, with his right arm still raised over his head looked bewildered over at Joe Leif and his wife and son. And then he stared down at the bodies of his bullet-ridden soldiers on the ground around him. He heard the sound of the Blackhawk engine gain RPMs as it began to inch off the ground. But then two final shots rang out and the engine slowed, whined down, and then settled slowly back to the earth unharmed. The pilot and co-pilot both slumped over, dead.

The officer then looked down at his chest and saw the green dot of light dancing slightly from left to right. He decided not to move. Joe saw the green dot on the man's chest, so he quickly looked down at his own chest. There was a green dot there as well. He quickly looked over at Marge and his son, and was quickly relieved to discover that they were not being targeted.

And then the bushes behind them exploded with white light as a dozen Shadow Militia soldiers came out from behind cover, their SureFire flashlights, mounted on the rails of their M4s seeking out and lighting up the night. Soon, all four prisoners were surrounded. Joe Leif and the officer were disarmed and proned out on the ground, and then their hands were zip-tied behind them before they were hauled to their feet again. In the background, Marge could be heard crying as she hugged her son closely.

When all was secure, General Rodney T. Branch strode crisply out of the brush and walked up to his friend.

"Hello Joe." And then he looked Sheriff Leif straight in the eyes. "You look surprised to see me."

Joe turned his face away, then back again. He tried to hold Rodney's stone-cold gaze but could not. In the end, he looked down at the ground and his zip-tied hands in disgrace. He said nothing.

General Branch turned to the soldier beside him. "Lieutenant Little, take this enemy officer back to camp for interrogation. Special Agent Arnett is waiting for him there. I will be along shortly."

The Blind Man's officer was lead away in silence. He didn't resist. Uncle Rodney turned back to his friend.

"Fifty of my men were killed by the Blind Man today, Joe. Along with Larry Jackson and Danny Briel." Joe turned his face away, looking out into the darkness.

"I've known about you for a while, Joe. But ... I just had to see it for myself before I did anything about it. You need to know that I used you for military gain. Normally I wouldn't do that to a lifelong friend, but ... under the present circumstances, you didn't leave me much of a choice. Besides, I'm in a real nasty mood tonight."

And then Uncle Rodney's voice softened. "I'm sorry it came to this, Joe. I know you never totally subscribed to my role as commanding general of the Shadow Militia, but ... that doesn't change the truth of it all." He hesitated. "You got a lot of good men killed today, and you're gonna have to pay for that."

General Branch looked Joe Leif square in the eyes as he talked, even though Joe was trying to avoid his gaze. "I am the general. And I am in charge. Soon, the Blind Man will realize that as well."

Joe Leif looked straight down and mumbled to himself. "I'm sorry Rodney. I ... guess I lost faith."

Rodney nodded. "I suppose that's one way of looking at it."

Just then two more men stepped out of the nearby woods and walked over. It was Colonel Ranger MacPherson, walking ram-rod stiff, followed by a more laid back Colonel Dan Branch. They both stopped to the left of General Branch and remained slightly abreast as both colonels snapped to attention and saluted. General Branch returned the salute.

"At ease, gentlemen. Let's get this over with." He looked over at another nearby soldier. "Staff Sergeant Cervantes. Take the woman and her son away for a short time. I don't want them to witness this."

The staff sergeant led them away at gun point with another soldier, and, when they were gone, General Branch turned back to his two colonels. "Let's get this over with."

Two soldiers brought out three folding chairs and set them up behind a portable, white plastic table. Sheriff Leif looked on, confused. A few seconds later, the general and the two colonels sat down in front of him.

"Bring the prisoner forward."

Joe Leif was led up to the table. He stood before them, head and eyes bent down. The flames of the bonfire still danced away, throwing shadows into the grass around them.

"Read the charges please, Colonel MacPherson."

Ranger MacPherson pulled up a sheet of paper and clicked on his flashlight before he began reading.

"The accused, Joseph R. Leaf, Sheriff of Iroquois county, is hereby charged with high treason, that he did willfully and purposely conspire with the enemy of Iroquois county, that he did willingly and knowingly enter into contract with one Jared Thompson, to give away military secrets and the transfer of those secrets to the enemy, and that these secrets jeopardized the safety and well-being of Iroquois county and its residents. Said actions were in violation of the oath of his office of sheriff and the executive order signed by Sheriff Joseph R. Leif, governing these criminal acts."

"Thank you, colonel." General Branch looked over to his left. "Colonel Branch, what evidence does this tribunal have in support of this charge?"

Dan Branch picked up a manila folder and opened it. "Sir, we have transcripts of these intercepted communiques between the defendant and the leader of the enemy forces, one Jared Thompson. We also have recordings between the defendant and his wife, Marge Leif, as they discussed the crime and their subsequent escape. We also have eyewitnesses of Mr. Leif and his wife as they rendezvoused with a known officer combatant of the enemy, this last evidence witnessed by everyone here tonight."

Dan laid down the folder and remained silent. General Branch moved his hands to the table top and folded them there. "How does the defendant plead? Guilty or not guilty?"

Joe Leif looked up for the first time. He tried to talk but was having trouble finding the right words. "I ... just ..." and then he managed a quick flurry of a response. "I request legal counsel."

General Branch looked over at Colonel MacPherson and nodded. Colonel MacPherson shook his head from side to side. Rodney looked over to his nephew, Dan, who also shook his head from side to side. General Branch looked back at the defendant before speaking.

"Request denied."

"But ... how can you do that? I'm a citizen! I have constitutional rights! You can't do this to me!"

Uncle Rodney sighed and looked down at his folded hands. "Listen Joe. I know this seems harsh, but ... you put all of us in danger, and you did it for financial gain. You betrayed us all, and, if we hadn't found out about it in time, all of us would have died because of your actions. As it is, two of my best officers and fifty of my men are now dead and buried in a sink hole. At least you're getting a military trial. They got nothing."

Joe Leif didn't say anything.

"Sheriff, you've disgraced yourself, this county and your office. The evidence against you is overwhelming, and, quite frankly, we don't have time to give you a trial that lasts six months. All that bullshit went out the window a year ago when the lights went out and martial law was declared. You have a right to a speedy and public trial. We've given you those rights. Is this not speedy enough for you? And you certainly can't get any more public than this."

General Branch leaned back in his chair. "Under martial law and the terms of your own executive order, your right to an attorney is waived. We have a war to fight, Mr. Leif." The general leaned forward again. "Now, this is the last time I'm going to ask you. Do you plead guilty or not guilty?"

Joe Leif didn't answer right away. He was still looking for a way out of this mess, but the general would not be denied.

"Joe, listen to me. This isn't just about you. Your wife is also guilty of conspiracy to commit treason, and we have plenty of proof to that as well. Conspiring with the enemy during time of war is punishable by death by firing squad." Rodney locked eyes with Joe. "Don't make me kill your wife too, Joe. Not in front of your boy. At least let him grow up with one parent."

Joe Leif finally nodded his head slightly, and then he spoke. "The defendant pleads ... guilty."

General Branch didn't waste a moment. "Let the record show that the defendant has pleaded guilty to the capital crime of treason. The tribunal hereby accepts that plea." General Branch stood and Colonel Branch and Colonel MacPherson followed him to their feet.

"This tribunal hereby sentences Joseph R. Branch to death by firing squad, a sentence to be carried out immediately."

Sheriff Leif's mouth dropped open in surprise. "But ... but ..."

General Branch immediately drew the Colt 45 caliber pistol from his holster and walked around the table until he was standing in front of the convicted. Rodney raised the pistol to his friend's head. "Sergeant remove the prisoner's badge of office."

The soldier closeby stepped forward and removed Joe's sheriff's badge, then stepped back again out of the line of fire. Uncle Rodney's right thumb moved to the safety release and clicked it off. Dan Branch looked down and then away. He was struggling, trying not to show any emotion. Colonel MacPherson looked dutifully on as General Branch moved his right forefinger to the trigger of the pistol.

"Does the prisoner have any final words?"

Joe Leif struggled with his mouth, and finally managed to open it and speak. "I ... I want to apologize to my community for the wrongs I've done. I let them down. I lost faith, and ... I'm very sorry." He looked down and then quickly back up again before Rodney could shoot him. "And I think most of all, I apologize for making my friend shoot me. I know you don't do this lightly, Rodney, and that it will affect you greatly for a long time to come."

Uncle Rodney pressed the trigger on his pistol and a loud boom rang out across the clearing. But the shot went over Joe's head and he didn't fall to the ground as expected. Joe began to cry and he suddenly fell to his knees, his ears ringing and his head hurting from the noise and the concussion.

"Joe, on behalf of Iroquois county, I accept your apology." And then he holstered his pistol. "In lieu of death, I hereby commute your sentence and replace it with banishment. You and your family will leave Iroquois county and never return."

Joe looked up and into Rodney's eyes. "If the convicted does return, then he will be shot on sight." Uncle Rodney bent down to eye level and looked straight into Joe's eyes. "Do you understand, Joe?"

Just then, there was a tiny flash of light just off the western horizon. It lit up that part of the sky for a few seconds and then began to fade.

Joe Leif looked out at the flash of light as did everyone around the bonfire, which was now beginning to fade into embers.

"What was that?"

Rodney lifted Joe to his feet, pulled out his knife and quickly cut the restraints from Joe's wrists. Rodney looked over to the west with the others. "I'd say that's probably Eagle River, Wisconsin being vaporized by the Blind Man."

And then he turned over to Mac. "I'll say one thing for the man, he doesn't waste any time and he always goes strong."

He quickly turned back to Joe Leif. "There were no nukes in Eagle River. That was disinformation designed to confirm your guilt, and you fell right into it."

He turned to Dan. "Colonel Branch, get Marge and the boy up here and let's get them on their way. We have a lot of work to do. I have a sudden urge to kick Mr. Thompson's not-so-blind ass!" And then he turned back to Joe Leif. "Up on the logging trail you'll find a cart filled with enough supplies to last a week. You'll also find an M4 for protection, a thousand rounds of ammo, ten ounces of silver, and we'll also return your sidearm to you."

He turned to walk away but then stopped halfway. He turned and made eye contact with the former sheriff. "Joe, you need to understand that I'm serious about this. If you come back before this war is over, then I'll put you down personally."

Joe Leif nodded. "I know, Rodney. This is all on me. I won't be back." And then he reached out to shake his hand. Joe's lone hand hovered there between them for several seconds. Finally, Uncle Rodney stepped forward, grabbed his hand and pulled him in close. After a brief embrace, General Branch turned and walked away into the treeline without looking back. Colonel MacPherson followed his general.

Dan Branch stepped forward and held his hand out to his friend. Tears welled up in Joe's eyes as he accepted it. The two embraced, and then Dan held out a small piece of paper.

"This is the name and address of a family with an extra house two counties over. They've agreed to rent it to you until this is all over. They know nothing of your crimes, so you can live with some measure of respect."

Joe took the paper and nodded. "Dan, will he ever forgive me?"

Dan smiled. "Hell, Joe, he's already spared your life twice tonight. If that's not forgiveness, then I don't know what is."

He turned and barked out orders to the sergeant and his soldiers. "Escort this man and his family safely to the county line, point them in the right direction and then return to base."

Without another word, Dan Branch turned and walked away from the clearing. Joe Leif looked after him until he disappeared into the trees. Then his wife and son arrived and were escorted to the logging trail and their supplies.

An hour later their escort peeled away and returned to

base, leaving Joe and his wife to face the night, their shame, and a lifetime of regret.

CHAPTER 17

<u>**August 26, Swearing in the New President**</u>

GENERAL BRANCH STOOD BEFORE VA SECRETARY Joseph Donnelly in a pasture just outside the wooden barn, surrounded by Shadow Militia soldiers, all bearing M4s and facing outward as if to ward off any physical threats.

"Let's get you back inside Mr. Secretary. I don't want to take any unnecessary chances in the home stretch."

Joseph Donnelly was dressed in a black suit that hung a little too loosely off his now slender frame. His hair was combed back neatly and greased into place with the only thing the soldiers had been able to find: a jar of Vaseline petroleum jelly. The two men walked back inside the barn, followed by several of the soldiers.

"The federal judge should be here momentarily. We played hell finding him. That's why it's taken so long before swearing you in."

Joe nodded impatiently. "Let's just get it done so we can get down to business."

General Branch smiled. "This has been a long time coming, and I'm just as anxious as you are. The sooner we get you sworn in, the sooner you can take charge of the military and get this country back on course."

The VA Secretary smiled. "To tell you the truth, general, I'd settle for a hot bath, a shave and a haircut."

General Branch laughed out loud. "Well, Mr. Secretary, I would think that the United States of America, even in its present diminished capacity, should be able to accommodate that request."

Joe Donnelly thought to himself. *The president of the United States doesn't make requests ... he issues orders!* But what he spoke aloud was something completely different. "I just want you to know, general, that I'm eternally indebted to you and your group for getting me out of Haiti." He hesitated, looking briefly into the general's eyes. "The country will be needing men like you to help us lead our way back to world dominance."

Colonel MacPherson stepped up behind General Branch and whispered into his ear. The general nodded and turned back to Joe Donnelly. "Mr. Secretary, the judge has arrived. Are you ready to become the President of the United States of America?"

Joe smiled broadly. He couldn't believe this was finally happening. He was going to be president of the United States, the leader of the free world! He smirked deep inside. And to think that just a year ago he was being investigated by the FBI for possible fraud charges. Of course, he'd been guilty, but ... it no longer mattered. Any evidence of his guilt was probably no longer available since the collapse. He was now free and clear. And then he thought to himself *America truly is the land of opportunity.*

They milled around for a few minutes and then US District Court Judge Edmond Roloefs walked through the barn door. He wore his black robes, but they were clearly in need of a good dry cleaning. He was carrying a large, black Bible in his left hand.

"Good afternoon, Mr. President."

Joe beamed inside, his emotions almost out of control. This was the first time anyone had used his new title. "Well, your honor, let's not get hasty. I'm not the president yet."

Judge Roloefs smiled as he replied. "Well, that's a technicality I plan on resolving right away. Are you ready to take the oath?"

Joe nodded, barely able to control his excitement. General Branch and Colonel MacPherson moved back a few paces, taking their rightful places in the background. Sergeant Donny Brewster moved up closer to his commanding officer, to the left and slightly abreast, his M4 on a one-point sling against his lean stomach. He didn't like the new president, but there was nothing he could do about it.

"Please raise your right hand and repeat after me."

Joe Donnelly placed his left hand on the Bible and then raised his right hand. His lips were dry, so he licked at them nervously.

"I do solemnly swear."

"I, Joseph Donnelly, do solemnly swear."

"That I will faithfully execute the office of president of the United States."

Joe's hands were sweating now. It was finally happening.

"That I will faithfully execute the office of president of the United States."

"And will to the best of my ability."

Joe could hardly speak. His throat constricted and his voice became suddenly very weak. But he pressed on.

"And will to the best of my ability."

"Preserve, protect and defend the Constitution of the United States."

Judge Roloefs waited for the VA Secretary's response, but it didn't come. He leaned in closer to Joe Donnelly and whispered. "Are you okay, Mr. President?"

Joe pointed to his throat and tried to speak, but nothing came out. Judge Roloefs turned to the small crowd. "General Branch, can we get some water for the president?"

General Branch motioned to Donny Brewster, who quickly walked forward, and handed his canteen to Joseph Donnelly.

The VA Secretary looked at it sceptically, wondering ... *did this sergeant put his dirty lips on this canteen?* But, despite his petty reservations, he reached down to unscrew the cap. He turned as hard as he could, but the cap wouldn't budge. Donny Brewster saw his problem and shook his head in disgust. He reached out and grabbed the canteen, unscrewed the cap before handing it back to the soon-to-be president of the United States. Joe grudgingly took a small swallow of the warm water. It was disgusting to him, but at least it moistened his throat enough so he could talk.

"Thank you sergeant."

Donny returned to his place beside his officers. Judge Roloefs turned back to the VA Secretary and gave him time to put his hand back on the Bible and to raise his right hand again.

"Just say the last phrase and we'll call it good, Mr. President."

Joseph Donnelly uttered the final words which made him the official president of the United States of America.

"Preserve, protect and defend the Constitution of the United States."

Judge Roloefs reached out to shake the president's hand. "Congratulations, Mr. President."

Joe smiled and shook the man's hand. Then he was congratulated by everyone there, going around the room, shaking hands and accepting praise and congratulations. After fifteen minutes the new president turned to General Branch.

"So what happens now, general?"

In response, General Branch turned to Colonel MacPherson and issued commands. "Colonel, you are to take the president to Dyess Air Force Base in Texas so he can better carry out the duties of his office." The colonel stood to attention and saluted sharply. The general returned the salute and then pivoted back toward the president. "Mr. President, that particular base has complete power and facilities to help you regain command and control of all military forces. This base is home to the Seventh Bomber Wing, composed of two squadrons of B1b Lancer Stealth bombers as well as the 317th Airlift Wing which is the largest force of C-130J Super Hercules remaining in the world. The base is over six thousand acres and should be able to serve you well until you can choose a more suitable command post. The commanding general of the base has been apprised of your situation and is eagerly awaiting your arrival."

The president nodded. "Very good, general." And then he hesitated. "One other thing, general. I require a satphone so I can begin my work right away."

"Absolutely, sir. The colonel will provide you with one immediately. And, Mr. President, with your permission, I'd like to return to my home. I believe the Shadow Militia has completed its mission and can be of no further use to you."

The president smiled and extended his hand to General Branch. "On behalf of a grateful nation, I thank you." The two men shook hands and Uncle Rodney turned and left the barn. Colonel MacPherson handed his satphone to the president.

"We'll be outside when you're ready to depart, Mr. President."

When he was alone in the barn, Joe Donnelly punched in the number and held the phone up to his right ear. When the call connected, he spoke in hushed tones.

"It's done. I am now the president of the United States." And then he paused. "What are your orders?"

On the other end of the line, Jared Thompson smiled. *He had won. He had beaten General Branch without firing a shot.*

Dyess Air Force Base - Texas

THE BLACKHAWK HELICOPTER CIRCLED ONCE OVERhead, then came down softly on the runway, followed closely by the two Apache gunships that were providing escort. According to the terms agreed upon by General Branch and

General MacDermid, newly sworn-in President Donnelly exited the Blackhawk as the base band played hail to the chief. Colonel MacPherson exited after him but stayed in the background in case he was needed. General MacDermid strode proudly up to the new president and crisply saluted him. Colonel MacPherson had given the president a quick private lesson on rendering salutes, and the president did a passable job his first time around.

"It's good to welcome you to Fort Dyess, Mr. President." There were several hangers closeby, but the president couldn't see the B1 bombers from this part of the base. There were about a thousand airmen standing at attention on the tarmac, and President Donnelly was visibly impressed.

"It's good to be here, general. So what happens now?" General MacDermid pointed toward the assembled airmen and the small stage at the head of the group. "Would the Commander-in-Chief care to address his troops, sir?"

Joseph Donnelly thought to himself. *Commander-in-Chief, I like the sound of that.* "Absolutely, general. Please lead the way."

General MacDermid walked briskly toward the small, portable stage and then up the steps where he approached the podium and spoke into the microphone. When the music stopped he addressed the troops.

"Thank you for coming today. It is with great pleasure and relief, that I introduce to you, the president of the United States of America!"

The general backed away and waited for the president to reach the podium. He saluted again and then Joe reached out to shake his hand. The thousand or so men roared with enthusiasm, but when the new president stood behind the podium and raised his hands, they gradually quieted down.

"Thank you so much General MacDermid, and thank you to all airmen and officers of Fort Dyess. It's truly an honor to serve as your Commander-in-Chief, and I will do my utmost to lead you with the dignity and honor that you are all accustomed to." And then he paused. "Now, it's been over a year since I've been on a US military base, and I can tell you I've never been happier, or felt more secure. All of you have sworn an oath to protect and defend the country, and your diligence is needed now more than ever as we seek to rebuild our great nation and continue to protect against all who would seek to destroy us.

"Over the ensuing weeks, I will work to form a new working government and to restore America to its former greatness."

The crowd erupted in applause and President Donnelly raised his hand and waved to them as he turned to leave the stage. Several other high-ranking officers lined up to shake the new president's hand and he accommodated them dutifully.

After several minutes, President Donnelly was led away from the blazing hot tarmac and into a waiting limousine. The limo was flanked on both ends by HumVees, armed with 50 caliber machine guns. President Donnelly could barely contain his delight as he drove away to begin reforming the United States federal government.

Colonel MacPherson looked after the motorcade as it pulled away from the stage. He nodded in satisfaction before getting back into the Blackhawk helicopter and flying away.

August 27 - Somewhere South of the Mason-Dixon Line

GENERAL MASBRUCH LOOKED DOWN AT THE MAP spread out on the table in front of them. "Where did you get all this information, General Branch?"

Rodney looked down at the map as well and smiled. "The Blind Man had a spy in his midst, and he didn't even know it. His name was Sammy Thurmond."

General Masbruch's tan face was lined with wrinkles, especially at the corners of his eyes. His bald head was shiny, but his green eyes seemed to glow with appreciation as he looked down at the plans that Colonel MacPherson and General Branch had explained to him in great detail. "Isn't he the one they called "the Blind Man's pet?"

Rodney shrugged. "I think so."

"What caused him to betray his boss?"

Rodney smiled. "He appeared to fall in love with my daughter-in-law."

General Masbruch looked up and out through the door of his tent. "So where is he now? I'd like to talk to this guy, especially if we're going to be risking everything based on information he's given us."

Colonel MacPHerson fielded the question. "I'm afraid that's impossible, General Masbruch. He's dead. Killed by the Blind Man."

The general sighed. "Most unfortunate. You say you confirmed all this information with boots on the ground?"

Mac nodded. "That's right."

Masbruch reached up with his left hand and wiped the sweat away from his bald head. "This damned heat and humidity is oppressing." And then he looked up and smiled at Mac and Rodney. "General Branch, I'll start positioning my people right away. We'll time everything and coordinate the attacks perfectly." And then he reached over to shake Rodney's hand. "Thanks Rodney. The Blind Man will never see it coming."

Rodney looked over at Mac. "Did you just hear what he said, Mac?" And then he looked over at General Masbruch. "General Masbruch, are you developing a sense of humor in your old age? The same thing happened to Mac just a few days ago."

For a moment the general looked confused, then a light seemed to go on in is head and he laughed out loud. "The pun was not intended, general. Though it does seem appropriate."

"We have to get going now, general. But we'll leave this part of the campaign in your capable hands. Please let me know if you need anything or get in trouble."

General Masbruch took a step back and snapped to attention. Then he saluted sharply as Rodney did the same. Mac and Rodney turned and strode out of the command tent and walked to their waiting Blackhawk. They had work to do.

The New Administration

"Gentlemen. I have some plans already laid out, and I'm going to need some support from the military to make it happen."

The conference room at Dyess Air Force Base was large and immaculate. The table was rectangular, and every seat was filled, bringing the total in the room to about fifteen. "My new Chief of Staff will be flying in tomorrow, and I need him to report to me as soon as he lands. I also need some office space as I plan on appointing cabinet members soon."

General MacDermid was seated to the president's right. He turned to his exec. "Make a note of it, John."

The colonel nodded and was already writing it down. "It'll be done, sir."

"The next order of business is appointing my vice-president. He'll be flying in from West Virginia at fourteen-hundred hours tomorrow. He'll be flying a Lear business jet with two F18s as escort. Please see that he's given immediate clearance as well as quarters appropriate with his office."

General MacDermid raised his eyebrows just a bit. "Is it someone we know, Mr. President?"

Joe Donnelly shook his head from side to side. "I doubt it. Most of the people we all knew a year ago are either missing or dead. But I've known this man for a long time, and he'll do a great job until we can get the country back on its feet and hold regular elections."

"I understand, sir. What is his name, Mr. President?"

Joe Donnelly hesitated for just a moment. "His name is Jared Thompson."

The general nodded to the colonel. "Did you get that, Colonel Frank?"

The colonel nodded. "Yes, sir. We'll see that he's given a proper greeting in accordance with his high office. Then we'll take him immediately to the conference room where the president can confer with him. If that's what you want, sir."

The president smiled. "That'll be fine, colonel. I'll be waiting for him. Please make sure there's a hot meal with the proper wine."

The colonel glanced over at his general and then back at the president. "The proper wine, sir?"

The president seemed perturbed by the question. "Yes, you do know what wine is don't you?"

The colonel nodded in military fashion. "Absolutely, sir. It'll be done, Mr. President!"

Joe Donnelly was enjoying the office of president, and he was just getting started. "See to it that you do, colonel."

And then the president stood to his feet, the chair scraping against the tile floor. "This meeting is over gentlemen. I'm off to take a nap before dinner is served. See that I'm not disturbed."

The rest of the people in the room rose up and stood at attention as the president walked out of the room. When the door closed behind him, General MacDermid turned and looked at his exec. "Well, Colonel Frank, I'm convinced. What about you?"

The colonel smiled. "I was hoping you'd say that, sir. I'll get General Branch on the horn and start the ball rolling." The two officers walked out of the room, each with their own missions to accomplish.

CHAPTER 18

The New Vice President Arrives!

"**T**HE **L**EAR **JET** **IS** **LANDING** **NOW**, sir. We'll be with you in just a few minutes."

Colonel Frank was about fifty years old. His hair was half-gray, but it made him look distinguished. He replaced the handset to the radio back in its place. Then he watched as the two F18s circled overhead on CAP and the Lear jet descended down into the glide slope. Five minutes later the door to the jet opened and the new VP walked out and into the blazing hot Texas sun. The vice president wore an immaculate grey suit with a red power tie. There were dark sunglasses on his head and he carried a cane in his right hand. He was helped down the steps by an aid. The colonel met him at the foot of the stairway. He saluted sharply, but the Blind Man didn't return it.

"Welcome to Dyess Air Force Base, Mr. Vice President! The president is waiting for you." The Vice President didn't say anything. He just turned toward the voice and his aid led him after the colonel. They got into the same limo that had transported the president the day before and drove to the conference room. The president was already there and seated at the head of the table. He stood to his feet when the VP walked into the room.

"Jared, it's so good to see you. I hope your flight was

good."

The Blind Man nodded. "It was well ... all things considered."

The president hesitated and looked at his new VP with a questioning stare. Jared Thompson leaned in close as they shook hands and whispered something into the president's ear. The president pasted on a smile.

"Won't you sit down beside me here, Mr. Vice President?"

The Blind Man sat down with the help of his aid, and then everyone else sat down as well. There was a dignified and official air to the room, and all fifteen chairs were once again filled with high-ranking officers from the air force, army, marines and the navy. They had flown in from existing bases and ships from all over the country for this very meeting.

"Well now. I'd like to introduce all of you to my new vice president, as soon as we get him sworn in. This is Jared Thompson."

General MacDermid stood and began to clap. The other generals, admirals and their aids rose and clapped as well. Finally, the president motioned for all of them to be seated.

"Let's get on with it, gentlemen. We have a country to run."

But before he could get started, the door opened and five men walked in. They wore dark suits with radio earpieces and took up flanking positions around the room. One of them spoke into his wrist. "Position is secured. Eagle One may enter."

President Donnelly rose to his feet. "What is going on here, general? Who are these men?"

General MacDermid smiled and rose to answer. "They are part of the president's secret service detail, Mr. Donnelly."

The president turned and looked over at the general. The look on his face was one of total befuddlement. But after a short moment it was replaced with anger. "You will address me as Mr. President! Is that clear, general!"

But the general just laughed, and this infuriated the president even more. He stomped his foot down hard and reasserted his dominance. "I said, general, you will call me Mr. President right now, or I will have you relieved of your command!"

Just then newly sworn-in President Townsend walked proudly into the conference room. At once, everyone inside rose and stood at the position of attention.

General MacDermid snapped to attention and turned to face Michael Townsend. "Good afternoon, Mr. President. We've been waiting for you."

Right behind President Townsend, General Rodney T. Branch strutted in, followed closely by Colonel MacPherson. Both wore full, army-dress uniforms. There were four stars on Uncle Rodney's collar.

"What the hell is going on here? Who is this man?"

Michael Townsend looked at Joe Donnelly and smiled. "You don't mean to tell me you don't recognize me, Joe? I guess it's been a few years since we've talked, but ... still. I'd think you'd remember a fellow cabinet member."

And then the color drained from Joseph Donnelly's face as he recognized the Secretary of Transportation. "But ... but ... you're dead."

President Townsend laughed out loud, followed by most people in the room. The Blind Man turned and looked at President Townsend and General Branch. An evil sneer formed on his lips.

"But, I was sworn into office first! It's too late! I'm already the president! You can't be president after I'm already president!"

President Townsend smiled and shook his head from side to side. "You were always such an ambitious and cowardly man, Joe." And then he looked over at General Branch. "Rodney, did you have this man sworn in as president of the United States?"

General Branch stepped forward. "I did, Mr. President."

"And who was the man who administered to Joe the oath

of office? Was he a federal court judge?"

"No, Mr. President. The man who administered the oath was the president of the Iroquois county drama club." Uncle Rodney smiled. "But he was very convincing, sir. We all thought it was his best performance ever."

The president slapped Rodney on the back with glee. "And who was given the oath first, Joe Donnelly or myself?"

"You were, Mr. President. The swearing-in ceremony of Joseph Donnelly was just a sham. He was never the president, sir."

Then Uncle Rodney looked closer at the Blind Man and frowned. He suddenly went on full alert and lowered his center of gravity. The Blind Man reached his right hand into his pocket and ran toward President Townsend. The secret service detail was caught off guard, seeing a blind man run as though he could see. Jared Thompson pulled out the pearl-handled thirty-two caliber pistol and raised it to fire.

A loud boom rang out and then another and another. The secret service men cleared their coats and drew their pistols, but it was too late. By the time they were ready to shoot, the Blind Man's body was already bleeding on the floor and Uncle Rodney was holstering his forty-five. The new Chairman of the Joint Chiefs had just administered two to the chest and one to the head.

President Townsend was being ushered quickly out of the room by his secret service detail, but he violently shrugged them off. "Stand down, you fools, Can't you see the danger's gone now!" The president looked down at the body, bleeding on the floor in front of him. Then he looked back up at Uncle Rodney. And then he laughed nervously. "Well, hell, Rodney, looks like I made the right choice for my new Chairman of the Joint Chiefs."

Joseph Donnelly's legs gave out and he sank back down into his overstuffed chair. And then he lowered his head down into his hands and cried. "I'm not the president."

President Townsend smiled, but he couldn't totally conceal his sympathy. He turned to General MacDermid. "General, will you please place the VA Secretary under arrest, pending formal charges of treason? I'll let the military handle the tribunal."

Joseph Donnelly was taken into custody. His hands were cuffed behind his back and then he was led away, still crying as he walked. The president started to walk to the conference table, but General Branch stopped him.

"Mr. President. We have a big problem."

President Townsend stopped and turned. "What is it, Rodney?"

Rodney bent down to the floor and rolled over the dead man on the tile floor.

"This man is not Jared Thompson."

The Blind Man's Lair

JARED THOMPSON HAD WATCHED THE LEAR JET LAND on the tarmac at Dyess Air Force Base and watched as his double was led away, seeming with all the honor and pomp ascribed to a man of his high office. It was possible that his extra caution had been unnecessary. But still ... extra caution and even paranoia had kept Jared alive for most of his life. He should be getting a call from the new president any moment now. He would wait to make sure.

Preparing for War!

"WE NEED TO GET THE PRESIDENT OUT OF HERE AS SOON as possible! We also need to scramble every jet you've got and prepare for attack!"

General Rodney T. Branch continued to bark out orders and all the generals and admirals around him rushed to carry them out as quickly as possible.

General MacDermid turned to Colonel Frank. "Get it

done, colonel!"

Colonel Frank turned and rushed out of the room. Rodney called out to Admiral Fletcher who was standing nearby. "Admiral, how many planes can we get airborne in the next two hours?"

The admiral met his gaze and thought for a moment. "I'm not sure what you need. We can get everything in the air, but that doesn't mean they'll have the range you need. I need more details."

Both Admiral Fletcher and General MacDermid sat down at the conference table with the Chairman of the Joint Chiefs. "I need to know what our assets are and where they're located and I need to know right away."

The general nodded. "Sure, we can do that for you, but it'll take about fifteen minutes. We'll write it up and have it on your desk. But, General Branch, there is one problem."

Rodney looked over at General MacDermid and frowned. "What is it?"

The general looked down at the table and fidgeted with his hands. "We don't have much in the line of ground troops these days. Most of them are still overseas, and many of the ones that are left here in the states went home to help protect their families after the power went out."

General Branch nodded. "That's okay. Just include what you have in the asset list. I already have enough foot soldiers to do the job. But what we really need is air support."

Both the admiral and the general smiled broadly. "Now that, General Branch, isn't a problem. Between the air force and the navy, we can give you plenty of airpower, sir."

Just then a siren started to sound all across the base. General Branch looked at General MacDermid with questions in his eyes.

"It's an air raid siren, sir. We're about to be attacked."

Rodney clenched his teeth grimly. "Did you get the president out in time?"

The admiral nodded. "Yes, sir. He should be landing on the aircraft carrier in the gulf any minute now."

Then he turned back to the air force general. "General MacDermid. Did you get everything scrambled?"

"We're doing it now, sir. Everything will shortly be in the air that can be in the air."

Rodney smiled grimly. "Okay then. Let's get farther underground to the Combat Information Center and see how the battle is going."

General Masbruch Attacks

COLONEL MACPHERSON STOOD BESIDE GENERAL Masbruch inside the mobile command post. It was just a big semi trailer filled with comm gear with soldiers running back and forth, delivering messages and sending their radio traffic. It was far from state of the art, but it got the job done.

"We're attacking on three fronts right now general. We are looking good in Georgia and in Montana, but the attack on the West Virginia complex is not going well. There were more forces there than we'd been led to believe, and we're being pounded by F16s and Apache attack helicopters."

The general rubbed his temples with the first two fingers of both hands. "What about our air support?"

"Nothing yet, sir."

The general looked at him in disbelief. "Nothing? Are you sure?"

Mac nodded. "Yes, general. I just got off the line with Colonel Branch, who is leading the ground assault. They're bogged down a mile from the complex and taking heavy losses from the air."

General Masbruch slammed his fist down on the table. A few soldiers looked up, but then quickly went back to work. "Get General Branch on the phone right now!"

Mac nodded and pulled out his satphone. "I'll do my best, general."

Colonel Branch - Spruce Mountain, West Virginia

"JEREMY, GET YOUR HEAD DOWN! DON'T TAKE SO MANY chances, son!"

Corporal Jeremy Branch looked over at his father and tried to smile. "That's a little bit like the pot calling the kettle black isn't it? I mean look at you, Dad. You keep running back and forth out in the open. There's a bullet hole in your boonie hat and another on your sleeve."

Dan Branch hunkered down behind an oak tree as more bullets ripped the ground around them. They were taking intense sniper fire, not to mention the fire from the air was beginning to intensify.

"I thought Uncle Rodney was going to send us some air support, Dad. But I don't see any planes up there except the ones shooting at us."

Dan nodded in agreement. They were being systematically exterminated on this ridge, and if they didn't take control of the air soon, they'd all be dead.

"Get General Masbruch on the line. We're going to have to pull back and regroup or else none of us will be left alive for the final assault on the complex."

Jeremy nodded and pulled out the handset to relay the information.

"Jason! Prepare the men to pull back. Pass it on down the line! Every other man will pull back one hundred yards at exactly 0937 hours. Then at 0945 the remainder of our forces will pull back. Make sure no one is left behind."

Jeremy looked over at his dad frantically. "Dad, I can't get through on the radio. I think we're being jammed or something."

Colonel Branch watched as another of his men went down as an Apache gunship made another pass with his M230 chain gun. Four more men were cut to pieces, their bodies shredded and their blood splattered against the trees around them. He yelled at the others out of desperation. "I said stay down! Get behind a big tree until we move out!"

Lieutenant Jason Little moved away quickly down the line, passing the word to everyone. But unknown to Colonel Branch, he would never make it all the way and many of his men would be left behind to die on the ridge. The .308 sniper bullet reached out and found its mark in the center of Jason's forehead, ripping away the top half of his skull. It was a painless end to an otherwise honorable and successful life. His big body went down hard onto the broken shale of the West Virginia mountainside, his blood seeping out into the rich, dark humus and brown leaves of the woods.

Donny's Last Charge

A HALF A MILE AWAY, ON THE NEXT RIDGE OVER, Sergeant Donny Brewster and his breaching force of 75 men didn't get the order to retreat. Some of his men carried M4s with plenty of grenades, while others had some variation of the older M16s. A few had simple AR15s, but none of them were prepared to take out Apache attack helicopters. The master plan put forth by General Branch had counted on overwhelming air superiority, so they hadn't bothered with carrying many heavy Stinger missiles with them. Their mission depended on speed, but they weren't going anywhere until their air support arrived.

"Get Colonel Branch on the line. We need to find out what's going on!" Donny could barely hear individual voices with all the sounds of gun fire and rockets going off all around him. He looked over at the radio man and saw the gaping hole on the left side of his chest. He was just now in the final stages of bleeding out. Donny grabbed the handset but the cord was no longer attached and half the radio had been blown away.

"Damn!" He looked around him and saw that a third of his men were dead or wounded. They would not survive if he didn't do something and fast. He grabbed the nearest living corporal and yelled at him.

"We're going to attack!"

Corporal Eric Olsen looked at him like he was crazy. "Are ya outta yer cotton-pickin' mind! Were gonna be kilt!"

Donny grabbed him by the shirt and pulled him in closer."You're already being killed! Besides, you're already ugly as a fish and half your teeth are gone. Do you wanna live forever that way? I said we're going to attack and we're going to do it right away. These are snipers and plenty of them. The longer we stay here the more of us will die." He looked out at the ones closest to him. "Everyone! Fix bayonets! We need to get in as close as we can as fast as we can. They'll have flank security with automatic weapons and claymore mines, so we're going to head straight down the gullet into the center of their line. We're going downhill, so we'll have the benefit of speed. Once we get inside their line we kill them all!"

He pushed Corporal Olson away, picked up a handful of mud and blood and smeared it on his cheeks. "Corporal Olson, you lead them down the left and I'll take the right. We don't stop until they're all dead!"

Corporal Olson looked down the hillside at the scattered dead and dying. He suddenly thought of his corn crop back in Georgia and wondered if it would ever get picked. And then he thought *What the hell. I'm already 55 years old. Do I want to live forever? Besides, if ya gotta go; this isn't such a bad death.* He took out a tub of Redman and quickly stuffed a pinch into his left cheek. And then he screamed and raised his carbine up over his head.

Donny laughed out loud and screamed as well. Soon all his men were screaming and shaking their weapons over their heads. Two more men went down from sniper fire, and then Donny headed down the hill, screaming like a maniac, thinking of Nurse Vanderboeg and her beautiful blonde hair, locks that he would never again touch.

CHAPTER 19

Inside the Blind Man's Lair

JARED **T**HOMPSON LOOKED OUT AT
the screen in front of him. It was all state of the art.
He knew exactly who was dying and who was liv-
ing, and, so far, he was winning this battle. His air force had
already destroyed the runways at Dyess air base in a surprise
attack along with half the buildings. He'd wanted to send another sortie to finish them off, but had been surprised to learn
that the Shadow Militia ground forces were attacking all three
of his major bases in Georgia and Montana and here in West
Virginia. This had forced him to conserve his airpower and
pull it back to protect his own position as well.

But now he was making General Branch pay for his arro-
gance. Unfortunately, he didn't even know where the general
was right now. If he had known, he would have sent one of his
precious nukes to take him out, just out of spite. His original
plan had been to meet the general face to face, to talk to him
first, and then put a bullet in his head so he could watch the
look of despair on his face and then to slowly savor the flow of
his blood into the ground. But ... to the general's credit, he'd
been a worthy adversary, and so, Jared would just have to kill
him at a distance, in a more impersonal way. So be it. Wasn't
it General Eisenhower who'd said that even the best war plans
only survived the first shot. He would have to improvise and

adapt.

By now the new president, Michael Townsend, would already be dead, killed by Jared's own stunt-double, assassin. He was proud of that one. As soon as he'd found out about the general's plans to reinstate the presidency, he'd been one step ahead of General Branch all the way. Jared liked dangling carrots in front of his adversaries, making them think they were winning, when, in reality, they'd never had much hope, even from the beginning.

No, this rebellion that the Shadow Militia had formed was now being systematically destroyed. They were leaderless and in disarray. He'd always wanted to bring the Shadow Militia out of hiding, knowing intuitively that he had them outmanned and outgunned. The only chink in his armor had been the sudden alliance with Dyess Air Force Base in Texas. He hated Texas. But now that he'd destroyed their airpower while still in their hangers, it was all done except the mopping up.

Jared looked back up on the TV screen above him. Now, it was time to shift some of his airpower to Montana and Georgia to finish destroying the attacking ground forces of the Shadow Militia. He reached down to move the mouse and press a button, but a sudden jolt threw him off his feet and he landed onto the couch several feet away. The explosion had rocked his facility even two-hundred feet down inside the earth. The wine glass on the mahogany table top spilled onto the floor and shattered.

He yelled at the top of his lungs. "What is going on out there?"

His assistant rushed into the room. "I don't know, sir."

"Well ... find out and find out now!"

Another explosion rocked the room and Jared was thrown to his knees. He got up slowly and leaned against the corinthian leather of the couch. He looked up at the state of the art computer screen and watched it flicker off and on several times. It no longer seemed to be updating in real time.

Another explosion, this one bigger than the first two rocked the room and Jared Thompson stayed on his knees. All he could think of was *Damn you Rodney Branch! I'm going to kill you if it's the last thing I do!*

Dyess Air Force Base, Texas

GENERAL MACDERMID RELAYED THE NEW INFORMA-tion quickly to his new Chairman of the Joint Chiefs, who was personally coordinating every detail of this attack. "We have direct hits with all the cruise missiles, General Branch. Their command and control is now severely damaged."

Uncle Rodney nodded his head in satisfaction. "Good. Now release the heavy bombers. I want Spruce Mountain leveled. Bury the Blind Man in his own personal tomb!"

General MacDermid passed down the orders and reported back. "The B1s and B52s are almost there, sir. The B52s will carpet the surrounding area with conventional 500-pound bombs. Each B52 has a payload of up to 70,000 pounds. They're flying out of Barksdale in Louisiana, sir. The BONEs are from here. The BONEs will drop GBU-37 laser-guided, bunker-busting bombs that can possibly collapse the concrete down on their heads. "

General Branch frowned. "What do you mean, possibly?"

"Well, sir, they are 4,700 pound bombs that are designed to break through hardened targets. They're pretty standard so far as bunker busters go."

Uncle Rodney reached up to stroke his chin. "So, how do we know for sure they'll reach down into the Blind Man's operations center?"

General MacDermid looked over at Colonel Frank and hesitated. "Well, sir, I guess we don't really know for sure. We don't have the specs on his facility. We don't know for sure the thickness of the concrete or even how far down it's buried in the earth."

Rodney Branch walked over to the general and looked him square in the face. "This man has a knack for surviving. I want Jared Thompson's guts blown all over West Virginia. Ya got anything for the occasion? Something bigger?"

Colonel Frank tried to stifle a grin, but couldn't quite do it. General MacDermid still wasn't used to Rodney's methods or demeanor. When he spoke it was slowly and with proper enunciation.

"Well, sir ..." But he hesitated. Rodney gave him an impatient look.

"Yes, general? You were saying?"

"Well, we do have Big BLU."

Rodney nodded. "And what is that exactly?"

"Big BLU is, more specifically, the GBU-57A/B Massive Ordnance Penetrator bomb, sir. They're 30,000 pounds a piece and can penetrate up to 200 feet of dirt and 20 feet of concrete."

Rodney smiled like a kid in a candy shop. "So, how many do you think we'll need?"

This was the first time General MacDermid laughed today. "Well, general, I think one should do it. We certainly don't want to blast clean on through to China."

General Branch nodded. "Ya know boys, what good are toys if you can't take 'em out and play with 'em once in a while."

He turned away and then back again. "Let's do it."

"Are you sure, sir?"

Now it was Rodney's turn to laugh. "Yer damn right I'm sure. Never underestimate the Blind Man, general. Today ... it's time to go strong or stay home!"

Rodney's smile was bigger than ever. "Give the order, General MacDermid."

Donny Brewster was still screaming when he reached the first sniper, who was proned out in a slit trench with rocks mounded up in front of him. The man tried to get up and turn his rifle toward Donny, but was quickly cut down with two, three-round bursts from Donny's M4 carbine. Donny ran to the next trench, firing his carbine as he moved, killing another and then another. By now other Shadow Militia soldiers had caught up with him and were killing enemy snipers of their own. Donny couldn't believe how many there were, but he just kept killing as quickly and efficiently as he could.

A sniper came up behind him and leveled his rifle before firing. The .308 round tore into Donny's left arm, spinning him around and throwing him to the ground. The enemy soldier rushed forward and lined up for the killing shot. Corporal Olson came out of nowhere, thrusting his bayonet into the man's back with a loud scream. He jerked back hard and pulled out the knife before thrusting it in again and again and again, until the man finally dropped to the ground, squirming just for a few seconds before bleeding out on the dirt and shale.

Donny jumped to his feet, blood dripping from the wound in his arm, but he kept moving forward. "Go men! Go! Kill them all!"

Two minutes later, totally spent, like a fired cartridge, Donny collapsed onto the leaves and stopped moving. The shooting had died down now, but Donny Brewster no longer had the strength to keep going. Corporal Olson hurried up close and plopped himself down on the ground beside him. He looked at the bleeding arm and then at Donny's pale skin and swore out loud to himself.

"Ya done got shot, Donny. Ya crazy son of a bitch!"

Sergeant Brewster lay back on the leaves, his mind floating in and out of consciousness. Corporal Olson worked quickly to apply the tourniquet, hoping above hope that he was in time. Donny reached up with his right hand and stroked Eric's dirty, greasy hair softly and tenderly.

"Thank you, Nurse Vanderboeg. I love you. I will never leave you again."

Eric threw back his head and laughed out loud. "Crazy bastard. I love ya too, sergeant, but don't be expectin' a wet, sloppy kiss from me!"

Suddenly, he heard the heavy bombers overhead, and the sound of bombs falling. The massive explosions began to erupt close to the underground complex. Corporal Olson yelled as loud as he could. "Take cova' men!"

And then he drug Donny's body down into a slit trench to wait out the pounding.

CHAPTER 20

The Blind Man's Concern

TWO HUNDRED FEET BELOW THE surface of the mountain, Jared Thompson began to realize that everything wasn't going exactly as he'd planned. Where was all this firepower coming from? He'd neutralized the air base at Dyess. He'd assassinated the new president. This should not be happening! But it was. The computer screen on the wall flickered off and on again. He cursed below his breath. Then he felt the concussion of 500-pound bombs as they detonated on the surface above. There were dozens of them going off every few seconds or so. And then the bunker busters began to hit, maybe a dozen in all. Suddenly, he started to doubt the impregnability of his underground fortress.

After a few, quick moments of reflection, in the mindless dizziness of the Blind Man's rage, Jared Thompson started to understand. He had not beaten General Rodney T. Branch. He had, indeed, underestimated his enemy again. He had killed Sammy Thurmond ... his right-hand man. Sammy Thurmond was dead and could not save him. But, more importantly, General Branch was alive! The Shadow Militia was now attacking all his installations and in great force, backed up by massive airpower, and he had no idea where it was coming from. All his intel, from day one, had told him that the Shadow

Militia had very little airpower. That was their weakness, and, therefore, that was Jared's big advantage.

The Blind Man swore out loud over and over again. He'd been planning this attack his whole adult life. He was born to rule! His mind and will were superior to any other. It would be a travesty if he could not rule unopposed. Another bunker buster went off and shook the room around him. Pieces of dry-wall dust fell down upon the Blind Man, and he tried to brush it off his Armani suit, but to no avail. And then he thought to himself, *My wine cellar. What is happening to my wine cellar?* He called out to his assistant over and over again, but the man was already lying on the floor, dead and motionless in the next room.

And then, after all these years of success, of winning every battle, after all these years of scheming, killing and controlling those around him ... it suddenly occurred to Jared that ... control was an illusion.

Colonel Branch Gets Through

"COLONEL BRANCH! THE RADIOS ARE WORKING AGAIN! I have General Masbruch on the line, sir. He wants to talk to you."

Dan walked over and grabbed the handset. He could hear the pounding of the 500-pound bombs falling onto the Blind Man's underground complex. "Yes, general."

"Dan, I need you and your men to fall back. Fall back as quickly as you can!"

Dan shook his head back and forth without thinking. "I don't understand, sir. Why should we fall back? As soon as these bombs let up we're going in for the final ground assault as planned. We need to get into position."

But General Masbruch laughed nervously on the other end of the line. "No, colonel. I am ordering you to retreat several hundred yards and stand by for further orders. Get up high where you can see, and then observe and report back to me."

Dan hesitated, He looked over at his son, Jeremy, just a few feet away. "Yes, sir. We are to fall back and watch. Anything else, sir?"

There was a moment of silence. "Well, Dan, you might want to tell all your men to plug their ears. Just watch the show, Dan. You're going to love it. Courtesy of General Rodney T. Branch."

"Yes, sir. We will comply immediately." And then he turned to his right and looked over at his son, Jeremy.

"What's wrong, dad?"

Dan Branch smiled. "He says Uncle Rodney has a surprise for us, and that we should plug our ears."

Jeremy looked out past the ridge, then back at his father nervously. "Dad, is he going to nuke them?"

Dan shook his head, "I don't know, son. But let's get back as far as we can just in case. You know your Uncle Rodney. He tends to get a little excited sometimes."

Colonel Branch turned to his men and began barking out orders, and soon they were all retreating off the ridge.

Desperation Sets In

JARED THOMPSON WAS NOT A GOOD LOSER, BUT THAT wasn't totally his fault. After all, he'd had very little practice at losing, and it was not something he'd set out to excel at in the first place. So, it was no surprise that, when the Blind Man realized he'd been beaten, that he would take it poorly.

Jared looked up at the computer screen hanging by its wires on one end, protruding out the wall. He looked around him at his corinthian leather couch, covered in plaster and debris from the ceiling, and he wondered to himself *How did this happen?* But, to be quite frank; it really didn't matter anymore. It wasn't like a football game where you could blame the referees, especially not when you ran a totalitarian organization.

The bombs had appeared to stop falling up top, but that

gave him little consolation. Most of his people had deserted him or been killed, and it was then, that Jared realized that he was almost useless without other people to do his bidding. He wanted to escape from this mess, but, he didn't know how to do it. Normally he would just order someone to take him away, but ... there was no one left to order around.

Jared looked at the empty bottle of wine on the carpeted floor beneath his feet. He bent down to pick it up. He read the label out loud. Domaine Leflaive Bâtard-Montrachet Grand Cru Chardonnay. It had been bottled in 2015. That had been a very good year for wine and for him personally. It was a white chardonnay out of Burgundy, France. It certainly wasn't the best of wines, but it was good for everyday. If memory served him correctly he'd bought several cases at an auction for only five-hundred dollars per bottle. He tossed the bottle back onto the dirty carpet.

First, General Branch had destroyed his palatial bunker in Pennsylvania, and now ... this.

Jared Thompson had no way to escape, no place to go if he did escape, and ... quite frankly ... not a whole lot left to live for. He'd wanted to meet Rodney Branch, but ... not as a vanquished foe, but, rather, as the glorious victor. But now ... what would happen to him? They wouldn't let him go, probably wouldn't even let him live, and, if they did ... he would be in prison, surrounded by common criminals. That was beneath him.

To go on living in a world that he did not control was ... unsupportable. He'd made his decision.

Jared moved over to what was left of his control station. Auxiliary power had kicked in shortly after the second wave of attacks, and the emergency klaxon was blaring away with the most annoying of sounds.

Thankfully, there were still lights on the control panel, which meant he could still do one more thing. He looked up at the dangling computer screen; it was dark and empty. He had no idea what was going on up at the surface, but this one thing he knew. They would be coming for him soon ... coming en masse, and ... there was one last gift he could give them. He just hoped that General Branch was up there, somewhere close enough to experience it. Jared had installed the twenty-kiloton atomic warhead device last year, just in case something like this happened. Jared prided himself in foresight, among other things.

The Blind Man punched several keys on the keyboard. The control panel screen hadn't broken, so it was easy enough to see what he was doing. The computer asked for his confirmation keycode. He took off his Rolex watch and smashed it on the table in front of him. The parts sprayed out into the room. Jared picked up the back plate; it was solid gold of course. He looked at the engraved numbers and smiled. Yes, there were always options to those who took the time to think ahead.

Quickly, he punched in the numbers and pressed "enter."

The countdown started.

Dyess Air Force Base, Texas

"So what's happening in Georgia?"

Colonel Frank smiled and gave General Branch the good news. "The fighters from the USS Ronald Reagan reached the battle and have turned the tide. We enjoy air superiority on that battlefield, and have commenced pounding the Blind Man's ground forces. It'll all be over in Georgia soon, sir."

Rodney nodded his head. "Okay then. What's happening in Montana?"

This time General MacDermid answered. "It's pretty much the same story there, sir. Carrier planes from the Nimitz and Enterprise have established dominance and the enemy is surrendering en masse."

General MacDermid waited for Rodney to say something, but nothing came out, so he went on. "For all practical purposes, sir, the war is over. The Blind Man's done ... he's finished. We beat him, general!"

But General Branch still remained silent. Even after all these years, after all this killing, especially after all these years and all this killing ... he found no glory in war. "Make sure the president is kept informed, General MacDermid."

The colonel nodded."He's listening to everything on board the USS Ronald Reagan in real-time, sir."

Rodney looked up at the bank of computer screens on the wall in front of him. The art of war had changed so much in the decades since he'd last fought in Vietnam, but ... one thing hadn't changed, indeed, never would change. When it all came down to it, no matter how advanced the technology, it was always one man against one man. And the wisdom of Sun Tzu would remain forever timeless.

> *"If you know the enemy and know yourself, you need not fear the result of a hundred battles. If you know yourself but not the enemy, for every victory gained you will also suffer a defeat. If you know neither the enemy nor yourself, you will succumb in every battle."*

200 Feet Below West Virginia

JARED LOOKED AT THE DIGITAL TIMER IN FRONT OF HIM. He could literally count off the seconds of his life, watch them tick on by like individual leaves falling from a tree or blades of grass blowing in the wind. In the end it was always about control. Control and power. Money bought him power, and power got him control. But now ... money was worthless. But still ... he had control of his own destiny.

And then he thought the most profound thing. How many people actually know the moment of their death. Only God knew that, and so, he thought to himself. *I am a god. I hold the power of life and death in my hand.* He glanced down at the digital clock and smiled. Forty-nine seconds to live. Forty-nine seconds to immortality. He hoped the general was close enough to watch it happen. He would love to meet him in hell.

Dyess Air Force Base, Texas

"BIG BLU IS ALMOST OVER THE TARGET NOW, SIR. He'll be launching any second now."

General Branch nodded his head in acknowledgment, but didn't make a move. He would not rest until he knew for sure that the Blind Man was dead.

And then he couldn't help but wonder if Dan and Jeremy were okay. Last he knew they were alive, but ... he needed to find out, but ... first, he had to focus on this one final task.

"Big BLU is on the way down, sir."

General Branch stood motionless, waiting patiently.

200 Feet Below West Virginia

THE DIGITAL READOUT SAID TEN SECONDS. THEY couldn't stop him now. He had no regrets. This was it. This was the end. The last glorious ... And then he heard the impact of something very large and heavy above his head. It seemed to be traveling toward him as fast as gravity could take it.

He looked one final time at the clock. Two seconds. And then ...

One Mile West of Spruce Mountain

THE FORCE OF THE BLAST THREW DAN BRANCH TO THE ground as it shook the earth like an earthquake. His son, Jeremy, reached out to grab a nearby tree and managed to stay on his feet.

"What was that, dad?"

Dan quickly got to his feet and looked to the east. There, rising above the treeline was a very large cloud of dust and debris.

"Holy crap that was loud!"

Jeremy looked at his dad with fear in his young eyes. "Dad, is that a nuke? Are we all going to die now?"

Dan searched back in time to Pennsylvania, to the day

223

when he and Donny Brewster had watched the malevolent mushroom cloud form over the Blind Man's underground headquarters after Uncle Rodney has used his one and only nuke. He calmed his son's fears.

"No, I don't think, so son. This is different than the nuke I saw from ten miles out with Donny." And then he thought to himself before continuing. "It's big though. No doubt about that. I didn't know we had non-nuclear bombs that big."

Jeremy walked up and stood beside his dad. "Where do you think Uncle Rodney got that thing?"

Dan Branch smiled. "Well, I'm pretty sure we can rule out eBay this time around." And then he looked at his son's face and laughed out loud. "Can you imagine the shipping costs alone on something that big?"

Debris suddenly started to fall around them, so the two men quickly took cover under a shale outcropping. The rest of Dan's command covered their heads and sought what cover they could as sticks and rocks and other objects rained down on them. A few minutes later the debris stopped as quickly as it had started. Dan looked around them and then stood up. Jeremy soon joined him, and they both began to walk, scanning the ground to make sure the men were okay.

"Hey dad! Look at this!"

Jeremy reached down to the ground and picked up a bottle. "Is this wine?"

Dan walked up and stood beside his son. "Yeah, I think so. It has a foreign language on it. What, maybe French or Italian or something?"

Jeremy nodded and handed the bottle to his dad who read it out loud. "It says Grand Vin de Château Latour, 1961." He thought for a moment. "I think that's French."

A few other men began gathering around them, brushing the dirt and falling dust off one another.

"Should we open it up, dad?"

Dan shrugged his shoulders. "I don't know. I guess you're old enough to have a drink now." He looked up into the sky.

The dust cloud was starting to settle back down now. "I'm glad this thing didn't hit us in the head. I think these bottles usually have corks in them don't they?"

Dan looked around at the men gathering behind him. "Any of you men got a corkscrew?" But no one answered. He turned to Jeremy. "You got a canteen, son?"

Jeremy nodded and took the small pack off his back. Soon he held out the plastic, military-style canteen. Dan unscrewed the cap and then rapped the neck of the wine bottle against the shale outcropping. It took two tries, but the bottle broke and he carefully poured the wine into the canteen before tossing the bottle back onto the ground beside them. Dan raised the canteen up high over his head and laughed out loud. "To victory!"

The men behind him cheered as Dan took the first drink. He lowered the canteen and smacked his lips together. Then he handed the canteen to his son. "Well, it's not as good as Mocha flavored Frappuccino, but ... it's better than water I guess."

Jeremy took a sip and made a face. "This stuff sucks, dad. I'd rather have a Mountain Dew."

Dan shrugged and passed the canteen back to his men who were waiting for their turn. Dan climbed up onto the rock outcropping and was soon joined by Jeremy.

"That's okay. There's no accounting for bad tastes, I suppose." And then he looked around at the wooded hillside and thought to himself. *I bet this place is awful pretty when people aren't blowing it all up.*

Just then a captain ran up to the rock. "Colonel Branch, my men need to know what to do. Are we going to attack now?"

Dan looked over at Jeremy and laughed. Then he looked down the mountainside at the giant crater left by Big BLU. "Captain, if you and your men want to attack, then go right ahead, but Jeremy and I are gonna have some lunch."

The captain looked confused, but didn't say anything right away. Then he looked at the giant hole in the ground and turned to walk away. "I guess we'll have lunch too, sir."

Dan reached over and put his right arm around his son. He squeezed it hard and then let up. "Well, son. What'd'ya say we pack things up here and head on back to Iroquois?"

Jeremy smiled and then wiped the dust away from his eyes so he could see better. "Yeah, that's a good idea." And then a thought came to him and he laughed.

"What's so funny?"

"I was just thinking, well, at least we won't have to bury the Blind Man. There's nothing left of him."

Dan nodded his head. "I suppose you're right, son."

And then a bright, red cardinal landed on a tree limb just a few yards away. Dan looked at it and smiled.

"Let's go home, son."

EPILOGUE

PRESIDENT MICHAEL TOWNSEND stood behind the podium on the flight deck of the aircraft carrier, USS Ronald Reagan. The USS Reagan was the ninth supercarrier of the Nimitz class to be built, and, prior to the fall, operated out of Japan. However, after the global collapse, all military personnel were eventually called home to defend America's own borders and to deter other nation's from attacking the crippled once-superpower.

The nuclear-powered aircraft carrier was a big ship by anyone's standards, almost 1,100 feet long, with 3,200 people on board to serve her. She was capable of launching ninety-plus aircraft from her decks, and remained one of the mightiest war machines ever built, especially now, in a world where most countries couldn't even power an electric light bulb.

"We are here today to honor both the living and the dead, the heroes of renown, those who fought and lived, as well as those who fought and made the supreme sacrifice to their nation.

"I feel it's only fitting to award that honor on the deck of the USS Reagan, on the deck of the ship which launched the final sortie of the last battle of that great war."

He paused long enough to look around. All the key players

were there. General MacDermid and Admiral Fletcher were seated off to one side. The general was now the new Chairman of the Joint Chiefs, while the admiral had been promoted to the president's cabinet as the Secretary of Defense. The new head of the NSA, Jeff Arnett, sat beside them. He was much happier since moving out of Uncle Rodney's pole barn.

Seated to the left of the president in the front row were Jackie and Dan Branch. Jackie held the new baby, a healthy boy who rested happily against her chest as she listened. Dan had a harder time, holding down baby Donna who was now a toddler and always trying to get down to play on the flight deck. Jeremy sat beside Dan. He had joined the US Marines and was now in his dress blues. Jeremy had received a battle-field commission and was now the youngest lieutenant in the US military.

Seated next to Jeremy was General Masbruch, who had stayed in the regular army for another three months until moving back home, south of the Mason-Dixon line. He was retired now and in a hurry to get back home to his vegetable garden.

Sparky Fillmore, the old man who'd walked from western Kansas to Davenport, Iowa in response to God's call, was seated in the third row beside his wife, Edna. Sparky's wife still had trouble believing that he'd traveled all that way just to vouch for the Shadow Militia on that first day with General MacDermid, but ... without him there, the entire course of history would have changed, and Jared Thompson would now be in control of the entire United States.

Sergeant Donny Brewster had reluctantly accepted a commission as a Captain in the Marine Corps, heading up the newly reformed sniper training school. He'd been a sergeant for so long, that the idea of people saluting him seemed too bizarre. But he was adjusting to it. His left arm still gave him trouble when the weather changed, but it had healed up well under the tender loving care of Lisa Vanderboeg. They'd been married now for six months and she was pregnant with their first child, a child who would be born in a free America.

Colonel Roger "Ranger" MacPherson, the Executive Officer and co-creator of the Shadow Militia, now wore three stars on his collar and was helping to rebuild the army after so many in America had died. It was indeed a daunting task.

Seated beside Mac was Uncle Rodney. He now wore a pair of clean blue jeans and a red, flannel shirt. The president's staff had tried to get him to dress up in his uniform, but Rodney had told them in no uncertain terms to bugger off. General Branch had stayed in the army long enough to ensure the rebuilding of the military was on track, before finally bowing out and returning to Iroquois county. At first he'd declined the president's request to attend this ceremony, but President Townshend was every bit as bull-headed as Rodney. When Marine One had landed in Rodney's front yard yesterday, he just hadn't had the heart to tell the man no. After all, both of them respected each other, and, to some extent, had fought a war together.

"And now, let us get to the heart of the matter. America would not be free without the sacrifice of an outfit called The Shadow Militia. Prior to the collapse, the FBI would have arrested this man." He nodded over at Uncle Rodney, who just smiled. "However, fate, it seems, is not without a sense of irony, because today, I am here to bestow honor on the very outfit that, in a more civilized time, would have been considered an enemy of the state." He paused and looked again over at Rodney.

"Rodney T. Branch, commanding general of the Shadow Militia. Will you please step forward."

Rodney stood to attention, did a perfect left face and marched to the podium. He stood in front of his president quietly. And President Townsend surprised the old man by snapping to attention and rendering him a perfect, military salute. Tears welled in Rodney's eyes, but he held them at bay behind dams of stoicism. Rodney returned the salute and the president quickly cut away as did Rodney.

"Thank you so much, my friend. America can never repay

you enough."

Rodney said nothing. He just nodded in reply.

President Townsend turned slightly and spoke into the microphone. "It is with great honor and humility that I do hereby award to the commanding general of the Shadow Militia, this Presidential Unit Citation for displaying overwhelming gallantry, determination, and esprit de corps in accomplishing its mission under extremely difficult and hazardous conditions. When America was down, the Shadow Militia was at its best, and you defended us all when we could not."

President Townsend shook Rodney's hand and then pinned the ribbon to his chest. Afterwards, he gave him an engraved plaque. Rodney accepted it, noting that it felt heavy in his hand.

And then the president moved back to the microphone and spoke again.

"Now, this next award is one that I didn't tell General Branch about, simply because I feared he wouldn't show up to accept it. However, I would be derelict as president if I did not recognize the general for his extreme sacrifice both in and out of uniform, because without him, we wouldn't be standing here today."

The president reached under the podium and pulled out a wooden box, ornately carved and inlaid with gold. He set the box on top of the podium and opened it up. Ceremoniously, he lifted the blue ribbon out of the box, a metal star hung from it with an eagle just above the star. Uncle Rodney saw it and his knees suddenly went weak, but he quickly steeled himself and remained at attention.

"For conspicuous gallantry and intrepidity at the risk of life above and beyond the call of duty, I award General Rodney T. Branch the Medal of Honor."

He stepped forward and draped the ribbon over Rodney's neck. Rodney didn't move. He didn't say anything.

"Would you like to say a few words, Rodney?"

Uncle Rodney looked down for a moment and then back

up again. Finally, he nodded and stepped up to the microphone. He looked out at the thousand or so sailors, marines and soldiers before him and cleared his throat.

"Thank you. Normally I don't tolerate this kind of showboating, but ... since the president is ordering me, I suppose I should put up with it." There was a ripple of laughter through the crowd, and the president himself couldn't help but smile.

"Listen folks ... I'm not a hero. I'm just someone who saw a need and filled the gap. That's all. The Shadow Militia was made up of Americans, just like you and me, and America has always been filled with heroes, so, it's no surprise that this unit is being honored today."

He looked down again at the plaque in his hand. "Some people would say that I was the leader of the Shadow Militia, but ... the truth is, when I thought I was leading them ... they were really leading me. In all, just over the past year alone, ten-thousand Shadow Militia soldiers died in defense of our country. But it wasn't me who died. It wasn't me who marched in the mud, killed the enemy, and stood neck-deep in blood, watching my fellow soldiers die around me." He looked out at his fellow warriors and his face grew stern.

"I was just the general."

And then a tear finally escaped the dam and trickled down his cheek. "I accept these awards, but only in the name of the people who really earned them. Men like Lieutenant Harold Steffens, who, at the Battle of Iroquois, dove his plane into two-hundred enemy soldiers, thereby sacrificing himself but winning the battle. Harold was 82 years old at the time. He didn't have to fight, but he wanted to, was eager to. And it was bravery from men like him that won this war. A general can only issue orders, but ... it's the officers and noncoms under him that carry them out, and it's the privates and lance corporals and airmen and sailors who do most of the fighting and dying."

He looked out over the crowd and then over at President Townsend. "Mr. President, I accept this honor on behalf of all the men and women who died under my command in service to our country. God bless their souls ... and God bless America."

With that, the soldiers and sailors stood to their feet and began clapping and cheering as loudly as they could. The applause lasted for five minutes until, finally, the president led Rodney back to his seat of honor and then closed out the ceremony.

THAT WAS THE LAST TIME RODNEY BRANCH SPOKE IN public. He returned to private life in what was left of Iroquois county and started to rebuild. Uncle Rodney lived another fifteen years after that, adapting to civilian life as best he could. His friends visited him often, and he enjoyed their company, but he was always equally glad to see them go, so he could get back to his privacy.

Dan and Jackie, along with baby Donna and their three children that followed, built a house closeby. Rodney worked hard at being a good grandfather, just like he'd promised he would. But most of the time, he took walks in the woods, went fishing at the Mill Pond, or just sat on his porch watching his bird feeder.

And when he died, it was with the smell of sulphur on his breath, and the roar of battle in his ears. He was a warrior until the end.

Twenty Years Later

JACKIE BRANCH STOOD OVER UNCLE RODNEY'S GRAVE. It had been twenty years since his death, but she missed him now more than ever. She was now an old woman, and not a day went by when she didn't recall the words of Uncle Rodney when she'd first moved to Iroquois before the war.

He'd seen her as a potential threat and had asked her: "So, young lady. What's it going to take to move you from the liability column to the asset column?" In retrospect, she had been a liability, but he'd given her the benefit of the doubt and the respect she hadn't yet earned. In the end, she had become the warrior he'd always wanted her to be, and, in the process, they'd earned each other's undying respect and love.

She remembered their fishing trip and the little talk at the Mill Pond just after the battle for the Mackinaw Straits. She had asked him if they were all going to die, and his answer intrigued her to this day.

"Well, truth is Jackie, we all know we're going to die. That's a given. We don't know when and we don't know how. But ... maybe the more important thing is to pick a cause worth dying for.

"I spent my whole life getting ready for this final moment in the world's history. Most people have the luxury of growing up and falling in love, getting married and then they spend the rest of their lives creating beautiful memories for their kids and grand kids.

"That didn't happen to us, Jackie. For whatever reason, it just didn't happen to us.

"It would appear that our job is to reset society to its place of normalcy. Our job is to win this war, defeat the tyrant, and rebuild."

And then Jackie had asked him what comes after that. His reply had been profound.

"I don't know, Jackie. By then I'll be dead and you'll be an old woman. I guess the only one who can answer that question is the baby in your arms and the one still growing in your womb. After all, they can only build on what we leave them. So ... let's leave them both the ability to choose a good life and the freedom to start over again."

Jackie looked down at the granite headstone in front of her. There was a US flag stuck in the ground beside it. There were four stars on the stone with an engraving of the Medal of Honor.

And underneath the name 'General Rodney T. Branch" were the words:

God ... Family ... Country

Jackie turned to walk away, but she would be back tomorrow. This time Dan would come with her ... the walk would do him good.

Skip Coryell lives with his wife and children in Michigan. He works full time as a professional writer, and *The Blind Man's Rage* is his twelfth published book. He is an avid hunter and sportsman, a Marine Corps veteran, and a graduate of Cornerstone University. You can listen to Skip as he co-hosts the syndicated military talk radio show *Frontlines of Freedom* on www.frontlinesoffreedom.com. You can also hear his weekly podcast *The Home Defense Show* at www.homedefenseshow.com

For more details on Skip Coryell, or to contact him personally, go to his website at www.skipcoryell.com

Books by Skip Coryell

We Hold These Truths
Bond of Unseen Blood
Church and State
Blood in the Streets
Laughter and Tears
RKBA: Defending the Right to Keep and Bear Arms
Stalking Natalie
The God Virus
The Shadow Militia
The Saracen Tide
The Blind Man's Rage
Civilian Combat - The Concealed Carry Book